BE SILENT

BE SILENT

DANIE BOTHA

Be Silent
Copyright © 2017 Danie Botha
All rights reserved

This book was published under Charbellini Press.
No part of this book may be reproduced in any form by any means without the express permission of the author, except in the case of brief quotations embodied in reviews.

This is a work of historical fiction. Apart from well-known actual people, events and locales, all names, characters and incidents are the product of the author's imagination. Any resemblance to actual persons, living or dead, is entirely coincidental.

www.daniebotha.com

Published in the United States by Charbellini Press

ISBN: 0995174806
ISBN 13: 9780995174801

*This book is dedicated to
Nico, Charlotte, Florence and David*

Signing up is easy! Simply go here: http://eepurl.com/cmmGCT

Author's Note:

The British Federation of Rhodesia and Nyasaland was created in 1953, consisting of Southern Rhodesia, Northern Rhodesia and Nyasaland. Those territories are now the countries of Zimbabwe, Zambia and Malawi, respectively. This Federation was dissolved on December 31, 1963. Zambia declared independence from the United Kingdom on October 24, 1964: Kenneth Kaunda was its first president.

The years leading up to Zambia's independence were marked by a growing awareness of African nationalism, leading to nonviolent resistance against the British colonial rule. During this same time period, a new church founded by Alice Lenshina, in the northeastern part of Zambia, flourished to the point of becoming a concern to the black African nationalists, who were just coming into power. The teaching of her Lumpa Church eventually created a situation of a state within a state bringing the church into perpetual conflict with local and national authorities, conflict which culminated in July and August of 1964 in the suppression of the church.

Against this backdrop, small numbers of South African missionaries continued to work on Mission stations throughout the country, as they had been doing for several decades.

Be Silent is a work of fiction. Madzi Moyo, Fort Jameson (Chipata) and Chinsali exist, but the characters and story herein are imaginary. Any resemblance to actual persons, living or dead, is entirely coincidental.

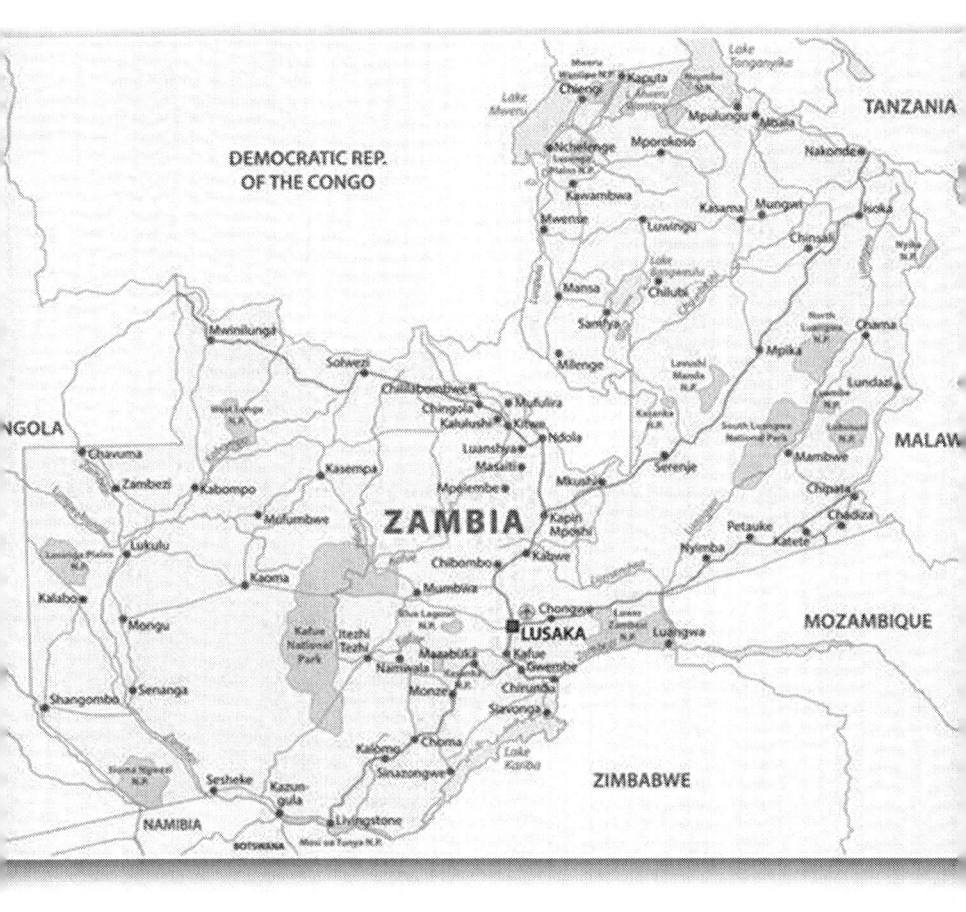

1

Lusaka, Zambia. Thursday, March 18, 2004

He was certain she was lying. The voice was indisputably hers, but deeper and wearied. Her frugal choice of words alarmed him. "I've carried the guilt for so long," she had said. She did not sound overcome with joy that he had tracked her down—or remorseful enough, not after all these many years. He wondered whether he would recognize her: Rianna. He found it peculiar that he had so little trouble with her voice. Try as he might, the veil would not lift from her face, except for the eyes. Her eyes were, as they always had been, dark pools that could shoot fire at a moment's notice.

"Lukas, I didn't know. Not that my statement could ever have had such a consequence. We were only children."

Was that her second lie? Lukas transferred the receiver for a moment to his left hand and closed the sliding door to the balcony, shutting out the street noise and evening heat. A tepid wind had propelled the mix of Chinyanja voices, jarring trucks and car horns, along with whiffs of *nshima* porridge from the street vendors, six stories below, into the room. The shirt was plastered to his back; he pulled it free as he listened to her hesitant voice and the air conditioner labouring to cool the night. How could she have remained oblivious to how everything had played out in the aftermath, after her sworn statement? She had left the country three weeks later, but she could still have learned the truth. There were her parents and brothers; they'd known all along and had stayed behind.

It was no coincidence that he had met her brother at the convention only yesterday: Minister P.J. Vermeulen, representing the government of Zambia—now the new Deputy Minister of Justice in Lusaka. It did not require much digging to confirm that Rianna Vermeulen and P.J. were brother and sister. He, Lukas Ferreira, was part of the UN delegation sent to observe the proceedings of the Truth and Reconciliation Commission. Rianna's brother was a grade behind him when they'd all attended the same Mission school in the Eastern Province in the year of the independence, 1964. Rianna, who was two grades ahead of him, had been thirteen.

According to P.J., his sister was on a week-long visit to the country, her first since she left. She'd come all the way from Oxford, where she was a professor of English Literature. She was divorced, with no children. She had wished to attend her brother's swearing-in ceremony as deputy minister, three days earlier. Their parents were both still alive but too frail to travel the two and a half thousand kilometers from their assisted living complex on the outskirts of Cape Town. Rianna and P.J. were the only remaining siblings; they had lost their younger brother ten years earlier to a brain tumor.

"Why did you come looking for me?" Her question was a mere whisper now.

"I wish I had, but I didn't."

He did not tell her that it had taken over twenty years before he managed to sleep through every night, but instead thinking about the three of them: Rianna, Anthony and himself–about what happened. He did not tell her it was another ten years before he was able to accept that he was not responsible for what had happened that second-last day of July 1964, and ten more years before he'd found the courage to return to the country.

Lukas did, however, tell her that her brother had filled him in on the missing decades. He also told her that this old friend of his, the African one, was now a school principal, nearing retirement, and was attending the T and R Commission proceedings. He mentioned that he thought that this—his meeting his African friend again—was sheer coincidence, but what had happened to the friend after Rianna, and later Lukas, left the country for high school was not. Not when the friend ended up imprisoned for a year, wrongfully convicted, because of her false statement.

He realized they had both chosen not to mention Anthony, his classmate of so long ago. It was safer for now not to. They would stick to discussing his African friend, the school principal.

"You have to speak to him before your return to Oxford," Lukas said.

"Have to, Lukas? I told you I didn't know."

Her third lie.

Lukas paused. "You know now—there are no more excuses. You have to make it right, Rianna."

"Perhaps it's too late for restitution. What exactly do you want me to do?"

"I want you to make it right, Rianna. At least speak to him."

"Lukas, how much do you know about guilt? Guilt and doubt that dissolve into your system, poison every bone and muscle, and in the end, shortly before it kills you, paralyzes your soul. Don't tell me about guilt. I have accepted my punishment years ago; I have carried it this long. Let me be."

Perhaps she was not lying.

"Rianna, you can change that. You were only thirteen!"

"I wish I still was."

Lukas had always been intimidated by the extent of Rianna's determination when they were children; it bothered him much less now. He returned to the balcony and leaned over the railing, inhaling deep, listening. This was his official welcome home. The receiver was still in his hand; he gave her the principal's number anyway.

2

Katete, Zambia. January 2, 1964

They would never understand.

This was her sanctuary. Up here she was invisible, the ground more than thirty feet below. It required little effort to scale the mango tree's thick trunk and follow its unevenness upwards as it grew slimmer until she reached her lookout branch. Her legs swung down on both sides, one arm wrapped around a side branch, her back rested against the coarse trunk that towered another thirty feet above her; it was heaven—the tree glue on her fingers regardless. At this height there was always a breeze coming through the green canopy, making the unforgiving summer glare more bearable, discourage the mosquitos from pestering her. She closed her eyes, savoring the ripe sweetness of the yellow fruit.

She dared not tell anyone she had become too heavy for her old spot higher up, the branches would sway dangerously, scaring even her. She'd been forced to find another lookout branch, ten feet lower. At least she had also grown taller, which made the climbing easier. Her body was growing fast, but still her mother was so hard to convince that she was old enough for a proper brassiere, to hug her young breasts.

When her mother had handed her the coveted piece of pink feminine attire, she had pleaded, "You are growing into a young woman, Rianna. When you need these, there should be no more tree climbing."

Rianna had only laughed and kissed her mother, put on the bra and run off to climb her tree.

From up here she had a view of most of Katete, their Mission station in Zambia's Eastern Province. The long firm leaves formed a natural clearance, a window, allowing her to look down from her lookout branch to the river, which ran though a narrow valley far below her. To both sides, she could see all the way, to where the ridge behind the Station disappeared into the forest. She had spent much time recently looking at the world that lay beyond that river to the south.

Not even the possibility of tree snakes deterred her as she rustled higher, dressed in crudely cut short pants. From here she could watch the world. She could see the comings and goings of everyone on the Station. In the tree she could *think*.

Leaning back against the trunk, she would take one baked peanut at a time out of a little fabric bag, break the shell open, roll it between her thumb and fingers until the thin baked skin rubbed off and then stuff the two nuts in her mouth. *Father wishes me to become a lady, demonstrate finesse, become someone of consequence perhaps. Mother would be content if I only managed not to break an arm or a leg or my neck.* She smiled as she stuffed four

BE SILENT

more peanuts into her mouth. She sniffed again: ripe mangoes and baked peanuts—paradise.

"Rianna, when are you ever going to stop climbing trees?" her father asked the next day.

"It's a mango tree, Father. And it's the only tree that I climb."

"You are not a little girl anymore, and the men on the Station are not blind."

"But, Daddy, I need the tree! It's my friend." She laughed at his concern. She had no fear of the heights she scaled. "Father, I am up among the leaves within seconds. You know I always change out of my dress and wear short pants when I climb. Those men can see nothing, and they can't even keep up with me."

She was not boasting. It was accepted as fact that she was the fastest mango-tree climber on the Station, perhaps in all of the province, Africans and missionaries included. She was even faster than her brother P.J., who was almost ten and just as tall and strong as she.

But that day, she had a pressing problem to unravel in her hideout.

The previous evening she had been with her mother and father in the dining room after supper. Mother had taken the bull by the horns. "Rianna, your father and I have heavy hearts. This will be your last year on the Station with us."

She, however, was bubbling with excitement. "I know, Mother dear. It's going to be so lovely. I'll be the oldest in the school!"

"Rianna, you'll see how fast a year passes. It will break our hearts to send you away for high school. Missions don't pay much for being Station maintenance man, but this is our calling. We would have it no other way."

Rianna was used to it, there never being money. Doing the work of the Lord in the tropics was not a lucrative affair and every missionary child grew up, knowing it.

Father took over. "Sending you to the South at the end of the year will place significant financial strain on us, in spite of the Mission's support. And, we won't be able to see you after the customary three years."

Her heart sank. That was it, then: she'd been forewarned about her end-of-year marching orders. She would be cut off from her family. They were, effectively, planning to abandon her by sending her far away. She wondered why there were no laws in the land preventing such actions taken by God-fearing parents. How could sensible parents commit such deeds? Perhaps the missions were a law unto themselves.

She had to wait a long time before she could slip away to her tree the next day.

It was the third consecutive year that she would attend the small, one-teacher Mission school on Madzi Moyo, staying in the school hostel during the week, coming home every weekend. Madzi Moyo, "water of life." That is what the local Chinyanja people called the place.

Rianna peered beyond the river toward the South.

The South is so very far away, and yet it's only eleven and a half fearful months away. There surely would be no mango tree to climb, and they would try much harder than Father and Mother to make a lady of me.

"I do not *wish* to become a lady!" she hollered from the thirty-foot-high branch, rocking her part of the tree. She was flying a pink flag. She'd had little difficulty slipping out of the garment and pulling it through her short sleeves, tying the elastic shoulder straps to a short stick, which she waved now from her tree-window for the world to see.

3

Fort Jameson, Zambia. January 3, 1964

The chiffon dress barely moved in the gust that pushed through the veranda's screen windows; the humidity had it glued to her breasts and thighs. Her knuckles were clasped white behind her back as she hastened her pace, refusing eye contact. The afternoon air was charged with her discontent and traces of wisteria, yellow oleander and sugarbush. *He cannot be allowed to get away with this. Not again.*

"Madzi Moyo. The boys are going to Madzi Moyo."

She had not been ready when he'd told her that. Not so soon. He would always plan everything, plot, toss the grenade and leave her to pick up the pieces. Every time. She kicked her slip-ons off with so much force that the projectiles thudded off the screen, making him jump to avoid them. She knew she was even more beautiful when upset, but she still refused to look at him.

BE SILENT

The pacing took her all the way down the wide veranda to where it ended against the wall of the kitchen at the back of the house, forcing her to make an about turn and pass him again as she followed the long porch around the corner toward the front, as far as it would allow, make another about turn at the mesh door and pace all the way back.

He reached out, unable to resist her fragrance—Morning Rose, it was called—his fingers merely brushing her warm skin in passing. She jumped.

"Do not *touch* me, Louis Ferreira!"

Her mother had warned her: "A lovely man, such a genuine soul, but be careful–he's very driven." Madzimoyo. Madzi Moyo. Was that another outpost in the hinterland of this Dark Continent? Louis was so entwined with the Missions Secretary and managed to pull off these ambitious arrangements in exotic locations. She was not certain whether she could ever bring herself to trust the old man, the Secretary, again, after his plotting with Louis behind her back all these months.

They were discussing the boys' future (or rather, she was being informed about it) on the secluded eastern veranda, not wanting to disturb the boys themselves with the news—well, not yet.

She halted abruptly. "Louis, do you realize that Madzi Moyo is a full twelve miles from Fort Jameson? The boys will be leaving our house as if they were going to university, and they are only going to grade one and grade five." He opened his mouth to respond but she had already disappeared around the corner on her pacing spree.

From inside the house, the boy could see only her silhouette. She was much taller than Father, even in bare feet. They were both, he knew, unaware of his presence in the sitting room, watching their every move, overhearing the deliberation. He had mastered the art of entering a room without a sound, of being a mere shadow, of sitting quietly in a darkened corner without moving a muscle. He was *Mthunzi*, "shadow"—the name the local people had given him.

It was easier at night, after lights-out time, when he couldn't sleep and everyone else was snoring softly. He would slip from his bed, glide from room to room in the dark without making a sound, watch each one of his family members—his mother, his father, his little brother and sisters—reassure himself that they were breathing and safe before he eventually returned to his room.

Most of the old Mission rest houses had been built with wrap-around porches, complete with low veranda walls and pillars. The porches kept the houses cooler during the tropical heat months, but also kept them somewhat dark. He found it, therefore, of little challenge to become a shadow even during the day, to slip in and out and listen. Born curious, he always needed to know.

"Maria, it's only twelve miles. We talked about all of this before we moved here. We were fortunate to have had them with us at home all these years."

Maria recalled the brief discussion they'd had mere weeks earlier, in the car, on their way here, to the Eastern Province. Louis had mentioned a boarding school that the two boys would have to attend, and that was all—no detail, no particulars.

"How can it be fortunate to send your young children away?" she said in challenge.

"At least we won't have to send them down to The South. Madzi Moyo is essentially around the corner."

"Louis, how can we send them to the lions and hyenas and people we don't even know?"

For the first time the boy in the inner room moved, going closer to where his parents were, but he remained in the shadows. Lions and hyenas—do they even have schools in the game reserve? Next to the window, he stood motionless. Father and Mother would not be impressed with him eavesdropping. Madzi Moyo? What a weird name. But, twelve miles? He had once walked five miles and he was dead tired. No wonder Mother was so upset.

"That is not entirely true, Maria. We worked with many of the staff when we were still in the Northern Province. They have an excellent boarding house, only a few steps from the little *Voortrekker* school."

She had stopped pacing and looked at his father, this time shaking her head. His father laughed. That was always a good sign. His father managed to touch her hands without her jumping away. The boy could see the struggle in her face.

"The school is run by the Dutch Reformed Church," his father continued, "which means we will have a say in what they teach the children. The state school here in Fort Jameson would be a different story—we would have no voice. More important, the children will be safe."

She pulled her hands back. "How can they be safe if they are no longer under our roof? Not with the upcoming election, not with the African nationalists promoting their civil disobedience campaigns. Louis, I am not sending my boys into the middle of the jungle on their own."

Her pacing started again, her bare feet making *swush-swush* sounds on the polished red floor.

His father was not giving up; he followed her.

"They won't be on their own," he said. "We'll drop them off Monday mornings into the care of responsible missionaries and pick them up Friday afternoons; and it's not in the middle of the jungle."

She halted, standing on tiptoes, the eyes closed, spreading her arms backwards, as if to fly. "Even if it is on the eastern border of the jungle," she said, "it's still the jungle. Did you forget, Louis, your son Wouter only turned six, and we're allowed to stay in this country only because of our workers' visas, through the church?"

His father sat down on the low wall. "The people have accepted us, Maria. They don't see color. And Lukas will look after Wouter."

"He's barely ten!"

"You know he's responsible beyond his years," his father said.

"Lukas is not supposed to take over his parents' role, Louis."

Lukas moved farther back into the shadows but still close enough to the open window to hear. He had to strain now to hear his mother speak. She often whispered once she'd conceded.

"Louis, we'll see them only on weekends."

"And during vacations."

"Louis, they're my babies. What about my babies?"

"Maria, they are not babies. And this is Fort Jameson, not Lusaka or Ndola. There have been no riots here, even less so on the Station. You'll see—Madzi Moyo is a peaceful little place that has been tamed, a pearl in the jungle."

"Louis, you can't tame the jungle."

"Maria." His father gestured with outstretched arms and she stepped into his embrace. She needed someone to hold her tight; she was shivering. His father held her for a long time. It was not often that Lukas had seen his mother's eyes fill with moisture, even less often her shoulders shaking as she sobbed silently.

Years later he would remember how long it could take for tension to flow out of a burdened body, a woman's body.

4

Madzi Moyo, Zambia. January 5, 1964

It was a Sunday afternoon when Lukas and Wouter arrived in Madzi Moyo. They came there in the middle of the official rain season, but that particular January, Northern Rhodesia's Eastern Province was dry and hot. There was little of the water of life.

Their mother and two sisters came along for the special occasion. Mother would not hear of staying in Fort Jameson with the girls; not even a government official or police officer or justice of the peace would have been able to keep her home when her boys were to be dropped off on the eastern edge of the jungle. Suzanne was old enough to sit in the back between the boys. Cecilia, who was only eighteen months old, remained on her mother's lap for the twelve-mile journey.

The six of them were ready to flee the unforgiving two-o'clock sun by the time their Opel Record stopped on top of the hill in front of the school boarding house in the shade of a giant *mopani* tree. The Opel had only two doors. Suzanne and Wouter waited patiently for their mother and baby sister to get out, untill Wouter could pull the little lever on the side of the left seat and flip it forward so they could climb out. Lukas had already slipped out on his father's side, and he and Father were waiting impatiently on the wraparound porch, at the front door.

The boarding house stood on the border of Upper and Lower Madzi Moyo.

Sixteen *mopanis* formed a small forest in front of it. A single mango tree stood as if shunned, on one side; it must have been quite old, for it was taller and larger than the *mopanis*. A bougainvillea had grown right into a *mopani* near the veranda; it had crossed the clearing, grabbed hold of a pillar and covered the whole length of the sloping veranda roof's supporting beam with purple patches. A frangipani welcomed them with its sweetness as they went up the six stairs to the front door. It was impossible not to crush the white propeller-shaped flowers scattered on the stairs; their fragrance followed the children around for the rest of the afternoon.

Lukas requested to do the knocking. There was no doorbell. He had to knock twice. The front door opened eventually, revealing the house mother: Miss Hannah. (They learned later there was no Mr. Hannah.) Miss Hannah was much older than their parents, a lady of plump and soft features, her long, silvery hair braided and tied up behind her neck. She moved slowly but gracefully. Her mouth didn't smile, but her eyes were friendly.

She received the six of them in the formal sitting room. Like most of the old Mission houses the rooms were large and dark.

It was a calming dark, not a fearful one. The adults had tee, the children were offered pre-mixed orange drink in tall, transparent plastic glasses. Miss Hannah apparently did not possess straws. The drinks were cold and sweet; each glass had two ice cubes. Next to the tray with glasses was a plate with Marie cookies, which Lukas quickly counted, dividing by seven and informing Suzanne and Wouter that they each could have four.

They embarked on a guided tour of the grand old place the moment the last Maries had found a resting place. Miss Hannah was not a lady to be rushed though; the tour was a painfully slow event. From the front door the Ferreiras trailed behind her large figure, working their way down the hallway to her quarters in the left wing. Lukas and Wouter grinned relieved when they were shown the full bathroom with indoor plumbing, further down the hallway; no outhouse visits would be required!

The dining hall was cavernous. Two long tables in dark wood were pushed end to end with eighteen chairs around them, completing the Spartan furnishing. The oiled furniture gleamed in the afternoon sun; it smelled of pine forest. Against the far wall stood an upright piano, hidden under a cloth throw. It didn't take long, listening to Miss Hannah's measured explanations, to realize they were inside an echo cave.

Lukas followed the procession through the dining hall with hands clasped behind his back, swaying his hips, mimicking Miss Hannah: "The dining hall seats eighteen people," he repeated. The room echoed his words and Wouter and little Suzanne followed suit, imitating his every move and words, making echoes. The three burst out laughing, bringing Miss Hannah, who was

BE SILENT

on her way into the kitchen with their parents, to a halt. She turned around and looked at them with a wounded frown.

The kitchen welcomed them with a medley of scents—fresh bread and rhubarb pie, mixed with a hint of overcooked cabbage. What caught the boys' attention however, was the pantry. Miss Hannah unlocked the door to the narrow room, which had floor-to-ceiling shelves on three walls. For a few seconds they were treated to the sight of the shelves, stacked with vast items of delight, before she abruptly locked the pantry again, slipping the copper key into her apron pocket. In the seconds the door had stood open, though, Lukas had been able to spot the rows of Marie packets on the second shelf. The message, however, was clear: locked it would remain. Over her dead body would probably be the only way in.

The children's sleeping quarters consisted of six rooms, three in each wing, each room accommodating four occupants. Miss Hannah allocated the two boys to different rooms. Wouter moved closer to his mother upon realizing that soon he was to be alone in a strange room in a strange house in a strange village. Mother covered his trembling hand with hers, shifting Cecilia to the other hip.

Not much later, Lukas stood next to Wouter on the veranda, watching the Opel with mixed feelings as it disappeared, far too soon, down the hill in a cloud of red dust toward Lower Madzi Moyo. Wouter gave a sigh and ran inside to his new room, obviously not wishing to let his brother see his damp eyes. Lukas remained standing on the veranda, peering into the distance where the trail of dust had faded into the simmering afternoon.

5

Madzi Moyo. January 6, 1964

By Monday morning the boarding house had come alive. Children's voices were everywhere. Most of the other children had joined the two boys during the night or in the early morning. The boys discovered with significant relief that all the girls had their own rooms, over in the left wing on the other side of the hostel, safely tucked away from them.

Lukas could not understand why the commotion made by the new arrivals, hadn't woken him. Only many years later did he realize missions did that to you: you became unobtrusive, thoughtful, considerate to a fault. It was easier to go unnoticed when you owned little, and demanded even less. This was the case with all Mission children—well, most of them.

Life under Miss Hannah was structured. She had a certain set of rules to govern her domain. By 7:15 a.m., she had every boarding-school child lined up in front of the hostel, faces and hands

BE SILENT

washed, properly dressed, fed and ready for the day. This was the best time of the day, she thought, breathing rapidly. The slightest activity would make her short of breath, but she still enjoyed it. She would never tire of the intoxicating mix of the frangipani and ripening mangoes, along with the subtle scent from the bougainvillea and *mopani* trees. It wasn't hot out yet, and already the cicadas were competing with the ever present cooing of the wood doves in the bush around them.

Command was then handed over to Rianna, a tall redhead, who was to accompany the children to school. Miss Hannah had instructed her, being the oldest of the boarding-house children, to not only lead the way, but also ensure that the *Kleintjies*, the youngest ones, reached the school safely.

Solemnly aware of her responsibility, Rianna tried to march them down the little hill like a drill sergeant, but her younger brother, P.J., had other ideas. He heckled her the whole way and was soon joined by Lukas and Anthony, who started dancing around her in circles, laughing and singing and clapping hands. Rianna wouldn't budge and shoed everyone on. Once they reached the school she whispered, with unhidden annoyance, "P.J. and friends, I will get you after school. You had better watch your backs!" P.J. and friends laughed at her as they ran off.

The teacher stood at the school's front door that morning, formally shaking each child's hand. She was much younger than Miss Hannah and it was clear that she loved smiling. Not only was she friendly, she smelled like the frangipani at the hostel's steps—pure and mysterious. Rianna herded the youngest ones together as they tried to step back from the unknown, including from the new teacher. She gently took Wouter and the others by the arm with a "Come on, guys, she won't bite. This is Miss Visagie."

Miss Visagie took Wouter's hand in both of hers and held it for a moment. She smiled and searched for his eyes, which were safely hidden behind thick, tinted glasses. "Welcome, Wouter," she said. His face started glowing and he pushed the fogging lenses higher up on his nose. Unable to make a single sound he simply nodded and escaped with the other children through the door.

The *Voortrekker* school consisted of a single large classroom, which also served as Miss Visagie's office. At the back were two smaller rooms, one a practice and reading room, the other, smaller one, an oversized closet with shelves all around it that functioned as the library.

Once everyone had entered, Miss Visagie appeared quietly at the front of the room. "Good morning, children. There is a desk for everyone. I have put your names on the desks I want you to sit at."

From the older children's corner one could clearly hear Rianna's voice: "That is so lame. I'll sit where ever I want to!"

Lukas was convinced Miss Visagie had to be deaf, for she continued undisturbed, "Grade ones and twos are in this first row, grade threes and fours in the second row, grade fives have a row to themselves and grade sixes and sevens are in the last row." Her gaze locked with Rianna's until the latter looked away. "Wouter, Sarel and Olga, your desks are over here," and she patted the designated spots. She wanted the *Kleintjies* right under her nose. Adam, the forth member of the grade-one class would only join them in a few day's time.

On the front wall was the largest blackboard Lukas had ever seen. He could not recall how many he had seen before, but never one that stretched across an entire wall of a large classroom. Along the two sidewalls were more blackboards, running the entire length of the room, underneath the windows. One would be able to draw so many things on all those blackboards! In spite of being ten years old now, he still enjoyed writing and drawing with colored chalk. He wondered how many boxes of board chalk Miss Visagie owned. He decided to ask her, at the first opportunity, if he could collect the small pieces of leftover chalk at the end of each day; he had ample room for them in his old threadbare canvas backpack, his faithful companion, which he loved carrying around.

Miss Visagie did not keep them long that first day. She explained in great detail how everything was supposed to work, with so many of the children being in different grades in one classroom. She talked about the importance of everyone's cooperation.

Convinced she was addressing only the oldest children who would much better fathom the depths of cooperation, Lukas started counting the blackboards on the sidewalls. Each blackboard was roughly as wide as a door. Twenty-two. Baffled by his discovery he did a recount; there was indeed one blackboard for each student.

And on a corner of Miss Visagie's desk stood a single shining brass bell with a dark wooden handle. The still smiling Miss Visagie explained that the bell would be used in the mornings only if one of the children was late for the start of the school day, at seven-thirty. But every Friday afternoon, she would give a different child the opportunity to ring the bell outside—to declare the end of the school week. Lukas stared at the bell, intimidating and inviting to him.

6

Madzi Moyo. January 1964.

At the end of each school day, the Station children who lived in Upper and Lower Madzi Moyo would gather in a single group for the walk back to their respective homes. This separated out the hostel dwellers as if by drawing an invisible line. The new children learned soon enough that the hostel children apparently were different; it was therefore prudent to observe a subtle distance.

By the end of the first week, Rianna had had enough of the segregation, which was mainly enforced by the Station children. Once they reached the top of the hill in front of the hostel, the Station children would split off to go their separate ways while the hostel children continued up the path to Miss Hannah's domain beyond the trees. Rianna turned to the departing Station children, pushed out her youthful breasts and addressed Barbara, also in grade seven. "Why are you guys so snobbish? You're not smarter simply because your parents live on the Station. *Ons is nie melaats nie!*"

BE SILENT

Barbara laughed, as if embarrassed. "We never said you had leprosy!"

Rianna was not satisfied. "Well, then don't treat us as if we have it. Shame on you, Barbara! What are these little ones going to think of us?" She spun around, ran up the six stairs and called over her shoulder, "Come on, guys, leave those snobs—let's go see what Miss Hannah has dished out for us!"

The rest of the hostel children followed Rianna up the stairs and disappeared through the front door. Only Lukas and Anthony remained, momentarily the captive audience of Barbara and the other Upper Madzi Moyo children. Lukas did not wish to publicly demonstrate his opposition to Rianna's scorn, but he was curious and he felt braver than usual, because he has had the privilege that day to ring the school bell at the end of their first school week. However, he would not be able to eat or sleep if he couldn't clarify the possibility of contracting the stigmatizing disease. A dreadful fate awaited the poor people with leprosy in the Bible.

"Why didn't you two run along with Captain Rianna?" Barbara took several menacing steps in their direction. "Aren't you afraid of contracting *melaatsheid*?"

Lukas noticed, as he took off his backpack and loosened the one strap, that Barbara was flat chested. He slipped his hand inside until it touched Miss Visagie's brass bell—he didn't even have time to tell Anthony about it.

Barbara took another step closer as the boys hesitantly stood their ground. Anthony piped bravely, "How can we get leprosy from living in the hostel if there are no lepers? That's not possible!"

Barbara wasn't going to let them off the hook without drawing blood. She lowered her voice, whispering, "How do you know

25

the boarding house wasn't a Leper colony before it became a hostel? Ask Miss Hannah, she'll tell you … Remember when you sleep tonight and you feel something crawling up your leg."

The other Station children started laughing, but Lukas jumped forward, pulled his hand free from the backpack and hollered, "You're plain mean, Barbara Wessels!" and he rang the brass bell inches from the bewildered girl's ear with all the strength he possessed. The laugh that was on her and the other Station childrens' lips died away as they turned around and ran off, baffled, leaving the boys in front of the hostel, uncertain about their victory.

Lukas and Anthony looked at one another, pulled up their shoulders and ran up the stairs. The matter of the leprosy, Lukas knew from his friend's puzzled face, was not closed—as, neither, was that of the school bell.

Embarrassing as it might be, input from Miss Hannah and perhaps even Rianna was required before Lukas would be able to close an eye that night. And he would have to run across to Miss Visagie's house to drop off the school bell, accompanied by a good explanation, before his father picked them up for the weekend—if he didn't want to find himself in big trouble.

With great difficulty, they managed to sit through the lunch hour meal, mostly pushing the food around on their plates, as they burned to speak to Miss Hannah in private. But it had to wait, Miss Hannah followed protocol: Missions Boarding School

BE SILENT

Protocol, which stipulated respectful silence and discouragement of frivolity during meals.

As soon as she granted permission the two jumped up and cleared their plates, taking them to the kitchen. They could not wait any longer. "Miss Hannah, we need to ask you something."

"What's so urgent, Lukas?" she said.

Anthony stood right behind him, one head taller. Lukas swallowed and whispered, "Miss Hannah, was this hostel a leper colony in the beginning? Before it became a hostel for the schoolchildren?"

Her large body shook as she laughed. "A leper colony! Where on earth did you hear that? Absolute nonsense. Now run along, both of you."

They were not at all pacified by Miss Hannah's response, but Rianna was nowhere to be seen, which meant they would have to ask her on Monday. She had told them her mother was a nurse who worked in a leprosy hospital before they moved to the Eastern Province. If there was anyone who would know with certainty, it was Rianna.

7

Fort Jameson. January 1964.

A surprise awaited the Ferreira brothers on their first Friday afternoon in Madzi Moyo. At exactly 2 p.m. there was a single loud knock on the front door. It was Father. (He came alone, and indeed had arrived much earlier.) The lime green Opel with its white roof stood waiting on the same spot in the shade of a *mopani*; it was time to go home.

The boys counted the stubby milestones, which once had been white, as they sped along, leaving a marooning cloud of red dust behind. Only a few short weeks before, the family had move into the Mission Rest House at Fort Jameson. The Rest House was in the middle of town on an unsightly, tree-covered hill, (back then the hill felt like a real mountain.) The grounds were vast and the house enormous, a relic of the British colonial era. Because of the steep gradient a set of large concrete stairs, one story high, led to the front door and a veranda that stretched along the front and sides of the house.

BE SILENT

Their father parked at the back, next to the office outbuildings. Armed with a single suitcase each, the boys passed the three-foot-high brick dollhouse, an exact replica of the homestead (miniature replicas were popular in those years.) Next they passed the donkey, a forty-four-gallon drum built into a brick contraption that resembled an ass when viewed end on, underneath which a fire was stoked as backup for hot water when the gas heater ran out of fuel. Lukas smelled the fresh ashes—someone had recently stoked a fire in the donkey's interior. He quickened his pace. Between the donkey and the backdoor stood the old mango tree. He stood on tiptoes and plucked two mangoes, inhaling the nectared yellow skin with its pale black dots, then handed one, the smaller one, to Wouter.

Mphatso, the kitchen boy was the first to notice them. *"Moni Mbusa*! Hallo pastor, how are you?"

Father, Wouter and Lukas all laughed. "We are all well, Mphatso!"

The laughing and talking brought Mother and Suzanne to the kitchen. Mother asked Mphatso to prepare tea for everyone, and, with her arms around her sons, she bundled them deeper into the house.

Even though those old houses were grandiose in size and style when they were built, the missionaries who lived there many years later were generally as poor as church mice. This did not dissuade the local population of Chinyanjas, who were even poorer, from seeking employment with the missionaries, since work was scarce in the land as their traditional rural way of living was slowly eroding. It was therefore not uncommon for several servants to work in one missionary household.

29

Traditionally the Chinyanja men would come work at the homesteads of the *Mzungu,* the white people, while their womenfolk stayed home tending to their own children. A particular hierarchy was observed. Kitchen boy, or cooky, was the most coveted position; next in line was the house boy, responsible for the remainder of the house, and least desired was the position of *bwalo* boy (garden boy), responsible for everything outside the house, on the grounds. Over time it was possible to work oneself up from *bwalo* boy to kitchen boy.

Mphatso, having been with consecutive Rest House families, engaged in his duties with pride; he had earned his position, having started out as a young *bwalo* boy decades before. Within minutes of Maria's request, he rang the tiny bell: tea was ready in the dining room. The lounge, or sitting room, was reserved for guests or important occasions. Even though it was only midafternoon, the dining room was in semi-darkness, the fifteen-foot-wide veranda being responsible.

Mother wanted to know everything, every detail, about their first week. Suzanne was simply overjoyed to have her brothers back, and danced and bounced around them.

Lukas was not impressed with the new school. "Mother, you will not believe it, but the whole school is squeezed into a single classroom. As if that is not bad enough, we only have one teacher. How am I ever going to learn anything? I can't believe we left Ndola for this. Father, when can we go back to the Copperbelt?"

Mother and Father smiled at one another. Father laughed. "Sorry, Lukas, we won't be going back to Ndola. This is where we're going to live now. It will get better, every week."

BE SILENT

Lukas decided it would be wise not to tell Mother, or even Father, that they, the hostel dwellers, could be the carriers of a dreaded disease, as Rianna and Barbara had implied. First he would try and determine how much truth there was to the story. He pondered whether they would also then be banished outside the city gates of Madzi Moyo and Fort Jameson like the poor lepers in the Old Testament. No, he dared not tell his parents.

That first night back home was filled with dreams. Lukas and his family were sitting in an old shoe store surrounded by hundreds of stacks of shelves, all reaching the ceiling. The shelves were stacked with thousands of boxes, each filled with a pair of new shoes. Lukas loved the smell of new leather. He would open a box, inhale deeply and then try the shoes on, one pair after the other. The shop assistant, an old man, sat back, giving Lukas free range. Soon, though, Lukas was forced to go to smaller and smaller sizes, as his feet continued becoming smaller; he was losing a toe each time he took a shoe off, due to the progressing leprosy.

As the night progressed, so did his anxiety, and his leprosy; he was running out of toes. Each time he took a shoe off, yet another toe would be rolling around inside. There was no blood; leprosy doesn't cause bleeding. It was not painful either, only terrifying. Mother kept a cool head. She would bend over each time and scoop up the toe that fell out of the shoe, fold it neatly in her handkerchief and put it in her purse with the greatest care. Lukas would then grab the next smaller pair of shoes, and the whole process would be repeated. It is uncertain how much sleep he had that first night back home.

8

Madzi Moyo. Monday, January 20, 1964

The boarding house in Madzi Moyo did not have the services of a kitchen boy. Miss Hannah insisted on doing all the cooking herself, she wished to be mistress of both her castle and her kitchen.

There was a house boy, though, responsible for the rest of the hostel. Charles Chombe towered above the children, tall and reassuring. Not even his white tunic could conceal his muscled physique. He always had a laugh and a happy word for everyone. His dream was to one day become a teacher, once he completed his matriculation exams. He was hungry for knowledge and read everything he could lay his hands on. It was impossible to walk away from the man without a glow in one's chest: he made everyone feel important. That was what drew Lukas to him the day they met.

BE SILENT

Lukas noticed on Monday during lunch hour that the Chinyanja man had something on his mind. He was uncommonly quiet and keeping to himself. As soon as they had cleared the dishes, Lukas sought him out.

It had been Charles who had started teaching Lukas some Chinyanja words whenever there were a few minutes to spare. When they had met for the first time, weeks earlier, Lukas had asked him, "Why is your name Charles? That's not an African name."

Charles had laughed. "Long ago, my parents believed that Britain would be good to our country; they were happy when they learned about the Queen and everybody in England, so they gave me this name. Things have changed since I was born, but it's still my name."

That Monday, Lukas had a different question. "*Zikuyenda*, Charles? What's the matter? Something is wrong."

The tall man smiled. "The *Mthunzi* looks deep. There is nothing wrong, I am only thinking a great deal. There will be an election on Wednesday."

It must have been obvious that Lukas had no idea what he was talking about, for he continued, "The people in our country will choose a new leader. Every grown-up in the land gets one vote, one chance to chose between two men. There are two parties, the ANC and UNIP. The people are tired of the Queen ruling them from across the sea, and they are asking louder and louder for one of our own people to lead, an African leader."

"A black leader, Charles?"

He nodded.

"Is that why you are worried, Charles? That the people will choose the wrong man?"

Charles was always pleased by the boy's ability to fathom a situation. The English-speaking people from the North came with many promises and delivered on very few of them, taking more than they gave; his people's distrust was vast. The *Amissioni* were different, though. Many of them came from the South, and most of his people trusted them.

But the *Amissioni* were few. And some of his people did not distinguish between white people from the North and those from the South, claiming they were all the same. Take this boy, for instance. He was different. He was *Mthunzi*—one who could be a shadow. "Yes," he said. "That's exactly why we are hoping more people will choose Mr. Kaunda, Mr. Kenneth Kaunda."

"Why Mr. Kaunda?"

"Oh for many reasons! He is one of us. He was born near Chinsali, in the Northeastern Province, not so far from here. He was a teacher and headmaster before he became involved with the ANC and later UNIP. He is working hard to get our own people to govern ourselves, and not the Queen. But the most important reason is that he believes we can change the country's government to an African one without violence, without killing people, similar to what Mr. Gandhi taught in South Africa and India."

"Who is Mr. Gandhi?" Lukas asked.

"Was. He was a wise East Indian man who taught and showed that one could protest peacefully and change a country and its government, without making war, without bloodshed, without killing and murdering. Mr. Gandhi was assassinated in 1948 but

BE SILENT

Mr. Kaunda still visited India in 1957 to learn more about how he achieved those goals."

"But why would they kill a man of peace, Charles?"

Charles laughed. "That was not the first time in history a man of peace got killed. Not every one agreed with Gandhi's peaceful methods and teachings."

Lukas didn't think again about the election-fever until he noticed Charles and Mavuto in a heated discussion on the stairs of the hostel two days later. Both were excited. Mavuto, the garden boy, was responsible for both the hostel grounds and the school grounds. He was also a Chinyanja, but kept to himself. He was even stronger and taller than Charles, but never smiled. He looked to Lukas like a very unhappy man.

Lukas smiled and greeted the two men on his way to the front door, and Charles called out to him, "Did you hear about the elections, *mwana?*"

Lukas shook his head.

"He won! Kenneth David Kaunda is our new prime minister!" Charles had great difficulty containing himself. They had been waiting for the day for so long, another step toward their liberation from Britain and the Queen's rule.

Mavuto, equally excited, added with awe, "And he is only thirty-nine years old!"

Lukas could not recall any of the grown-ups he knew ever mentioning the January '64 elections or ever discussing the rapid growth of African nationalism. Not Miss Hannah, not Miss Visagie, neither Olga's father, Reverend Ulrich Wessels, nor his own father or mother—none of them, discussed the hopes and aspirations of the local people, the Chinyanjas, amongst whom they lived and worked.

Even though he could spell *nationalism*, it was several years before Lukas understood what *nationalism* meant and many years more before he became alarmed by how *nationalism* could be exploited. The grown-ups must have believed that the children were too young to understand, on top of not being aware of what was busy happening around them. Perhaps it was none of the white people's business; perhaps they were afraid to ask the local people to where it would all eventually lead.

Perhaps the people from the South were not so different from the people from the North after all. Why would you want to discuss such matters with a six- or ten- or thirteen-year-old anyway?

9

Madzi Moyo. February, 1964

It was always hot in summer. That January as the heat increased and the rains stayed away, the red earth turned to dust. By the time February arrived, the people of Madzi Moyo were talking about changing the town's name to Madzi Pangono: "place of little water."

The talk about "Madzi Pangono" was all Miss Visagie needed for her wear-a-hat-all-day-long campaign. She was adamant that every one of her students would wear a hat when outside, from ten in the morning until five in the afternoon, an hour before sunset. She was especially concerned for the children who had far to walk to the outskirts of Upper and Lower Madzi Moyo.

"I promised your parents that I would ensure that you wore your hats. Since it is often a hundred and ten degrees, even in the shade, it is so important to protect you all from getting sunstroke."

Rianna just rolled her eyes at Miss Visagie's instructions; she flatly refused to bother with a hat of any kind. She believed, and frequently voiced, that the sunstroke story was only an excuse for Miss Visagie to wear her vast collection of exotic broad-rimmed hats. Not being Rianna, meant that the other children had to follow the hat rule. But the early mornings, when they walked to school after breakfast, were often cool, making it simple enough to forget the head cover they would need in the scorching afternoon.

One such day was chiseled into Lukas's memory. It had been a cool February morning with no indication of the heat to come later. As always, Miss Visagie did her hat-check at the end of the school day, just before the children left the building. Rianna amazed everyone that afternoon, for she had a hat in hand. It is still a mystery whether the hat was actually her own. And there Lukas stood, the only one in the whole school without a head cover. Even little Wouter was ready with his hat. As the children filed through the front door Miss Visagie motioned Lukas to the library.

The airless little room had, over time, developed a secondary function: it had become a place for rebuke and confession. Today Lukas met a total stranger in the library, an unsmiling Miss Visagie.

"Lukas, where is your hat?"

"At the hostel, Miss." He started counting the shelves. There were eight, equally spaced, from top to bottom.

"Lukas, look at me! Why is it at the hostel?"

"I forgot it there, Miss."

The third wall had a window in it, that was never opened, which meant that several of the shelves were very short.

"Do you want to get sunstroke Lukas Ferreira?"

He wondered why he tolerated her treating him like a grade-one pupil. Perhaps Rianna was smarter than he had been giving her credit for, when she openly displayed her contempt of the ridiculous rules.

"No, Miss," he said. He started counting how many books were on each shelf.

"What am I going to tell your parents when you get an attack of sunstroke, Lukas?"

He had no idea what she would tell his father and mother. They would be devastated, his sister Suzanne even more so. He pulled up his shoulders.

"Do you realize that sunstroke can kill you?" Miss Visagie continued, raising her voice. "I am not making this up, young man—it is that serious!"

The room was small, making them stand close to each other. Lukas looked at his teacher. Her face was flushed: she believed every word she spoke. From the first day, he had thought she was pretty, their Miss Visagie. She was even prettier when her cheeks glowed from excitement or from being upset, like his mother. The aroma of flowers filled the musty library, swathing poor Lukas. She wore one of her clingy dresses, which she wore only on special days. Like the other day, when Olga's father had visited the school, Miss Visagie was all flushed and flustered. She had never stammered but then.

Lukas didn't have the slightest idea what sunstroke was, other than being something very deadly and bad, according to Miss. He tried hard to image the sun striking a person down, and how the flimsy little cloth hat would prevent that from happening. He wondered whether it was as deadly a disease as leprosy. It had to be very bad if Miss Visagie made such a big deal of it and you could get it from just being outside.

He wondered whether you would be protected against it if you were a Station kid, like Barbara and her sisters, instead of being a hostel dweller. For the briefest of moments he regretted being a hostel dweller. The most appalling thought, though, was that his family would be very upset, if he was to drop dead from sunstroke, just because he refused to wear a stupid hat. That would be really silly.

"I think I understand, Miss," he said. "I will remember my hat tomorrow."

"Run along then, Lukas. Remember to keep to the shady spots as you go up to the hostel!"

"Yes, Miss, I certainly will."

He took her admonitions literally, making a game of it, and jumped from shade to shade, crisscrossing the long path up the hill to the hostel. In several places the shadows were simply too far apart for him to reach directly from one to the next, even with his biggest jump; he was forced to dart through patches of sunlight until he eventually reached the safety of the large shade of the *mopani* where his father's Opel would park. His chest was burning and his heart pounding from the shadow jumping, and he dropped down on the stairs, faint-headed. The relief that the sun did not strike him down washed in waves over him; he started laughing. Silly Miss. Silly him.

For the remainder of Lukas's schooling in Madzi Moyo, the hat was never forgotten again. He would take it off only at the dining

BE SILENT

table, when getting into a bath or into bed or inside the school or church buildings. Lukas is convinced that if you look closely and feel with your fingers, even today you can find the slight ring, an indent, around his head, just above his ears, from wearing the stupid hat. After his one-on-one visit to the room of rebuke, he even briefly considered sowing the hat to his scalp.

That afternoon Lukas added a second item to his list:

1. Leprosy
2. Sunstroke.

10

Madzi Moyo. March 1964

As the weeks flowed, the children became accustomed to life on the Station and at the boarding school. It also became clear the single biggest obstacle that threatened their existence was Miss Hannah's fortnightly cabbage pie: *purple* cabbage pie.

Before Madzi Moyo, few of the children were familiar with purple cabbage. As far as Rianna was concerned, cabbage was a light green leafy vegetable, had a foul smell when cooked, was to be avoided if possible and should be consumed only when no other option was left and scurvy stared one hard in the face. Purple cabbage was therefore twice as intimidating. Rianna realized she must have led a very sheltered life.

Purple cabbage pie was Miss Hannah's new specialty, for the election year. It is still uncertain whether she served the cabbage pie as a special treat or as a strange punishment, payback for the trials and tribulations she endured looking after all the boarding-house children. In her defence though—she always added vast amounts of sugar and cinnamon to the pies. One particular evening, the portions of purple cabbage pie were especially large, and accompanied by only small servings of sausage and mashed potatoes. The children were famished, and barely allowed Miss Hannah to say grace before attacking the food on their plates, all but the cabbage pie.

Few of them could keep up with Rianna, though. She finished first, pushing her plate, with the generous helping of cabbage pie still on it, with some force to the middle of the table, hissing something under her breath that sounded like "*varkkos.*"

Miss Hannah jumped up from her seat at the head of the table. "Rianna! Did you just say pig food? What kind of example does that set for the little ones? Take your plate back immediately and finish your food!"

Rianna glared at the house mother and folded her arms on her chest without touching her plate. "I have finished my food. I am actually trying to protect the little ones."

Rianna wondered why she had ever had to leave Mother and Father Vermeulen in Katete. *They* would never have tried to feed their children purple cabbage pie—the cinnamon failed miserably to hide the foul smell. She was convinced the educators in the South, where she had to go next year, would also choose not to demean themselves by subjecting growing teenagers to questionable edible items.

"Rianna," Miss Hannah said, "you did not touch your cabbage pie."

"Purple cabbage is not food."

"Rianna, how dare you! I baked it specially."

"*Pers kool is nie menskos nie.*" Purple cabbage is not human food.

Miss Hannah's voice rose by several decibels. "Rianna Vermeulen!"

None of the other children moved. They dared not blink, nor breathe. Rianna and Miss Hannah had never locked horns to this extent. They glared at one another, Miss Hannah's eyebrows raised in surprise and Rianna's lowered in defiance.

"It's true," Rianna said. "At home we feed all the purple cabbage to the pigs. *They* seem to love it!"

Lukas couldn't help himself. He giggled and kicked Anthony in the shin.

Anthony snorted, and tried unsuccessfully, to drown his laughter in his hands. Miss Hannah's eyes fell on him and he began coughing. The younger children around the table seemed to take that as permission to start giggling.

"Lukas and Anthony," Miss Hannah said. "Stay out of it!" She gave each child a look that could drop a horse dead in its tracks. Silence returned to the table.

Miss Hannah's face had changed in hue when she turned back to Rianna. "I am not feeding you children pig food. I will phone the Station chairman *and* your father!" She marched around the table.

Rianna jumped up, knocking her chair over while yelling, "Please, go phone them both! I am sure Reverend Wessels will demand an explanation of why you feed us purple cabbage. What if the little ones become ill? And don't forget to ask my father why he feeds the purple cabbage only to the pigs!" Without asking for permission she gave a sob and stormed from of the room.

The purple cabbage pie remained on the menu fortnightly, but only in tiny portions, except on Rianna's plate. Whether Miss Hannah refused to acknowledge defeat or whether she believed that she could desensitize the children's emotional allergy to purple cabbage by feeding them small amounts of the hated substance over a prolonged period of time, was a fair question.

11

Fort Jameson. May 1964.

Every Friday afternoon Lukas and Wouter were picked up by their father and driven the twelve dusty miles back to Fort Jameson. The tree-covered hill appeared the moment they reached the outskirts of town, and it became a game to see who would spot the small red triangle of roof of the Rest House, where they lived, first. The abundance of mature trees made it impossible to see anything but the piece of roof. Not until the last moment, on the way up the winding gravel road, when the shrubbery suddenly fell away, would the house appear, its three wings towering above them.

It always caught Lukas by surprise, when they got out of the car on those Friday afternoons—the chanting of the *adhan*; the midafternoon hour call to prayer from the mosque. It remained a strange welcome back home, as if the chanter had been waiting for his arrival. Try as he might, peering down the hill to where the

BE SILENT

chanting came from, he could not even see the tip of the mosque's minaret. If he ran up the stairs toward the front door, he could at least see the tip of the bell tower of the Roman Catholic church and the steeple of the Presbyterian church. The three places of worship stood within a block of each other, in a neat triangle. The cathedral's bells would chime the hour around the clock—as if unperturbed by the calls from the minaret.

Away during the week at the boarding school, he would forget all about the muezzin's daily call: calling the faithful to pray, five times a day—at dawn, midday, mid afternoon, sunset and again two hours after sunset. Every day his parents had to listen to the chanting. Lukas knew his mother was inside the house this very moment and she would be pausing, as she did each time the adhan was heard, but, as she said, she would "pray to the God of the Bible."

It became tradition, once they had greeted his mother, that the three of them– Father, Wouter and Lukas—would go down to Youssef's shop. (The boys called him Joseph). They did not mind at all that it was only for ice cream on a stick. They usually gave Youssef fifteen minutes after the adhan's call to finish his prayers. They would take their time walking down the slippery gravel road. Once they reached the very bottom of the hill there were two streets to cross to reach the shop.

The moment Youssef saw them, he would smile and call out, "*Muli bwanji, Mbusa!*" Good afternoon, Pastor!

They always waved in return and called back. "Hallo, Joseph!"

"I see you brought the boys for their treat, *Mbusa*. Just a moment—let me finish up here then we can go through to the back."

Lukas always relished in the kaleidoscope of fragrances that twirled around them as they waited—mysterious, intoxicating and soothing. He was convinced that Youssef was of East Indian heritage, but Wouter insisted that he had to be from Arabia. He dressed in a long white knee-length tunic made of thin cheesecloth, with matching pants. On his feet he wore brown leather sandals.

Youssef's house was at the back of the large square building; a spacious courtyard and a garden stood right in its center, and the shop was out front. Youssef, Father, Wouter and Lukas would leave out the shop's back door and walk through the garden to the house, where the ice cream freezer was kept. A sliding door opened onto the dimly lit room. Youssef carefully opened it and then gently closed it behind them again, before leading them into the room. The freezer must have been in the family for decades; the faded white letters spelling *Coca-Cola* were barely legible on its red sides.

Wouter stopped two short steps of the freezer, holding his breath, waiting for Youssef to grab the handle of the sliding lid. There was always a moment of hesitation before the lid gave way, allowing a cold mist to escape from its inside, twirling upward like burnt incense—filling the room with the stale odor of well-preserved ice, as if it had been frozen from the dawn of time. The moment of decision had arrived. Youssef had little trouble reading the boy's mind—he played along.

"What will it be today, Mister Wouter?"

There were four choices: chocolate on a stick, vanilla on a stick, strawberry on a stick and banana on a stick. Wouter's routine was to alternate flavors each week; it was banana flavor's turn.

BE SILENT

"Excellent choice, Mister Wouter," Youssef said as he placed the chilled ice cream in his hand.

Lukas and his father accepted their usual treat: chocolate on a stick. They never varied their choice, week after week. They remained spellbound as Youssef pushed the heavy lid back, cutting off the white plume of cold air; it disappeared as if sucked into the hollow stomach of the red freezer machine.

"Let's go back to the shop," Youssef said. "You can pay me over there."

They followed Youssef through the garden, which was surrounded on all four sides with pillars and open hallways with arches, like an ancient Roman mansion. Bougainvillea creepers covered the pillars, following the arches.

Exactly in the middle of the garden was a stone fountain, twelve feet in diameter, and almost twelve feet high, with water that sprayed in a perfect three-hundred-and-sixty- degree arch from the central figurine's crown. The smiling maiden also poured water from a narrow pitcher held on her hip; the water tumbled down below into a deep circular pool. Lukas paused and watched. He closed his eyes and listened—the water was now falling hundreds of feet to below, into an iridescent pool, complete, with no bottom. He startled himself and looked closer: the stone figure pouring the water, he discovered, had no clothes on, and was about as old as Rianna. For a moment he forgot about the ice cream.

"Lukas!" His father made him jump and he quickly rejoined the group. He looked back at the stone figure; she was still smiling at him. He was certain, however, that she had blinked.

By the time they were halfway back up the winding gravel road, most of the ice cream was gone. What was left ran down their hands, which only made them lick faster—their sisters were not supposed to know about the ice cream: this was their little secret.

12

Fort Jameson. May 1964.

Saturday morning saw the six of them heading down the hill in the Opel to Kapoor's Bazaar. The general store was located on Main Street, in the town center, right in the middle of the triangle formed by the church, the cathedral and the mosque.

Suzanne went on her father's hip, Wouter carried Cecilia and Lukas would help his mother push the ramshackle shopping cart through the store. They had to move fast—Cecilia could be amused for only so long before she would start whining. Their mother didn't believe she was old enough to be left at home with the brothers, which suited them just fine: they wouldn't miss an opportunity like that.

The moment Lukas entered the store, even before it was possible to find a shopping cart, the aroma of incense, spices, curry powders and all things secret and sugary engulfed him. It lured him in (as it did all visitors), as if hooking him in on a fishing line, pulling him in with invisible hands, the line taught, the hook not giving. On both sides of the aisle, as far as he could see, high up against the walls, tucked in behind two long wooden counters with glass tops, sloping shelf after sloping shelf was filled with flat rolls of fabric, in out-of-the-world designs and patterns and colors. Lukas paused to take it all in and breathed deep.

"Lukas," his mother said, "*take* the cart and keep going, please—we need to get to the food section." He grabbed the cart and his mother took the necessary items from the shelves or had them weighed and measured. Their boisterous group inched forward as his father, Wouter and the two girls circled around them.

As they headed toward the exit of Kapoor's Bazaar with their purchase, the sound of shouting, loud and vicious, came from outside. Lukas repositioned his hand under the paper bag of groceries and walked through the door. The angry shouting intensified. A crowd milled around, gathering down the street.

Father, Lukas and Wouter were craning their necks to see what the commotion was all about, when their mother called out, "Louis, the children. Get the girls into the car. Wouter, Lukas, now!"

The boys packed the groceries into the trunk fast, while their dad scrambled to help Suzanne, Cecilia and their mother into the car. Lukas slammed the trunk close and looked up the street. Two groups of Africans were facing off against each other, each side trying to shout the other side into submission.

The smaller group was holding placards, banners and sticks, and chanting, "Lumpa! Lumpa! We serve God, not the government! Sioni! Sioni! We will school our own children! Lumpa, Lumpa!"

The larger and more aggressive group chanted, even louder, "UNIP! Independence for all of Zambia! U-N-I-P! Support

UNIP! Respect the government! Away with the traitors!" "Serve your country," read some placards. Some of the protesters even carried spears.

The groups surged toward one another, just one block away from the Ferreiras' car, and ran into one another like waves, the placards and banners becoming battering rams. Spears and knives were pulled out. People were falling and being trampled upon; some bled from fresh wounds. The shouting turned into cries of terror.

From within the car, Lukas's mother cried again. "Louis, get the boys into the car!" The panic in her voice was unmistakable. As Father bundled Lukas and his bother into the back of the Opel, two police vehicles arrived, sirens blaring, driving straight into the melee. Policemen burst out and stormed into the mob, firing warning shots into the air, commanding order.

"*Gwirani!* Stop! Stop the fighting you idiots!" Several more shots into the air followed before a degree of calm returned.

Maria touched her husband's arm. "Louis, please take us home." He backed up cautiously, avoiding the still simmering mob and took a quieter street back to the Rest House on the hill.

Lukas peered through the rear window to where the police officers continued to push the two factions apart, yelling their orders in Chinyanja, applying their batons. Another warning shot hit the air.

13

Fort Jameson. May 1964.

Two hours later there was an urgent knock on the front door of the Fort Jameson Mission Rest House. Lukas followed Nixon, the house boy, whose job it was to answer the door.

It was an East Indian man, in uniform. "Good afternoon. I'm Sergeant Rangarajan, from the police station. Is the *mbusa* in?"

Nixon looked at Lukas. "*Mthunzi*, your father, please?"

Lukas ran off to call his father. He was in the office outbuilding, fiddling with the Mission's small printing press. Lukas paused for a moment inside the door—he found the penetrating smell of printer's ink reassuring—an association with home, with Father. Then he spun around and ran after the disappearing figure of his father.

Louis Ferreira took the police officer through to the formal sitting room at the front of the house. Lukas became part of the shadows and slipped out onto the veranda, inching closer to an open window.

BE SILENT

"What happened this morning in town, Sergeant?" his father asked. "I thought we were hundreds of kilometers away from Chinsali?"

"*Mbusa*, we were equally surprised. We did not anticipate that the Lumpa Church people would bother with a demonstration so far from their safe villages in the North."

"How did UNIP manage to get such a big crowd together to take on Alice Lenshina's followers, Sergeant? Did they know about the visit? That would mean there must be a third party that wanted them to clash. How many were injured?"

Sergeant Rangarajan laughed, holding up a hand. "Too many questions, *Mbusa*! The local UNIP leadership seems to be quite embarrassed by the fighting. The instruction from the national government is clear: *no violence*."

"That's what they preach to their followers," Louis said. "That's the theory, Sergeant—we know. But we were there. We saw."

"So I understand. The UNIP people claim the Lumpa people attacked first and that the UNIP supporters only retaliated. No one was killed, but I'm not allowed to tell you how many were injured."

"Are we under surveillance?"

Sergeant Rangarajan laughed again, "*Mbusa?*"

"Whose side are you on, Sergeant? UNIP's?"

"*Mbusa*, I'm not here to take sides, but guard the peace—maintain law and order."

Lukas melted deeper into the shadows. He was not sure he understood the policeman. The six of them had all seen what happened. He could tell his father also had his doubts when he asked, "What *is* the reason for your visit?"

55

The Sergeant grinned, "You are a direct man, *Mbusa*. As station commander here in Fort Jameson, I just wanted to make sure you and the missus are aware of the political turbulence here in the northeastern part of the country, which today has shown its ugly side. We're asking everybody to keep their eyes open and avoid unnecessary travel, especially at night or alone."

"We are quite aware of the situation. Are you placing us under house arrest?"

"Don't be ridiculous, *Mbusa*! This is the recommendation to *all* the residents in town."

"Are the white people in danger?"

Lukas wasn't sure he liked the policeman's laugh. "You are direct, sir! We're informing everybody. I did not expect trouble so far south, but this is reality. There is a restlessness in the land; everyone—well, apparently not everyone is yearning for independence from England. That will probably happen later this year. In the meantime…" He stood up.

"Oh, one more thing," he added. " Your staff—the cooky, house boy and garden boy—can you trust them?"

Father also stood. "I thought you weren't here to take sides? Yes, I trust them."

"How well do you know them, *Mbusa*? Do you know where their sympathies lie? You've only been here six months—"

"They are all Chinyanja and all sworn African Nationalists. Is there anything else, Sergeant?"

"Actually there is, *Mbusa*. Please let me know at the station if anyone of you, including your staff, has to leave town and if you notice anything suspicious. *Anything.*"

BE SILENT

As his father and the policeman were leaving the sitting room Lukas slipped around the corner, down the veranda's eastern steps and around to the back of the house. He would ask Mphatso about the sergeant's unsaid words; it might be wiser not to bother Mother or Father with such questions.

―――

Rahul Rangarajan sat behind the wheel; he did not turn the key in the ignition. In spite of having both side windows open the Land Rover remained boiling-hot—the idle wind was hesitant to bring reprieve. It carried the heady mix of pineapple, banana and mango from the small plantations on the far side of the Rest House—on such sweltering days he found the aroma overbearing. He looked back at the stairs leading up to the Rest House, which towered above him. It was past its glory days. He thought about the *mbus*a he had just spoken to, living in the house with his young family, and the local people working in the house. *Mbusa Ferreira arrived here not so long ago from the Copperbelt. He thinks he knows the local people, the Chinyanjas, but he's in for a surprise, an awakening.*

He, Rahul, had lived in this country for most of his life. He had been a little boy of three when his parents left India. He spoke Chinyanja much better than his mother's tongue, Hindi, and also better than the English he had learned in school. And yet, he still did not understand the soul of the African, of the *Chichewa*. Then again, he had trouble understanding his *own* soul.

He had sympathy for and understood the quest for independence and the African nationalists' aspirations. India had suffered similar injustices under the Royal Crown. Oh, his country had developed and been dragged out of the dark ages, but at a price: the soul of his people. Some of his own people, the fortunate ones, became powerful and affluent, but the majority was still in poverty and hopelessness, from which there was little chance of escape.

Perhaps the new African Nationalists would be able to deliver on their promises to offer a better dispensation to the locals than the Queen. He had his reservations given all the political rhetoric and vote-buying schemes he has seen in his life—empty promises as often as not. In the end, one tyranny simply replaced its predecessor, often under the cloak of democracy.

Then there were today's events, the clash between the Lumpa Church members and the UNIP supporters: brothers fighting brothers, brothers by birth.

Only a few days earlier, he had shared his concerns about a potential conflict here in the Northeastern Province with the commissioner of police. The commissioner, Mr. Deepak Subramanium, also East Indian, a large, unhealthy man, brushed them off with a snort. "Rahul, its your imagination! Perhaps you should cut back on all that curry, hey?" The commissioner's enormous stomach shook as he waddled off, laughing.

14

Fort Jameson. May 1964.

Mphatso was in front of the stove, preparing the evening meal. It didn't take him long to realize there was something bothering Lukas, who followed him around the room. Lukas was particularly interested in a pot Mphatso had simmering in the back. Inside it was *nshima* (the odor was unmistakable)—the Chinyanja's traditional staple diet: maize porridge. If he played his cards well, Mphatso would let him have some—Mother and Miss Hannah were inclined to rather feed them oats porridge in the mornings at home and at the hostel.

Mphatso was chopping carrots and paused with the big knife in midair to look at Lukas. "*Mwana, ma ku funa chiyani?*" he said—Boy, what do you want? He put the knife down and smiled when he didn't receive an answer immediately. "I see the *mwana* has a big question."

Lukas leaned against the wall next to the wood-burning stove. He blinked and swallowed. "This morning in town—we saw the fighting between those people. And the policeman who was here to speak to my father?" He blushed. "I heard what they were saying."

Mphatso was still smiling, "Ah, *Mthunzi*. I have noticed the *mwana* is like a shadow in the house, the shadow that listens. I'm almost done getting everything on the stove for this evening, then we can go out to the old mango tree and talk."

Lukas wandered outside and sized up the mango tree; it was about twenty paces from the small porch at the back of the house, not far from the dollhouse. He tried to climb the tree several times but could not get a grip with his sandaled feet on the V-shaped trunk, and kept sliding down. As the year had progressed, it had become habit to wear sandals outside, and they weren't helping. The tree towered sixty feet above him, its clusters of long, glossy leaves touching the kitchen's galvanized iron roof. The firm leaves gave him the goose bumps at night when the wind scraped them against the metal.

Lukas was so deep in thought, disappointed with himself, that he didn't notice the tall kitchen boy coming up behind him, until he spoke.

"*Mwana?*"

Lukas jumped, coughing in embarrassment.

"Mphatso ..." he said. "The policeman—why did he come and speak to father?"

Mphatso laughed. "You were the one hiding and listening, *mwana*! You tell me. What did they say?"

Lukas told him everything he could recall from the conversation as well as the one he had with Charles on Madzi Moyo. "Who is Unep ... Unip and the Loempa people, Mphatso?"

BE SILENT

"UNIP? That is the United National Independence Party. Mister Lukas, these things are for grown-ups, for adults—you should not worry too much about them. You are only in the primary school. You learn many new things about life and the world every day. There will come a time when you will have to learn about politics, but not yet."

"And the policeman?" Lukas insisted.

"The policeman came because of the fighting this morning in town. Nixon told me about it. It is strange that the Lumpa people came to Fort Jameson, because they live in villages in the North, far from here. They feel that obedience to their church is more important than following the rules of the government in Lusaka."

"Will there be a war with the Lumpa people, Mphatso?"

"No. But I'm convinced the sergeant thought that one of us knew why the fighting broke out, that we sympathized with one of the sides, perhaps with the Lumpa people."

"*Do* you?" Lukas didn't blink.

"We all want independence for our country, but we don't want fighting—not with England and not with our brothers. Run along, Mister Lukas, run along. I'm sure the *amayi* is looking for you. I have to get back to the kitchen."

Lukas remained behind under the mango tree—there was a great deal to think about now. He was certain his mother was not looking for him.

15

Madzi Moyo. July 1964.

Little encouragement was required at the end of each school day for the children to grab their hats and journey uphill to where lunch was waiting. They were barely past the tire-swing in front of the school one day, when Anthony turned to his friend and said, "Do you hear that, Lukas?"

Both boys turned around quickly and ran toward the sound, past the school, past the dilapidated tennis court where figures now appeared, running in the distance, obscured by the underbrush. As the boys got closer, they could hear the Chinyanja men yelling, urging their dogs on. Wouter and his friends now caught up with Lukas and Anthony, insisting that they didn't want to miss any of the excitement, and refusing to turn around on Lukas's instruction and return to the hostel. The boys still had no idea what was going on, but that did not matter: what did matter was to catch up with the men and become part of the commotion. Lukas grabbed hold of his little backpack straps and only ran faster, but Anthony remained half a pace ahead of him.

When Lukas turned around to take a breath, he could barely make out the school building far behind them. Wouter, Sarel and Adam were falling behind. Lukas was surprised to see the timid little Adam still with them. The little boy always disappeared back home as soon as he could escape the classroom. He was like a little broken-winged sparrow, and Rianna had, from the first day, taken him under her personal protection. She had made sure every child and adult in Madzi Moyo was aware of it, too. Perhaps that was why Wouter and Sarel allowed him to tag along, their fear of Rianna's wrath was greater than their reluctance to let the boy join them.

Lukas and Anthony followed the men and the dogs along the course of a creek, shadowed on both sides by scores of sausage trees with very little foliage. Suddenly Anthony stopped.

"Come on Anthony," Lukas said. "Let's catch up and find out what they're after!"

"What about Miss Hannah? She is going to be very mad if we're late."

"Never mind Miss Hannah—we're not the only ones who'll be in trouble. Run faster!"

By then they could hear the excited voices quite clearly: "*Khoswe! Khoswe wamkula!*" Rats! Big fat cane rats!

A group of men armed with long, sturdy sticks and dogs had surrounded one of the trees. There was something in the middle of the tree. It looked to Lukas more like a strange cat than a rat. The men's leader jumped forward, hitting viciously at the creature in the tree and yelling, *'Khoswe wamkula!'* The words send shivers down Lukas's spine.

The boys crept closer, close enough to see that it was definitely not a cat but a large rat, which craftily sidestepped the hunter hitting with his stick and literally jumped across the small clearing into the next tree, then the next. The excited entourage followed, shouting and yelling, their dogs barking. Five trees further down, a second group of men with dogs yelled victoriously. One man held up an unfortunate rodent by its tail. They had killed the first rat of the day.

The two boys split up to join the two men's teams. Lukas glanced back. Wouter, Sarel and Adam were nowhere to be seen. They must have turned around on Adam's account, he figured. Seconds later, Anthony's voice rose above the din: "They've killed a second one!"

One of the hunters in Lukas's group who looked like Mavuto, the hostel's garden boy, also held his first rat of the day up high for everyone to see.

A young Chinyanja man was now tasked to stay behind and keep an eye on the dead rats, to make sure that stray dogs didn't help themselves prematurely to the catch. After half an hour of running around following the men, the two boys were running out of steam. The fleeing rats constantly changed direction among the trees in an attempt to outmaneuver their pursuers; the men and dogs left the boys behind several times as they chased the lithe animals up and down the trees along the small river.

The next moment the hunting party took off, this time right across the creek, following the rats. Anthony came to a decision: "Let's stay behind and help this man keep an eye on the dead river beasts, instead of running like fools along with the rat-catchers!"

BE SILENT

It was much easier to keep up a running commentary on the chase from under the tree. "Number four coming. Oh, and number five!' Anthony ran ahead to meet the proud hunter, who carried the two rats by their tails and threw them nonchalantly onto the grass next to the other bodies. One rolled in Lukas's direction, causing him to jump backwards. Anthony laughed. "They're dead, my friend—they can't bite you anymore!"

Even though his lips trembled, Lukas hissed back, "I know that very well, Mr. Buffalo Hunter!"

Anthony just laughed again and joined them under the tree.

Armed with a long stick each, the boys carefully approached the five motionless bodies. It was a daunting task to try and roll one of the creatures onto its back with a four- foot-long stick, without getting too close—not that they were scared, but one had to be careful. Their putrid odor didn't make matters easier—dried blood and spilled guts mixed with a sewage existence, simmering together in the African heat.

The Chinyanja man, meanwhile, sat in the shade of the *mopani*, watching them with a bored grin—he wasn't planning on moving a finger.

"What do you think the rats eat?" Anthony said.

"Probably little mice?" Lukas volunteered. "They're the same size as a young cat."

Anthony grinned. "I'm not so sure they eat meat, but my father would try to convince us that twenty of these ones could kill a lion if they found him alone!"

"A lion?" Lukas said.

"Yes. If ten hyenas can kill a lion, I think twenty of these brutes can kill a lion. Well, maybe an old, sickly lion."

Carefully, they rolled the rat away from its former compatriots, making it possible to measure its total length, from nose to tail tip. Anthony did the stepping down, right alongside the carcass, counting as far as he paced: "One, two, three ... four."

He halted and looked at Lukas. "The rat is four, big size-five sandals long." He laughed and stepped away, "You want to feel how heavy the rat is, Lukas?"

"Not really," Lukas said. He had always thought of himself as an ordinary boy—one who wasn't easily scared, especially of stupid rats. But *these* creatures were no ordinary rats.

"I dare you!" Anthony said.

"What do I pick it up with?"

"Come on, Lukas! With your hand of course! Take it by its tail like the men do."

"Why don't *you* pick it up then?"

"I stepped its length." Which was true enough, but Lukas still felt he was being taken advantage of.

He was, however, willing to negotiate. "What if it has a deadly disease?" he said.

"Do you think these men would eat these rats if they had deadly diseases?"

Lukas found it inconceivable that someone could want to eat a rat, especially rats the size of a cat. "I thought they just killed them because they are pests?"

"Pick up the rat," Anthony insisted.

Lukas wasn't ready to do that: he would have to buy time. "Why would they want to eat them?"

"Because the rats have a lot of meat on them."

BE SILENT

Rat meat. Lukas shuddered.

"My father says many of the people here are quite poor," Anthony explained, "and it is a way out for them. Protein is protein, he says. Come on, pick up the rat!"

Lukas had always thought *his* family was poor, but they never had to eat rat meat. Perhaps they were not so poor after all. He looked hopefully at the young man sitting in the shade. He was obviously enjoying the situation: there would be no offer of an escape route from there.

He stepped closer to the rat, his hand outstretched. "We are certain that it is completely dead?" He looked at Anthony and the African; both nodded.

"Lukas," Anthony said, "you've been here the whole time. It's been dead for half an hour!"

Lukas touched the tail. It was scaly and almost as long as the rat's body, and it felt like a gecko he'd once held—cool and clammy. Almost like touching a frog. It was impossible not to inhale the fetor of the dead animal, soaking wet from crossing the creek several times and then covered with its own matted blood. Another shiver ran through him. He began to lift it. The beast was heavy; he had to step closer and support his outstretched arm with his free hand, and he lifted the bloodied corpse high enough for the other two to see. The stench was overwhelming.

A faint squeak escaped the rat's throat and the head turned in Lukas's direction.

The squeak that escaped his own throat was all but faint: it made the rat-hunters across the river turn to face them. Lukas dropped the rat and a moment later was standing under the tree behind the young Chinyanja man, who had jumped up. The rat squeaked again.

"Hit the *wamkula* rat!" Lukas yelled. "Hit him over the head! Hit him until he's dead!"

The youth needed no second invitation. His heavy stick came down over and over on the not-so-dead-yet rat. Anthony by then had joined Lukas at his safe distance away under the *mopani*. Lukas elbowed him hard in the ribs. "Dead for half an hour."

Fifteen minutes later, the men returned carrying six more rats and satisfied looks. It was time to go home and cook the evening meal. Everyone chattered and laughed as they scooped up the rest of the kill. Mavuto was one of those bending over, grabbing one of the rats by the tail, holding it high. He called out, "Hey Mapopa, what did you do to this poor rat? I heard you guys yelling and saw you hitting something."

Everyone gathered around Mavuto who was holding the well-clobbered rat. The men were laughing. Mapopa—the young man who has come to Lukas's aid when the rat had squeaked—stuttered, embarrassed, "The rat wasn't quite dead, so I hit it again."

Mavuto laughed. "You beat the head into a bloody pulp! Sorry, you'll have to take this one," he said and threw the rodent into the wild grass at Mapopa's feet.

Mapopa reluctantly handed the rat he'd previously chosen to Mavuto and picked up the now very dead, flat-headed rat, mumbling, "I had to kill him because you guys only knocked him unconscious." The men laughed even louder and patted Mapopa on the back.

Lukas and Anthony followed slowly at the back of the triumphant hunting party, the hostel and Miss Hannah still belonging to a different world. There was so much to digest. It was Anthony who noticed the wooden shed—it was easy to overlook if you were in a hurry. The shed was tucked in amongst the trees, with creepers and a bougainvillea covering most of its old structure. The boys were gradually falling behind the men and dogs, who kept up a brisk pace, and that only made the shed so much more interesting.

The shed had a heavy door at the front, with a rock rolled against it. Little remained of the original path; grass grew over most of it. Lukas followed Anthony along the narrow channel in the path where several feet had recently flattened the tall grass—the pungent smell of moss, rotting trees, leaves and wild mushroom inundated them.

Lukas stopped Anthony when he stooped to roll the rock away: Miss Hannah, he suddenly remembered, was waiting for them. "Anthony! I can barely see the men. Let go of the rock. We can come back tomorrow after school. We'd better run if we don't want Miss Hannah to kill us. Come!"

He didn't wait: he turned around, took hold of his backpack and ran. Anthony kept up with him as they started gaining on the men. When they reached the tennis court, the men had just disappeared around the school. The boys ran up the hill to the hostel and took the stairs to the front door together, ready to face the housemother.

Miss Hannah was waiting in the formal sitting room. It was impossible to slip past to their rooms without her seeing them. "Boys! In here!"

The boys slouched into the room, still catching their breath.
"Anthony and Lukas! Do you have any idea what time it is?"
"No, Miss Hannah." Which was the honest truth.
"Allow me to tell you. It is almost *five* o'clock. I was on my way to the Station chairman to report you all as missing. I have already informed Miss Visagie. Did you tell anybody where you were going?"

It always amazed Lukas how adults asked questions they already knew the answer to. "We did not, Miss Hannah," he said.

"And Lukas—you brought the two little ones with you, although I heard even little Adam got dragged along. The two of you should have known better!' It behooved Lukas and Anthony both to drop their gaze and play We-are-innocent-ten-year-olds-who-didn't-mean-to lead-the-little-ones-astray-please-forgive-us.

Miss Hannah was not allowed to spank them, but there were other ways of dealing with troublemakers. They had to forfeit their late lunch and walk over to Reverend Wessels' house to explain themselves.

As the boys turned around to leave, she called them back, and sniffed them over, pulling up her nose. "What *is* that disgusting smell? Where *exactly* have you two been?"

They told her about the cane-rat hunt until she held up her arms and shoed them out. "Oh, just go. Go tell Mr. Wessels. *Then*, come back, and take a bath!"

Olga Wessels and her family lived at the far end of Upper Madzi Moyo. Outside the house, in the shade of a *mopani*, stood Olga's father's old motorcycle, which he used to get around on the Station. As chairman, he had many responsibilities and, though it was possible to walk everywhere, the Station was six miles wide.

BE SILENT

It was almost six by the time they returned to the hostel. At least they hadn't had to face little Olga or her irritating sister, Barbara. Olga's father explained to them that the adults were so concerned because of what had happened in Fort Jameson a few weeks earlier when the Lumpa and UNIP supporters had clashed. "Things are changing in the country. It is safe here on the Station, but we need to know where you boys go. You cannot simply disappear. Do I make myself clear? I am ultimately responsible to your parents for your well-being."

That supper the two ten-year-olds each received a double helping of Miss Hannah's famous purple cabbage pie, and Miss Hannah kept a hawk's eye on them until they'd eaten the last crumb.

Rianna furrowed her brow—something had happened right under her nose.

16

Madzi Moyo. July 1964.

"I don't want to end up at the Chairman's house again, Lukas." It was early the next afternoon, and Anthony and Lukas were standing outside the school.

"Anthony, we won't. We'll go for lunch at the hostel first. That way Miss Hannah won't become suspicious. Then we can run down to the shed, have a look and come straight back. No one will miss us. No one will even know."

It was a solid plan. They made sure to be on time for lunch and quietly ate everything Miss Hannah dished up. Lukas was aware throughout the meal of Rianna's constant stare. He was certain she had noticed they were finishing everything on their plates, as they did the previous evening. He did his best to ignore her.

No sooner had Miss Hannah dismissed the two boys than they left the hostel, trying to be unobtrusive. They lingered at the crossroads to Upper and Lower Madzi Moyo. They were in no need of curious bystanders and once they reached the school they paused again, then walked slowly around the building, just to make sure. Then it was off to the hidden shed. It felt much farther than the day before, perhaps because they didn't run. Again they walked single file down the grass footpath to the door. The rock still blocked the door. They carefully looked around.

Lukas bent down to roll the rock aside but barely managed to move it an inch. Together, the boys wiggled and rocked the stone away from the door. To Lukas's surprise, the heavy door didn't make a squeak when they opened it inch by inch. He was so eager to see what was inside, but equally terrified of what they might come across. The interior was dark. Only a sliver of light came from a narrow window at the far back of the single room. The boys remained in the door entrance for several minutes. As Lukas recounted afterwards, "You have to let your eyes get used to the dark."

His first reaction once they stepped inside was disappointment. He had expected it to smell like old forest—moldy and stuffy with a telltale of rot—but not that there was nothing worthwhile inside. Nothing but a few empty crates in one corner and some firewood stacked neatly in another. Only after their eyes grew accustomed to the darkness did they notice two flat wooden containers at their feet.

Anthony crouched down and opened the lid of the top one. "Lukas," he said, "where's that backpack of yours? Did you bring the flashlight?"

Lukas swung the pack off his shoulders, fiddled inside and extracted the flashlight. The beam fell on something he had only seen in pictures. This one was different though. It had to be brand new—the woodwork was all polished and shiny; the roaming light reflected off the glistening black metal.

Anthony whistled. "It's a machine gun!"

Lukas stretched to touch the rifle, but Anthony called out softly, "Don't touch it!"

Lukas jerked his hand back. "Why not?"

"You may leave fingerprints!"

"Who's going to see my fingerprints? You're making stuff up Anthony. That's what you get from reading all those silly detective stories."

Anthony wasn't giving up. "Their owner might see our prints on the rifles for all we know. Let's not disturb *anything*."

Lukas carefully closed the lid. "That is no hunting rifle, Anthony. I've seen my dad's, the one he used to kill kudu with."

"I *told* you it's a machine gun," Anthony reminded him. "It's not for hunting; this kind is used by soldiers, I think. But who would have put it in this shed? Let's get out of here," he pleaded.

Lukas kneeled back down. "Help me move the top box, Anthony."

"Lukas, we should leave!" Anthony's whisper had become louder.

Lukas shook his head. "We'll leave in a moment, but we need to know what's in the bottom one. Please, help."

Together they pulled the top box down and opened the lid of the bottom container; it produced an identical brand-new automatic rifle. Much more effort was needed to get the two boxes on top of one another again in exactly the same position they had found them.

Lukas suddenly felt less brave. "There are no soldiers on the Station, Anthony. Someone must be hiding the rifles here. They look brand-new. Shall we tell my father?"

"It is only Tuesday—you won't see him until the weekend. What about Mr. Wessels?"

"The Station chairman?" Anthony had to be kidding, Lukas thought. "Then we'll be in deep trouble again. He told us not to wander off on our own, not without telling an adult where we went. No, Mr. Wessels will kill us." Lukas said.

"What about Miss Visagie?" Anthony ventured.

"No, she's only the school teacher—she won't know anything about rifles."

A twig snapped outside. The boys froze. Even the cicadas went quiet for a moment. Lukas turned the flashlight off and wondered what possessed them to have come there in the first place.

"Perhaps it's the owner of the guns," Lukas whispered.

They remained motionless for a good three minutes.

"It must have been a cane rat or something," Anthony finally offered.

They stepped outside and closed the door, taking great care not to make a sound, glancing furtively around. The crickets, cicadas and wood doves had resumed their background symphony—nothing was the matter.

Lukas volunteered, "Can we then at least tell Charles, the house boy?"

"What if *he* was the one who stored the machine guns here in the first place?"

"I don't think Charles would do that," Lukas said. "He's my friend. He's a gentle man."

Anthony snorted. "How would you know? Just because he taught you a few Chinyanja words doesn't mean he might not have secrets!"

Lukas looked at his friend in utter amazement; *he was jealous*! Jealous of his friendship with Charles. That was so ... how would Rianna have put it: *so stupid*!

The rock was much harder to roll back in place. It suddenly gave way, rolled over and struck the door with a clang, making both of them jump backwards. The noise was probably heard on the other side of the Station thought Lukas. They glanced around again.

"We had better go back, before Miss Hannah notices we're gone," Lukas whispered. "Come on, Anthony, let's run!"

They only stopped to catch their breath after they reached the school. But as they rounded the building, Rianna suddenly stepped in front of them, arms folded across her chest. She was also breathing fast as if she had just run a long way. She was not smiling. The boys retreated several feet.

"What do you want?" Lukas wheezed.

"I know your little secret, boys." She stepped closer.

They stood their ground. "What secret?" Lukas asked.

"Don't play dumb with me, Lukas Ferreira. I saw the two of you at the shed. Do you realize everyone on the Station heard it when you guys rolled that rock into the door? What were you thinking?"

Lukas glanced at Anthony. "Well, it was very heavy, and we're not telling you. Anyway, it's none of your business!"

Rianna had caught her breath and now stepped even closer. Lukas had never stood so close to an older female, except his

BE SILENT

mother and grandmother. He could see every freckle on her nose. Her mop of red hair almost touched his head. He could tell she used an avocado-scented shampoo.

"Then I will tell Miss Hannah as well as Mr. Wessels," Rianna hissed. "You know what will *then* happen to the two of you."

With that she spun around and started walking fast up the hill toward the hostel, swinging her arms. Anthony looked at Lukas with big eyes. Only years later did Lukas fully grasp the meaning of blackmailing, but he knew now Rianna had them in a corner; she had *power* over them. They ran after her. They had to come to an agreement before she reached the hostel.

"Please, Rianna!" Lukas pleaded, jogging alongside her.

She stopped. "Please, *what*?"

"You can't tell Miss Hannah or Reverend Wessels."

"I sure can, unless you tell me what you saw in the shed, or better still, *show* me."

"There was *nothing* inside, except some empty crates and some firewood."

Rianna stooped down until her nose was six inches from his. Lukas could now smell her breath; it smelled of almonds. It was nice. But he couldn't avoid her eyes, dark pools that burned with intensity. "Then why, boys," she said. "did it take you almost *twenty minutes* to look at that nothing? And why did you use your flashlight for so long? I don't believe you. You *saw* something."

She turned around and started walking even faster. They were already at the crossroads, close to the hostel. Time was running out, and they had to tell somebody about the guns, Lukas realized. Perhaps Rianna would know what to do.

"Rianna, *please*." She stopped, frowning menacingly. Anthony looked at Lukas and pulled up his shoulders in surrender.

"So tell me," she said, "or I walk down to Reverend Wessels' house right now!"

"I can't tell you but we *will* show you," Lukas said. "Then you can see for yourself. Otherwise you'd just say we're making it up."

"Let's go *now*, then," she said and jumped around the other way.

"No!" Lukas said. "Rianna, it has to be another day. Anthony and I have to go inside, Miss Hannah is waiting for us. We will go and show you, but not today. Please?"

Her face broke into a smile. "All right, but don't think you can get away with not showing me. Do I have your word boys?"

"Yes!" they both insisted, and ran inside, relieved, without waiting for her further permission.

17

Madzi Moyo. July 1964.

The next morning Miss Visagie announced that the schoolchildren were to perform a small play for their parents and the Station staff, in four weeks. Time was of the essence; therefore, they would start with practicing that very afternoon, right after school, and every afternoon. Every child would be given a part, however small. Lukas and Anthony looked at one another in alarm; they would not be able to go and show Rianna their discovery.

And now they had this silly show to prepare for.

For the next seven days, the boys carried the secret of the shed on their slim ten-year-old shoulders. Rianna seemed like a new person: she practiced the piano in the hostel dining room, every day after school. She had disappeared into a world neither Lukas nor Anthony was familiar with. And she appeared to have forgotten about their promise to show her the inside of the shed.

Lukas wouldn't give up. "Then let us tell Charles, at least?" he suggested.

Anthony shook his head. "I still don't think we can trust him, Lukas."

"But *I* trust him. We have to tell *somebody*."

"No, we don't. The guns are none of our business anyway. They're for grown-ups, for soldiers. We can just forget about them, pretend we never saw them."

"Anthony! You know that's impossible. How can we forget? We should tell."

"Who? Not the Chairman again." Anthony laughed.

"*Evangelist Miyanda*," Lukas said, emphasizing each syllable.

"Patrick Miyanda? But he lives on the other side of the station."

"So?"

It didn't take Lukas long to convince his friend that the evangelist might be the best person to share their secret with. He was a Chinyanja, not a parent of one of the Mission-school children (though he had a sixteen-year-old son, Peter), or the chairman or a friend, but a respected person on the Station never the less. Evangelist might just know what to do.

The boys stood outside Miss Visagie's small, circular, two-story thatched-roof apartment, a *rondavel*. Lukas was holding her black bicycle. Concert practice was over, and all the other children had already left. Lukas had asked Miss Visagie on the spur of the moment, right after practice, whether they could borrow her bicycle to ride to the evangelist's home. Evangelist lived on the outskirts of Lower Madzi Moyo, a three-mile journey there and back. Miss Visagie was probably too surprised by the request, he figured, to deny them.

The black monstrosity was a 26-inch men's bike with a sturdy chrome carrier at the back. A light for riding after dark was mounted to the front handle, the size of a large man's fist; it worked with a dynamo that one had to clip down onto the rear tire. Lukas was always amazed by how easily the tall, trim Miss Visagie swung her long limb over the saddle and pedaled down the road.

Even Anthony, who was a head taller than Lukas, was still too short to sit on the saddle and reach the pedals. They had to both stand upright and pedal, very careful, so as to not crush their young manhoods on the crossbar as they negotiated the slippery gravel roads. The plan was to take turns standing and pedaling, with the other sitting on the carrier as a passenger.

Anthony, being taller, would pedal first. Lukas took hold of the back of the saddle with one hand and ran alongside the rear wheel as Anthony took off, then jumped onto the carrier, and grabbed the saddle with his right hand as well. Anthony protested bitterly as they almost crashed into the red earth, just managing to keep them both upright by pedaling harder. Past the hostel, the bicycle accelerated rapidly down the steep hill.

Both boys hollered at the top of their lungs as they went faster and faster. Lukas spread his legs sideways. "See if you can go faster, Anthony!"

"I can't! I'll lose control!" His knuckles were white as he clasped the handle bar to control the drifting front wheel, pinching the crossbar between his thighs and keeping his feet planted on the pedals. He tried to keep to the firmer tire tracks made by the motor vehicles, and succeeded, at least until they reached the bottom of the hill. There the firm gravel surface ran into a pit of loose sand, which gripped the front wheel and threw the boys into the air. The bicycle didn't go far; it toppled right over.

The previous boisterousness was now absent from their panicked yells of terror. "Lukas!" and "Anthony!" they each managed before they thudded into the hot sand.

Shaking the sand from their clothes was the easier part. It took considerable longer to brush it out of their hair with their hands. The sand had even ended up in their eyes, their noses and ears. Both of them sneezed as they walked over to the bicycle lying on the side of the road. It was no longer black; instead it was covered with thin film of red-brown dirt and sand.

"She's going to kill us!" Lukas moaned as they stood the bicycle up. He spit into the sand, licking and wiping his tongue on his short sleeve—he couldn't get the disgusting red earth taste out of his mouth. He spit again.

"This is a Mission station. Miss Visagie isn't allowed to do that," was Anthony's calm logic. "We can't let Evangelist see us like this. Let's wipe the bicycle down at the hostel and take it back to her just before supper. She doesn't need to know we didn't get there."

18

Madzi Moyo. July 29, 1964. 3:30 p.m.

On the way to lunch the next day, Rianna easily caught up with Lukas and Anthony. "You remember where we're going during Miss Hannah's naptime? You haven't forgotten your promise, Lukas Ferreira?'

"No, Rianna, we have *not* forgotten. We will meet you here, on the stairs, as soon as we're sure she's asleep. About half past three."

She made them wait a full five minutes before she showed up. "Boys, you can run along to the school. I'll meet you there. No need to draw unnecessary attention to the three of us."

Anthony must have accrued some boldness, because he responded before Lukas could say anything. "So it *is* true; you're ashamed of being seen even with grade fives! Perhaps we *shouldn't* show you what's in the shed if you are so high and mighty. I don't think you're any different from Barbara!"

Rianna spun around, "Anthony Benade, a promise made is a promise kept; I'll meet you there." For a moment she paused and looked embarrassed. "Please."

Lukas played with a small piece of colored chalk from his backpack while they waited for Rianna to join them at the old tennis court behind the school. As soon as she came around the corner, he bent down and drew on the concrete slab.

They fell into a single file with Rianna at the back, and walked briskly but in silence.

Near the shed Rianna called out, "Exactly why could you not just tell me what's inside the shed, Lukas?"

"I told you. There are empty crates and firewood."

"Yes, but you wouldn't tell me about the *big* thing you saw!"

"Because you wouldn't believe us if I did!"

At the shed the boys glanced around. It was easier to roll the stone away with Rianna's help. Before opening the door they glanced around once more. Rianna had enough. "What's it with all this looking all over—open the door!"

Lukas whispered, "Someone might see us."

"So what if someone sees us?" she said out loud.

"Wait till you see what's inside," Lukas whispered again.

He swung the door open, with Rianna and Anthony a short step behind him. As they waited a few seconds to get used to the

BE SILENT

dark, Lukas pulled the flashlight from his backpack and turned it on. For a moment, as the light played against the walls, he thought the two rifle containers were gone. But they were exactly where they found them before, at their feet.

"What's that terrible smell?" Rianna whispered.

"Ratdroppings." Lukas said.

He fixed the beam of light on the top box and instructed Rianna. "Open the lid."

She hesitated, for only a split second, then crouched down and pushed the lid open. Quickly she stepped back, clasping her hand in front of her mouth. Her eyes were large as she turned them on the boys. "Who else knows but you? Did you tell anybody?"

They shook their heads.

"These are *automatic rifles* boys, AK-47s. They're used by soldiers and guerilla fighters."

Lukas and Anthony nodded in agreement, although neither of them had ever seen gorillas with rifles.

She bent down and rummaged through the box. "Here are the magazines and ammunition as well." She stood up, now talking more to herself. 'What's it doing in this shed?" Then, looking at them: "Is this the only one?"

"There's another in the other box. It's identical to this one," Lukas said.

"Come—we have to go and inform Reverend Wessels *immediately*," Rianna said. "This is very serious!"

Lukas could swear Rianna appeared pale, but perhaps it was only the poor light in the shed. Together, they put the lid back on and repositioned the containers.

"*Gwirani!* Stop! No one is going anywhere!" The order came from the door behind them. They spun around. A tall man filled the door opening—Mavuto, the garden boy. And in his hand, pointing right at them, was a handgun.

19

Madzi Moyo. July 29, 1964. 5:15 p.m.

At a quarter past five, Miss Hannah walked over to Miss Visagie's rondawel. This problem was too serious for the telephone; it would be better to speak in person. She had to inquire about the whereabouts of *three* of the children in her care.

Miss Visagie opened the door immediately. She quickly stepped back as Miss Hannah steamed in, trying to catch her breath.

"Miss Visagie," Miss Hannah said, "Have you seen the two boys, Lukas and Anthony and that rebel girl, Rianna?" She tried her best to ignore the always-present fragrance that wafted around the schoolteacher—like spring blossoms. Her soaked back and wet armpits were impossible to hide—she hoped to heavens it didn't smell—she loved the station, but the humidity was killing her.

"Well no, not since school got out," Miss Visagie said. "They walked up the hill to the hostel."

"They did have lunch," Miss Hannah said, "but disappeared immediately after. I assumed they had a rehearsal and I took my nap shortly after three."

"No, there was no practice today—I wanted to give the children a break. It's barely a quarter past five. Shouldn't we wait a bit before we become too worried?"

"Gerda, don't be fooled by their youth—those two boys had to go see Reverend Wessels not so long ago. They ran off with the men during the cane-rat hunt, without telling anybody, and returned only before dark. As for Rianna—she always pushes the envelope. She's capable of *anything*. The other hostel children have no idea where they all went. We even searched the hostel three times, from top to bottom."

"Miss Hannah, but we don't know that the three are together, do we?"

"No, but I am convinced they are up to something. I can feel it in my hip." Miss Hannah touched her thigh.

Gerda Visagie turned her face away in an attempt to hide her smile. "Why don't we wait until half past five?" she said. "I'll walk over to the hostel then. If the children are still not there, then we can inform Reverend Wessels."

Gerda watched the older woman walk back to the hostel, across the road, clearly uncomfortable. It was a greater weight on one's shoulders to be responsible for twelve boarding school children from one in the afternoon until seven fifteen in the morning, keeping them not only fed but also safe. She was happy with her own choice to rather teach. She waited fifteen minutes and slowly walked to the hostel.

BE SILENT

Miss Hannah opened the door, no longer short of breath but still anxious. She blurted out, "Still no sign of any of them!"

Gerda smiled. "Don't worry, Miss Hannah, I'll go see the Wesselses. I need the exercise."

Miss Hannah stepped outside, closed the front door and leaned against it. Her eyes followed the lithe figure of Gerda Visagie as she walked below the *mopanis* with a bounce in the direction of Upper Madzi Moyo. "I need the exercise," she repeated in Gerda's bubbling voice, and snorted. The wind accentuated the clingy fabric of the schoolteacher's dress, hugging her healthy body. Miss Hannah groaned as she turned around and went back inside, mumbling, "Exactly how much resistance do you think the poor Ulrich Wessels will have against your charm, sweet girl?

———

Olga answered the front door. "Hallo, Miss Visagie! Do you want to come in? Oh, Miss, you smell so nice." Her grade-one student gave her a firm hug.

"Thank you, Olga," Gerda said. "Can I please see your father? It is urgent."

As Olga ran off to find her father, Rina Wessels, a little unkempt and with a baby on the hip, took the schoolteacher through to the living room, sending her young ones out, and handed the baby to Olga to look after.

Reverend Ulrich Wessels listened patiently as the prim teacher relayed Miss Hannah's concern about the three unaccounted-for children. He had difficulty concentrating; the subtle aroma of frangipani drifted through the room. He was certain Gerda Visagie did it on purpose, to punish him; he hoped his spouse didn't notice his discomfort.

"Have we ruled out the possibility that they could be with one of their friends on the Station," he asked, "those who don't live in the hostel?"

"No, Reverend, I came directly to you. Miss Hannah insisted!"

Rina Wessels laughed. "Ulrich, there are only ten schoolchildren who don't stay in the hostel, and four of the ten are ours!"

That's exactly why your husband is so appreciative of ladies who don't neglect, but look after themselves, sweatheart, Gerda Visagie thought.

The Reverend laughed, blushing. "You are right, my dear, that leaves us with only six who might know something."

Rina would phone the Koks, the other Station parents with a telephone, and also ask Evangelist Miyanda to come over and discuss the situation, while Barbara headed out to ask the other children.

The sun was red on the horizon when Barbara took her bicycle from behind the house, past her father's motorcycle, which was parked under the big *mopani*. She cycled down the gravel road on her blitz of houses. She wasn't particularly fond of Rianna, but she didn't wish it on anybody to go missing in the jungle. She pedaled as hard as she could.

Barbara returned, flushed and energized, reporting dramatically, "None of the other children have seen them since school let out today." Little Adam Kok knew nothing either.

A gentle knock was heard on the side door. It was Evangelist Patrick Miyanda. The sun had disappeared; the red horizon was turning grey.

"*Moni, Mbusa* Wessels."

"Hello, Patrick. Please come in." He led the Evangelist through to the living room where Gerda Visagie and Rina Wessels were, and briefly sketched the situation.

"It's ten minutes past six," he said at the end. "Within twenty minutes, it will be completely dark out. Evangelist, we have to quickly check every house and building on the Station before I phone the police in Fort Jameson and the children's parents; I don't want to raise the panic alarm—not yet. How old is your eldest son?"

"Peter is sixteen, *Mbusa*."

"Do you think he will be able to ring the church bells for us?"

Patrick Miyanda smiled proudly. "Definitely, *Mbusa*! I have shown him before. He is becoming a young man now."

"That will be excellent. Ask him to start ringing the bells, and just keep ringing it until we tell him to stop. I'm going to phone Mr. Kok and ask him to bring his truck, and to get the message out that we need all the men, each armed with a flashlight and a sturdy walking stick. We don't want to step on any snakes in the dark during our search."

"And the bicycles, *Mbusa*?" Evangelist asked.

"No, perhaps not. We'll have the two trucks and a motorcycle. I want all the men on the Station to gather at the church, on the front steps. There should be twelve of us– I'm not aware of anyone who is away. We can split into three groups and work systematically through the Station; one truck with five men to

Upper Madzi Moyo, one with another five to Lower Madzi Moyo and the third group of two men on the motorcycle down to the hostel, school and clinic."

As if on cue, everybody jumped up. Barbara was quite proud to be included in the group of adults and become part of the search party. Her job would be to accompany Miss Visagie back to the boarding house, where Reverend wanted Gerda to stay with Miss Hannah and help her look after the remaining children. They dared not lose another.

20

Madzi Moyo. July 29, 1964. 4:15 p.m.

Rianna bolted forward. "What's it with you, Mavuto! Of course we're going. Excuse me, please. Let us past!"

Mavuto gestured nonchalantly with the muzzle in Rianna's direction and she scurried back. "I'm sorry, Miss Rianna," he said, "but none of you are going anywhere. This was *not* part of my plan. I didn't ask you children to snoop around where it does not concern you. Now things have become complicated."

Rianna stood her ground. "That's exactly the point. We're only children—let us go. Nothing is complicated, Mavuto. We won't tell anybody. We saw *nothing*." She again moved toward the door.

"No!" Mavuto declared. "You did see. You cannot leave!" He turned his head and barked, "Mapopa, come here!"

Just outside the door was the young man who had kept an eye on the dead cane rats. "Take the rifle containers outside," Mavuto ordered him.

As soon as the boxes had been removed, Mavuto stepped outside, turned around and yelled through the open door, "Don't think of making a sound! Even if you do cry for help, no one will hear you way out here."

He slammed the door shut, with the three children inside. They could hear him and Mapopa deliberating heatedly just outside the door, switching between English and Chinyanja. Mapopa did not sound happy at all with the sudden arrangements.

And he wasn't. Mapopa had to bite his tongue, but he knew it was wiser not to speak up when the much older and stronger Mavuto was speaking, especially when he was upset. Mapopa had never seen him so unraveled, and that covered their whole lives together. They had grown up in the same village, Paishuko, in the northern Chinsali district. Their mothers were sisters, and when Mapopa's mother had succumbed to brain malaria while he was still a young boy, Mavuto's family had accepted him as one of their own.

Mavuto had became the older brother he'd always dreamed of, the twelve-year age difference just adding to Mapopa's admiration of his cousin, now his adopted stepbrother. Mavuto often acted as his protector against the taunting of the other village children over Mapopa's albino depigmentation blotches on the side of his face, one arm and legs. He often ended up running toward Mapopa as a last resort, with the village children trailing behind him, calling, "Mapopa is a freak, a freak with funny spots. Mapopa is a freak, a freak with leopard spots!"

The relationship between Mavuto and his own mother, Fatsani, Mapopa's aunt, had become strained in recent years, ever since she had openly declared her support of the Alice Lenshina Church and her wish to move to one of their safe villages in the North. Her eldest son was heavily against the move, especially with the growing tension between the Lumpa Church and the government. The Church openly preached obedience only to God, with total disregard of the political governance of the country, denying the legitimacy of government officials. Mavuto was a dedicated African Nationalist and had joined the UNIP many years ago. He wholeheartedly supported the strife for independence from England.

Mapopa, who had turned eighteen only a few weeks ago, found himself torn between his two loyalties; his love for his adopted mother and for his older stepbrother. Still torn, he had followed Mavuto six months ago to Madzi Moyo, when his brother accepted work as garden boy on the Station, a move Mapopa still didn't completely understand. It seemed nothing like the direction Mavuto had been heading in his life.

During the previous two years, Mavuto had often disappeared for months on end, each time returning more driven and serious about the course his country should take to rid itself of the yoke of the British Empire.

Mavuto never confided in either Mapopa or his mother in where he went. And until ten minutes ago Mapopa had no knowledge of the automatic rifles in the shed. He was never aware that Mavuto had a special "plan." Now his stepbrother was explaining, in an agitated tone, why these children had to come along on their mission to the Northern Province, a mission that was being expedited. Mapopa himself was willing to follow his stepbrother almost anywhere, but he wanted nothing to do with rifles or with forcing the *Amisionni* children to join them.

"The *mtsikana*, the girl, was right Mavuto," he insisted. "They're only children. Let them go."

"You're a fool, Mapopa. That girl is a clever one, and she is no longer a child–she has two beautiful *bere*." He held his cupped hands in front of his chest. "If we let them go, they'll run to Reverend Wessels, and before you can say Mapopa Lisulo, we'll have the whole police force on us. Do you want to spend time in the jail in Fort Jameson? Do you?"

Mapopa shook his head. This was a Mavuto he had never met before. How do you argue with an angry man, twice your size, holding a handgun, when you are unarmed?

He tried once more, "But they're only children—let them go. *I* will come with you."

Mavuto was furious, "Are you not *listening*? The girl is not a child. And they saw the guns, all three of them. We can't leave them behind!"

In the shed, Rianna whispered, "Lukas, where's that chalk that you're so fascinated with? Quick, give me a piece."

She grabbed the piece of chalk and scribbled on the wall behind the door in Afrikaans, until the door opened. They all jumped and turned around as one to face the two men. Lukas was trembling and tried hard to remember why Anthony and he had thought they'd had a good enough reason not to go tell Reverend Wessels about their discovery.

"Listen, children!" Mavuto said. He had the one automatic rifle in his hands and his pistol was tucked into the front of his pants. "This is how things are now going to work. Mapopa is going to keep an eye on you. He has a gun and will shoot if you try anything. I have to arrange our transport. You will all wait here until I return. Believe me, we *will* shoot!"

He gestured Mapopa into the shed and handed him the pistol. "If they try to run away, shoot them. Do you understand me Mapopa? If they escape, I will have to shoot you!" The young man nodded solemnly.

Mavuto hesitated at the door and turned back. "Children, turn around and hold your arms behind your backs."

He took a long piece of thin rope out of his shoulder knapsack and cut three pieces. "Come on, we don't have time for games, hold out your hands. Now!"

When he tied Rianna's wrists she glared at him over her shoulder, hissing, "You monster. Shame on you, you big bully!"

"You don't know what you're saying," Mavuto said. "You have endangered my whole mission. Hold still. I am doing this for my country!"

Lukas was so dumbfounded that he simply held his arms out backward as ordered. Mavuto must have done this before, he thought; within minutes he had all their wrists tied behind their backs. Then he pulled a piece of cloth out, ripped it into three pieces and turned to Mapopa. "If they so much as make a squeak, gag them."

On his way out, he paused in the door. "Do *not* disappoint me." The next moment he was gone.

Mapopa instructed them to move to the corner where the empty crates were stacked and light from the back window would fall on them—making keeping an eye on them easier. He closed the door and pulled a piece of firewood against the far wall for him to sit on.

Lukas thought he and Anthony at least, had something in common with Mapopa, having together looked after the dead rats. Perhaps he would have a soft spot for them.

"Mapopa," he said, "can you not untie the ropes, please? They're biting into our skin."

Mapopa just barked, "Silence! No talking!"

"Or just loosen them a bit?"

"Silence!"

Lukas cast his eyes down and slumped together with his friends in the corner.

21

Madzi Moyo. July 29, 1964. 4:30 p.m.

Mavuto stuffed the rifle back into the wooden container, grabbed both boxes and carried them around to the back of the shed, where he pushed them as deep as possible under some creepers, completely out of view. He repositioned the branches and carefully raked the ground with a fallen twig. He stepped back, satisfied: no one would know. He still had another pistol in his knapsack to use if confronted.

Mavuto had suspected all along that the two boys had visited the shed the previous week, but until now hadn't been certain. When he saw them with the smart-mouthed girl heading for the shed this afternoon, though, he knew. The boys must have discovered the rifles and were taking the girl to show her.

It was four-thirty, an hour and a half before sunset; he dared not take possession of one of the two pickup trucks sooner— he needed the cover of darkness. The two trucks were the only roadworthy motor vehicles on the Station. Most people used bicycles. He ran past Reverend Wessels' house to verify the one truck was still there, before heading toward *Bwana* Kok's house where the other truck was kept.

He was still furious. The children had almost derailed his plans. What Mapopa would not understand was that he could not let the children go free. They would immediately run off to the Station chairman, who would phone Fort Jameson, and the next moment they would have Sergeant Rangarajan interviewing everybody, and that would be the end of Mavuto Lisulo and his plan.

Mavuto knew he was deviating from the instructions given him by the Eastern Province UNIP Headquarters, but there wasn't time now to contact them and request a modification. He was effectively on his own. The rifles had been his idea, anyway. His instructions from UNIP were to simply act as an extra set of ears and eyes on the Station, and to report suspicious activity. Headquarters reiterated their philosophy: *no violence*. But it was one thing to work undercover, as a garden boy for the *Amissioni*, but another altogether to sit and wait for something to happen, as he has been doing the past six months.

For Mavuto the philosophy of no violence meant only one thing: *no action*. He was restless after six months on the Station, playing dumb, tending to gardens. He knew the Lumpa people were going to be trouble, they were making plans—he could feel it in his bones. Talking to his mother and her Lumpa friends had given him some insight into what they were up to. He had noticed the low scale movement of the Lumpa people in the North. His superiors did not believe him when he reported back each week.

And so he had acquired the two rifles. He had decided a few weeks ago to put his own backup plan together, not to wait until chaos erupted. He had to be prepared. He was a trained soldier, not a baby sitter, and least of all a *bwalo* boy. With independence finally beaconing on the horizon, nothing that might derail their long struggle for freedom from England could be left to chance. Now the children's discovery had accelerated his plans. He was certain Alice Lenshina's people were marking the end of July as their final days of breaking away. He was ready.

He decided to use the remaining time until sunset to rework his plan; he had to account for every contingency. He would pick up provisions from the small house he shared with Mapopa in Lower Madzi Moyo. They would need extra warm clothing and sleeping gear, especially if the children were coming along. He hoped Mapopa would not lose his nerve guarding the children.

He had been reluctant to make Mapopa part of all this, but with the children involved now, he needed an assistant, even if that meant someone without military training. He had a soft spot for his stepbrother but wasn't sure that Mapopa's heart would be in this mission. Mavuto was not planning on killing, but he was prepared to use force and intimidation to achieve his goal if he had to. If he was successful, he might earn the respect of the military and even a promotion. Just think: *Captain Mavuto Lisulo.*

Once Mavuto finished packing two large military backpacks, with a canvas water bag tied to each one, he headed toward Mr. Kok's house, keeping to the forest's deep shadows. He would sit it out there until after sunset, claim the Kok's truck and follow an abandoned forestry road back to Reverend Wessels' house on the opposite side of the Station. He was not stealing the truck, he reminded himself: he was claiming it for the cause.

He would only have a few minutes after borrowing the truck to get to the second one and immobilize it, preventing anyone from following them. Then he had to get back to the shed, again using the old forestry roads, and pick up Mapopa, the rifles and the children. By that time it would be completely dark—dark enough to disappear.

22

Madzi Moyo. July 29, 1964. 4:45 p.m.

It was one thing to sit quiet for an indefinite time when you were barely ten, another to sit against the side of an upturned crate in an abandoned shed in semi-darkness by no choice of your own, and a totally different thing again when your hands were tied behind your back, and you tried hard not to breathe too deep in an attempt to not be overwhelmed by the fetid aroma.

Mavuto hadn't even troubled himself to remove Lukas's backpack when he hastily tied his hands. Lukas was still trying to comprehend what exactly has happened, and why they were being kept in the shed, guarded by Mapopa. He'd always thought Mavuto was only a loner, an unhappy garden boy who kept to himself.

The late-afternoon sun, coming in through the slatted window, shifted its bands of light across their faces. Lukas welcomed the light. Rianna's eyes were closed against it. He was amazed, almost disappointed, that Rianna hadn't put up a bigger fight. Even now, sitting between her and Anthony, he wondered why she remained so quiet; her eyes remained closed. She was resting with her back against a bigger crate; it looked as if she was sleeping, her breasts gently moving up and down.

He decided that if Rianna was going to play dead, he and Anthony would have to come up with a plan—they couldn't stay in the shed. What would Miss Hannah do if they were late a second time? The two of them would be in even bigger trouble than before. Perhaps if they spoke in Afrikaans, Mapopa wouldn't be able to understand them.

Lukas whispered in Afrikaans, "Anthony, what do you think Mavuto and Mapopa are going to do with us?"

Anthony whispered back, "I don't know. I thought they were playing, but this isn't funny. And why is Rianna so quiet? My hands are feeling weird—my fingers are going all tingly."

"Mine too. My one hand is completely asleep. I'm going to wake Rianna," Lukas decided. "We have to make a plan to get out of this shed and away from these men. I don't know what they want to do with the machine guns."

He gently kicked Rianna on the shin.

Her eyes flew wide open and she hissed. "What's it with you, Lukas Ferreira? Are you looking for trouble?"

"No, Rianna," he replied in Afrikaans, hoping she would understand why, "but I don't want to stay here. My hands are falling asleep. Do you think we can try and get out?"

She smiled. "You want to escape?"

Mapopa leaned forward from where he sat on his piece of firewood. "Silence! No talking!" He waved the pistol at them.

Rianna ignored him and repeated, "Shall we make a plan and escape?"

Lukas nodded. "But how?"

She leaned forward, looking at Lukas and Anthony, and whispered very softly, "I don't think Mapopa is as clever as Mavuto. I wasn't asleep—I was planning. I'm going to pretend that I'm feeling sick and get a convulsion."

When she saw the boys' blank faces she repeated, "I'll pretend to be having a fit, a seizure. Falling-sickness. I'm going to fall forward and shake my body. You guys can tell Mapopa I didn't take my pills this morning. We can try and convince him to untie our hands, at least. Once our hands are free, we can plan our next move."

"But he has a gun," Lukas protested.

"I don't think he'll use it," Rianna said. "He looks uncertain, and very unhappy. All right, here we go."

She swayed from side to side as she slowly sat forward and slid down to the dirt floor, rolled on to her side and started to slowly jerk one side of her body. Both Lukas and Anthony stared at her with genuine concern, even though she had warned them—this looked *real*.

Mapopa jumped up. "What are you doing, Missy?" He stepped closer, piercing the boys with his look. "What's she doing? What's wrong with her?"

The boys looked at their guard with innocent faces. "She said she felt sick," Lukas said. "She gets this falling disease, then she does *this*."

Rianna made terrible sounds in her throat and started foaming at the mouth. Her shaking increased steadily.

Mapopa became more alarmed. "*What* is this falling disease?"

Anthony asked with a sweet voice, "Do you think she can *die* when her body shakes like that Mapopa?"

"I don't know!" Mapopa said, raising his voice.

Lukas volunteered, "It might help if you untie her hands. Maybe she can't breathe properly with her hands behind her back?"

"Mavuto said I had to gag you if you made too much noise." Mapopa insisted. "Look what's happened now!"

Rianna shook violently with both her arms and her legs, making more gargling noises. The boys were becoming as alarmed as Mapopa. What if this was real?

"Mapopa! Please do something!" Lukas begged, not acting anymore. "Please cut the ropes so she can breathe better. She didn't take her medicine," he remembered to add.

Mapopa shoved the pistol inside his belt, took out a small pocketknife, knelt down at Rianna's side and cut the rope around her wrists. Rianna slowed her shaking down as she remained on her side and stopped making the terrifying throat sounds. She pulled into a small bundle and whimpered softly. She did indeed feel sick now from being on the dirt floor, inhaling the repelling air and powdery dirt she had kicked up with all her antics.

Lukas stood back. "Thank you, Mapopa. My hands also, please. I think she'll be okay now. I'll sit next to her."

The still stunned Chinyanja man bent down and cut both Lukas and Anthony's ropes, and the boys went and sat on the floor next to Rianna. Lukas gently started stroking her hair. She opened one eye and winked at him, then closed it again.

BE SILENT

"Mapopa, why can't we go back to the hostel?" Lukas asked.

"Because Mavuto said so, and he has a plan! He is coming to get us. Then we will all leave. He said, *because* you saw the rifles we have to take you with us."

"But *why* Mapopa? We won't tell anybody." Lukas persisted.

Mapopa laughed nervously, afraid about what Mavuto would do when he discovered their wrists were cut free. "You will tell the Chairman and the police and then *we*'ll get in trouble. They'll put us in jail. So you are coming with us!" Lukas wondered if he was afraid of what Mavuto would do when he discovered their wrists had been cut free.

"But Mapopa—"

"Shut up! No more talking or I tie your hands!"

The children remained silent in their small huddled group on the dirt floor. The light through the window was waning. Rianna slowly sat up and pulled the boys against her, one on each side, resting their backs against one of the bigger crates. She smiled grimly; she was so dirty now, and reeked of the shed—disgusting.

23

Madzi Moyo. July 29, 1964. 6:15 p.m.

Mavuto became impatient waiting for the sun to disappear behind the *mopanis*. It took even longer for full darkness to set in. He sat hidden among the dense vegetation, barely ten yards from the path to Mr. Kok's house, with a clear view of the house and the truck.

He knew he ran a terrible risk in waiting for the cover of darkness, that the house mother would certainly have raised the alarm by now. And the moment Reverend Wessels phoned Mr. Kok to warn him, his plan would be derailed. He had no other option, though. At least he could take the truck quickly: it was the practice on the Station to leave one's keys in the ignition—everybody trusted everybody.

By six-fifteen, he found it impossible to remain in his hiding place. With one backpack strapped to his back and the second in his hand, he walked alongside of the path, keeping in the deep shadows. Crouching low, he reached the rear end of the truck, loosened its canvas flap and dropped the two backpacks into the back with a soft thud. Then, silently, he snuck around to the passenger door, the side facing away from the house.

He kept his head down, below the window and reached for the door handle. But when the truck door sqeaked in the quiet evening, he froze. Silently, as he slipped into the cabin, he cursed Mr. Kok for neglecting his truck like that.

No movement was coming from the house. He slid as low as possible across the long front seat, slouched behind the steering wheel and felt for the keys. It would serve him best, he reasoned, once he started the engine to make a sharp U-turn to his left, without headlights, and disappear down the winding path before someone ran out of the house—backing up would take too much time.

The engine started with the first turn of the key, but he struggled to get it into gear; the truck screeched and emitted a cloud of smoke. Mavuto's foot slipped off the clutch, and the truck jumped forward and died.

"Oh shit!" he said out loud.

He got the engine going again and controlled his footwork on the gas and clutch pedals. A glance into the rearview mirror confirmed his hope that he had managed the theft without being noticed. He laughed, relieved at his achievement as he took off down the two-track dirt road.

Within minutes he reached the old forestry back road and continued without headlights, slowly circumnavigating the Station toward Reverend Wessels's house. He must immobilize the second truck. He pulled the truck off the forest road near the house and, now on foot, cut through the bush to where the second truck was parked in the back.

People were leaving the Wesselses' house. Mavuto stepped back, standing motionless in the shadows. *That must be the search party.* He would have to be very careful, but he couldn't wait; he crouched even lower as he snuck toward the truck, revising his plan as he went. He had intended only to deflate the tires, but that, he now realized, would only slow them down, not prevent them from following him.

Slashing a tire is hard work, even with his forged-steel hunting knife, he discovered. It took several thrusts and jabs, using both hands to prevent the knife from bouncing off the rubber. The sidewall of the tire just above the rim turned out to be the most vulnerable part. The truck sanked three inches as the front tire emptied.

He crouched by the rear wheel on the same side, took hold of the knife in both hands and drove it straight into the sidewall. The knife penetrated the rubber, slicing it open. The air escaped with a mighty hiss, but then the tire pinched the blade tight. Mavuto couldn't get his knife out. He mumbled under his breath, "Shit, shit, shit!"

Voices were coming his way, around the house from the front. He needed the knife. He pulled harder. The voices came closer. As the blade came free, he lost his balance, stumbling forward, his right knee moving into the path of the knife. He could feel the knife cutting into his flesh just above the joint. The pain made him collapse as he grasped the knife with both hands. The voices were just on the other side of the truck as he pulled the blade from his leg. He bit his tongue on purpose, desperate not to make a sound, and tasted blood in his mouth. The voices became quieter; the people were starting to head back to the house.

For a moment he felt lightheaded as he righted himself. It was almost impossible to crouch now as he slunk back toward cover; warm sticky fluid ran down his calf. His leg was on fire. It seemed like a miracle that he didn't sever the muscle from the bone. He managed to reach the bushes and shadows as the group of people reached the house. He limped into the forest; a few minutes later, he was back at the borrowed truck.

Mavuto preferred to think of the stolen vehicle as borrowed, since he was planning on returning it to its rightful owner, after his mission was completed. He was not a criminal. He swore softly in Chinyanja at his own stupidity, searching through his main backpack for the first aid kit. Firm pressure with a bulky dressing stopped the bleeding. He wrapped a tight compression bandage around his leg and wriggled in behind the wheel. If he was serious about leaving the Station tonight, he would have to break into the clinic and disinfect the wound and probably put some sutures in. Headlights off and in growing darkness, Mavuto followed the barely visible track, concentrating as he navigated the unfamiliar vehicle. It was impossible to ignore the throbbing of his leg.

The clinic back door had a single lock, which opened once he forced a crowbar he found in the back of the truck, into it. He'd been inside the clinic only once before, and recalled the layout of the place as best he could in the dark. He stumbled until he found the dressing room—it was easy following the disinfectant smell. The place was simply too dark; he had to turn a light on.

Rummaging through the cabinets he found what he needed: gauze, alcohol, sutures, scissors, rolls of crepe bandages and aspirin for pain. He dropped his pants and climbed onto an examination table and set to work. He yelled in agony as he poured the alcohol onto the wound; it started bleeding again. He grabbed the suture and put two crude stitches through the wound, pulling the gaping sides together, all the while whimpering like a little boy.

He poured more of the alcohol on the closed wound, dabbed some iodine on it and put a new dressing on, wrapping it tight. The iodine veiled the sickening smell of his blood that had soiled his trouser leg. After pulling his pants up, he fell back against the examination couch, grasping with both arms to get a grip on it. This was the second time he'd felt dizzy. It took Mavuto several minutes to compose himself and be able to stand up. He cleaned up his mess and stuffed some medical supplies into a small, covered rattan basket he found lying on a counter.

An open cartboard box near it was three-quarters filled with canned food. He went through the contents: beans and small sausages, probably destined for needy patients. Mavuto felt very needy. The rattan basket joined the canned food in the box, which he grabbed with both hands as he made for the back door, taking great care to put as little weight as possible on his right leg.

Old forestry tracks led from the back of the clinic to the school, and on toward the shed. He was not a little proud of his accomplishment, finding the path in the dark without headlights. He would proof to his UNIP commanders that they were wrong about him, wrong to have given him such a demeaning task on the Station—garden boy.

He realized he would have to be grateful if Mapopa and the children were still waiting on him in the shed, though. For all he knew they could have been discovered by now.

24

Madzi Moyo. July 29, 1964. 6:16 p.m.

Ulrich Wessels waited patiently for the Koks to answer the phone. The hands of the wall clock in his office stood at six-sixteen. Finally, someone picked up.

"Hallo, Kobus," he said, "this is Ulrich. I'm calling again about the children— Lukas, Anthony and Rianna."

"Still no sign of them?"

"I'm afraid not. We're commandeering all the adult men now to meet at the church. We'll split into three groups and search the Station systematically. If we don't find the children, I'll alert Fort Jameson and let the parents know. I'd appreciate it if you could bring your pickup truck, to get searchers from one point to the other more quickly."

"I'll be on my way in a few minutes, Ulrich."

Ten minutes later, Ulrich Wessels was about to step out the front door, when the phone rang again. It was Kobus Kok.

BE SILENT

"Ulrich, my truck has disappeared!"

"What do you mean?"

Kobus Kok was an accountant, the Mission treasurer: few things ever ruffled him. But now he sounded baffled. "The truck is gone. Someone took it. You know we leave the keys inside. Anyway, it's not where I left it late this afternoon. It's *gone!*"

Ulrich Wessels paused, but only for a second. "Can you still come, Kobus?" he asked. "With the bicycle? Please? Bring your flashlight and a sturdy walking stick. Front steps of the church. We need *every* man."

For a few moments Ulrich sat in his study, his hand still on the handset. What was going on? Were sinister forces at work here on the Station? He was suddenly acutely aware of the ancestral worship and sorcery that were still practiced in parts of the country.

He bent his head and prayed. Then his eyes flew open. Was it his imagination or had he just heard a motorcycle? *There's only one motorcycle on the station—mine.* It dawned on him: the missing children, Kobus Kok's truck just went missing … Someone was stealing his motorcycle!

He ran outside, yelling, but when he rounded the house he could see his motorcycle disappear down the driveway on its way to the main gravel road, too far away to tell who the driver was. He ran back to the house. Barbara and Olga were all standing at the front door with their mother, their eyes wide. The church bells started tolling.

"Ulrich, what is going on?"

"I don't know, Rina! Somebody just took off with my motorcycle and Kobus Kok's truck has disappeared!"

115

"Did you see who was on the motorcycle, Dad?" Barbara took her father's arm, pulling him inside.

"No, my dear, I was too late!" Ulrich Wessels said as he bundled his family inside and closed the front door. "But the battle is on—someone has declared war!"

25

Fort Jameson & Madzi Moyo.
July 29, 1964. 6:28 p.m.

The Fort Jameson police was in no hurry to answer the phone. Ulrich Wessels was a very patient man, but this was ridiculous. How could no one be manning the phone at police head quarters? He hung up, waited five seconds and called again. He had to wait almost another minute before someone picked up.

"Fort Jameson Police, how may I help you?"

"Good evening, this is *Mbusa* Wessels from Madzi Moyo. Could I please speak to the station commander?"

"I am very sorry, *Mbusa*, but it is after six and the station commander is not on duty anymore. How can I help you?"

"To whom am I speaking? I need to speak to the person in charge!"

"This is Constable Pillay. I am in charge for the night, *Mbusa*. What seems to be the problem?"

"Three Mission children have disappeared, as well as one of our trucks and a motorcycle, all in the last hour. I believe the incidents are all related. Would it be possible to send a team immediately to Madzi Moyo?"

The Fort Jameson side went quiet.

"Consatable?"

"I am still here, *Mbusa*. Were the children kidnapped?"

"That's a possibility, but we're not certain."

"You want a police team to come out tonight?"

"What do you mean, 'tonight,' Constable?" Ulrich Wessels said. "We need someone from the police *right* now!"

The line went quiet again.

"Constable Pillay?"

"*Mbusa*, do you realize how long it will take us to get a team together and then get over there? Our main team has already been commandeered by Lusaka. This is not going to be so easy."

"Constable, in that case I need to speak to your superior. This is urgent!"

The line went quiet a third time.

Ulrich Wessels had reached his limit. "Constable Pillay!"

"Sorry *Mbusa*, I'm still here. I was thinking for a moment. Are those *white* children who went missing?"

"Constable …? Three children from our Mission station are missing. Yes, they are white, but why is that important?"

"I just needed to get my facts straight for my report, *Mbusa*. How old are the children?"

"Two boys aged ten, and a girl aged thirteen."

"When were they last seen, *Mbusa*?"

BE SILENT

"I told you—they went missing an hour ago!"

"Thank you, *Mbusa*. What is the make of the truck?"

"It's a 1958 Chevrolet truck, navy blue with a brown canvas canopy. Constable, your superior, please."

"*Mbusa*, I will phone Sergeant Rangarajan at his home immediately. We'll send a team as soon as possible."

Ulrich Wessels fumed out of his study, bumping into his wife. "Sorry dear, but those police people, what are they thinking? Perhaps I'll take the truck over to the church—the men must be waiting already. Goodbye, love. Please keep the doors locked." He gave her a kiss on the lips and grabbed his flashlight and a walking stick.

Rina Wessels locked the front door and turned around to find Barbara in the hall.

"Why are we locking the doors all of a sudden, Mother?" her daughter asked.

Rina smiled bravely. "It's just until we know what is going on, dear."

A loud knock on the kitchen door made her jump. It was followed by the mbusa calling from outside, "Rina, dear, please open up!"

Ulrich pulled her outside, urgently whispering, "Someone has slashed two of the truck's tires!"

"Are the tires not simply flat, Ulrich?"

"No, they were slashed! I could see the cuts. We're stranded. I don't want to scare the children but this situation is becoming serious." He pulled her into the kitchen and locked the door.

"Perhaps you should take the hunting rifle with you?"

He attempted to smile. "No, I don't think it is that serious yet. You know where the rifle is: please get it and keep it at hand and ready. Keep all the children with you in *one* room, and keep the doors locked. Barbara will help you. I love you."

She received a firm hug and a lingering kiss. She tried to remember the last time he kissed her with so much passion. She would show that little vixen of a schoolteacher: Rina Wessels, in spite of six children, could get her act together and be desirable to her husband again.

The *mbusa* disappeared into the night.

26

Madzi Moyo. July 29, 1964. 6:28 p.m.

Charles Chombe was finishing his last duties in the boarding house for the day when he overheard the schoolteacher at the front door, trying to reassure Miss Hannah about the absence of the three children and volunteering to walk over to the Wesselses to report them as unaccounted for.

He had helped search the hostel. He found it odd that the children weren't there. The two boys were often involved in some form of mischief, and the young lady overstepped the boundaries of propriety—but for them to all simply disappear? That was unlike them.

Charles made his way home deep in thought, enjoying the red glow above the *mopanis* and the baobabs—it was not difficult to fall in love with this land: the tree giants dwarfing the *mopanis* as the elephants dwarfed the antelope. He would never tire of the bougainvillea that grew like weed throughout the Station, splattering the bush with reds and purples, emanating only a hint of fragrance. He had already started preparing supper in his little kitchen when he paused and put everything down. Something was out of place. He could not shake the feeling. He would walk over to Reverend Wessels's home and find out whether the children were now safe and sound; otherwise, he could forget about sleep that night.

The shortest route from his sleeping quarters in Lower Madzi Moyo to the Wesselses' house was along a footpath that ran between the clinic and the school. As the path crossed the old paved strip of road leading from the school down to the river, he noticed the truck behind the clinic and a light on inside; someone was working late.

The doctor owned an old Volkswagen van, which was in Fort Jameson for repairs. It was very likely him, though, still working at this hour. But whose truck was it? Dr. Harold Brown was long past due for retirement, but year after year he stayed on, renewing his contract with the Mission. He refused to return to England, his country of birth, which he left fifty odd years ago with his then young wife. She had succumbed to a stroke two years ago. Charles was convinced the old man was trying his best to literally work himself to death—he had little else left to live for, not even relatives back home.

As Charles hastened up the footpath's slight incline toward Upper Madzi Moyo, the truck passed him to his right. That was indeed strange using the old forestry road.

He recognized the truck now, though. It belonged to Mr. Kobus Kok. He would recognize the truck anywhere. (He

BE SILENT

smiled—there were only two on the Station!) Mr. Kok was often away from the Station on work-related matters, and was left with little time to tend to his own house. He and his wife asked Charles to give a hand after work, with minor repairs. Charles loved it. Even little Adam had started to enjoy having him around. And Adam's mother, Magda, had become a good friend of his. There were many things to fix, and then they would talk. Still, to the outside world he was only the House Boy.

The vegetation was too dense to see the moving vehicle clearly, but Charles was certain it was being driven with the headlights off. That wasn't right. He broke into a jog—it was another five minutes to Mbusa Wessels' place if he pushed himself hard. He ran faster.

There was no sign of the truck once he reached the forestry road. He paused and listened. He could not hear the truck's engine anymore, either. He knew a little of becoming-one-with-the-shadows, of moving without making a sound, stalking prey—he's been on a few hunting trips before. He continued along the forestry road, keeping to the deepest shadows, until he could see the *mbusa's* house. Then he disappeared into the bushes, working his way toward the clearing where the house was.

Charles paused on the edge of the forest, watching carefully. The *mbusa's* truck was parked at the back, close to the kitchen. He ran closer. The truck stood lopsided. Even in the little light coming from the house he could see the slashed tires.

Next to the rear tire was a small pool. Charles bent down, dipped his finger in it and smelled: it wasn't motorcar oil. *Blood.* And it was still sticky. The tires must have been slashed only minutes earlier and the slasher injured himself. The truck at the clinic had been Mr. Kok's, and had been driven without the headlights on. The light in the clinic—was that perhaps not Doctor Brown after all?

The church bells tolled. It would serve little purpose to knock on *Mbusa* Wessels' door now; the children were definitely still missing. Instead, Charles decided, he would have to catch up with the person who drove Mr. Kok's truck, slashed these tires and visited the clinic—find out if he knew where the children were.

If he was fast, the *mbusa's* motorcycle could help him. Reverend Wessels certainly would not give his permission, though, even if he was still home. Charles ran around the house. The motorcycle stood on its usual place, under the old *mopani*.

27

Madzi Moyo. July 29, 1964. 6:28 p.m.

Lukas discovered that he and Anthony had both fallen asleep sitting on the dirt floor, leaning against Rianna's sides, her arms wrapped around them when the approaching truck woke him.

Mapopa jumped up. "Turn around quickly that I can tie your hands, otherwise Mavuto will skin us all alive." He was not entirely stupid, Lukas thought.

A feeble light came through the small window. Mapopa was still tying the knot on Rianna's rope when the door was flung open. Mavuto stood in the opening, an automatic rifle in his hand and a second one hanging over his shoulder.

Mapopa gestured the children toward the door with his pistol.

But Mavuto held up a hand. "Everybody wait! Mapopa, where are those pieces of cloth? The children could raise the alarm outside. We have to gag them."

The cloth bit into Lukas's mouth. It hurt, and smelled like unwashed socks.

"Follow me to the truck," Mavuto said. "Mapopa, you walk at the back with the pistol."

A cool breeze welcomed Lukas the moment he emerged from the shed. Patches of indigo night sky were visible between the canopy of trees, and a few stars even blinked. Lukas realized he was terribly hungry when his stomach churned, in spite of the filthy gag in his mouth. He would settle for two large pieces of Miss Hannah's purple cabbage pie.

Mavuto closed the door and rolled the rock in front of it. "Come! Not a sound!"

A night creature barked not far from them in the darkness, and Lukas jumped. Mavuto laughed. "Hyena. Come!" Lukas required little encouragement to stay on his heels as they stumbled in the dark over the uneven ground toward the truck he had heard.

Mavuto lifted the two boys up into the back of the truck. Rianna declined his help and jumped onto the flat bottom with her hands still behind her back. Then she glared defiantly at him, mumbling. "You monster!"

Mavuto ignored her. He took his two military backpacks and rushed to put them on the passenger seat in the front. "Jump in the back, Mapopa," he ordered. "Keep an eye on them. Remember, children, Mapopa will shoot. We'll eat once we have some distance between us and this place."

Mapopa climbed in, and Mavuto fastened the canvas flap to the tailgate.

BE SILENT

It was darker than inside the shed. It smelled better though—of leather and canvas and flour and gasoline. The children crawled to the front of the truck bed, and sat with their backs against the cabin, facing Mapopa, who settled in a far corner.

The little light that entered was enough to make the pistol lying in Mapopa's lap visible. Lukas tried to reposition his threadbare backpack to serve as a makeshift cushion, but something kept jabbing him in the spine. It took a while before he remembered the packets of Marie cookies and the bag of dried peaches, which he and Anthony had borrowed from Miss Hannah's pantry only days ago. The cookies had probably been ground to powder by now. But at least they might not die of hunger after all.

Mavuto started the truck. They had just pulled away when Rianna turned her wrists to face their guard and mumbled through the gag, "*Maphopha, dhe dhopes dhease.*"

"No! Sit down!"

"Maphopha, *dhease!*"

"No! You wait! We have to be much farther, before I can cut the ropes and take the gags off." He added, "You have a big mouth and will warn the *Amissioni.*"

Rianna snorted at Mapopa and huddled back in with the boys. They had to use their legs to keep themselves from toppling over as Mavuto maneuvered the truck, swerving from side to side.

As Mavuto made a sharp left turn and careened down a hill, the children toppled over into a bundle in one corner. *Mapopa* and the cardboard box with food skidded over to the other side.

Hungry and scared as they were, they giggled helplessly as they righted themselves awkwardly, with tied hands, kicking outwards with both legs. The piece of canvas flap that Mavuto had tied down in his haste had come undone, allowing light from the surrounding night sky to fall on his face, showing his white teeth.

Rianna's mouth gag had slipped off and was hanging around her neck. She whispered, "Lukas, what is it with you and the backpack? What's in it that is so precious?"

Lukas mumbled back. "Small pieces of chalk, a piece of rope, a pocket knife, an old flashlight, two packets of crushed Marie cookies, a bag of dried peaches and one candle." Speaking with the filthy cloth in his mouth was not easy: he had to repeat it several times for her to understand. He coughed as he ran out of breath.

She smiled, "And where exactly did you find the cookies and peaches?" She must know the answer, he thought, but he answered truthfully nevertheless.

She laughed, "Does dear Miss Hannah know?"

Lukas shook his head—of that he was dead sure. Miss Hannah had been snoring on her bed when they took it.

"Did Anthony help you?" Another nod, though Lukas was reluctant to implicate his friend.

Rianna was silent for a moment. "If you don't mind, Lukas," she finally said, "when Mapopa unties our hands, I would like to borrow the pocket knife and keep it in my dress pocket. It has a little flap and a button—I shouldn't lose the knife. I don't like the way Mapopa is looking at me. I'd like to be able to defend myself if he tries something funny."

Lukas nodded. He wondered why anyone would want to hurt Rianna.

Pieces of the nighttime Madzi Moyo landscape flew past through the gap in the canvas as they raced down the gravel road.

BE SILENT

They were leaving the Station, Lukas realized from what he could see. For a few seconds he thought he had heard a motorcycle behind them, even see its headlight, but then it simply disappeared into the darkness. Lukas wondered if the motorcyclist was chasing them, and if so, why he gave up so quickly? He wondered what his mother and father were doing.

Mavuto could not have told his parents he was taking the children somewhere. Not in the middle of the week, not in the middle of the night, not without feeding them and packing their pajamas. He tried to imagine the scolding he was going to get from Miss Visagie and Miss Hannah.

He had to go to the bathroom, but fear made him hold out. There was no need to make the men even more upset. Anthony and he had obviously messed up some plan of Mavuto's. It could not have been a clever plan if Mavuto had to hide guns in the shed.

For a moment Lukas forgot about his full bladder, and held on for dear life as Mavuto drove more and more recklessly, like a madman. The truck's tail careened from side to side over patches of loose sand. Even Lukas's father, who loved driving fast, never drove the Opel like this. Never.

Lukas wondered about Rianna. He recalled how his mother made Cecilia and Suzanne sit on the toilet or potty when they had to pee. They could not simply stand, like boys. What was Rianna going to do? It could be awkward.

For a moment he wished his father or Charles or even Mphatso was nearby to help them get away.

28

Madzi Moyo. July 29, 1964. 6:30 p.m.

As Charles Chombe turned where the driveway joined the main gravel road that led past the church, he wondered if it had been wise to grab the motorcycle without asking permission. He was going too fast: loose sand grabbed the front tire, and the rear end swung out. He counter-steered and put his feet out, prepared to kiss the ground, but the bike righted itself and he gratefully regained control, and accelerated immediately, passing the church on his right.

The bells were tolling as if it were the Last Days. People standing on the steps of the church hesitated as they waved at him; he waved back and headed out in a cloud of dust into the night. He wondered how Reverend Wessels managed to ride the motorcycle without goggles. The wind and dust irritated his eyes, forcing him to squint and blink.

It was a good question which route would be the best to take to apprehend who ever was driving Mr. Kok's blue truck. He

BE SILENT

turned the motorcycle's headlight off. He knew the layout of the Mission's gravel roads, even in the dark. If he took a left at the crossroads and head down toward the school and clinic he could try and pick up the scent from there.

The person who stole the truck had to be the same one responsible for the missing children. What if he had an accomplice? Was he a white man or a Chinyanja? The boarding school approached on his far right; Miss Visagie's rondavel would appear any moment on his left.

The next moment he heard and then saw the pickup truck. It came racing up the hill on his left without headlights, bursting onto the scene. The driver almost overturned as he took the sharp turn left toward Lower Madzi Moyo, close to the hostel. Charles could barely make out the driver, but it was definitely not the small figure of *Bwana* Kok.

The stars shone down, throwing just enough light on the back of the speeding truck that for a moment, as the canvas cover flapped partly open, Charles thought he saw figures in the back. He turned the motorcycle's headlight back on as he turned to take the downhill curve and follow the disappearing truck. The light didn't help much: the cloud of dust and the enveloping darkness made visibility almost zero. He was forced to slow down as he followed and turned the headlight off again.

He was confident that he could catch up on the open road. There was only one way out of Lower Madzi Moyo. The kidnapper (he was now convinced that the children were being kidnapped) would unlikely take the road southwest toward the capital, Lusaka. He would much rather escape north, toward Fort Jameson and Chinsali, or turn east and try to cross the border into Malawi.

But that was a long way. What if he was wrong about the whole thing?

He would need supplies and money from his sleeping quarters and he would have to drop by Mr. Kok's home and make sure the truck had indeed been stolen.

He almost toppled over in his haste as he brought the motorcycle to a standstill next to his little house. He turned the headlight back on: he couldn't see much without it, and he couldn't afford to drop the bike. He ran in and threw some crucial items into a large shoulder bag. He owned no firearm; the hunting knife would have to do.

He started up the motorcycle and seconds later, skidded into the Kok's property. He had already prepared what he was going to tell Magda Kok:

"*Amayi*," he would say, "I saw the thief driving the truck, only minutes ago. It was not one of the *bwanas*. Please phone Reverend Wessels's house and tell him that I borrowed his motorcycle—I did not steal it. I am going to follow the stolen truck. I suspect that the missing children are in it. It was in a great hurry going down the Lower Madzi Moyo road. I think they will head north toward Fort Jameson. Please excuse me, dear madam, but I have to be on my way! Please ask *Mbusa* Wessels to also phone the police. And, ask him to forgive me."

The Koks' truck was not outside their house.

He paused for a moment, with the motorcycle's engine still running. He could see Magda Kok through the kitchen window—his dear, dear friend. She was six months pregnant, he remembered. No, he was not going to knock on that door after

BE SILENT

all. He couldn't afford another second: the kidnapper was gaining too much of an advantage. He kicked the bike into first gear, turned sharply to his left and took off, with gravel flying. He thought he saw light falling on the earth behind him—from an opened kitchen door—thought someone called after him, but he had made up his mind. There was no more time to lose.

It was twelve miles to Fort Jameson; he just might be able to catch up with the truck by then. He would push *Bwana* Wessels's motorcycle to its maximum. The gas tank was full. He hollered into the night as he accelerated, "*Mthunzi* and friends, Charles Chombe is on his way!"

29

Madzi Moyo. July 29, 1964. 6:40 p.m.

Ulrich Wessels was furious. He swung the flashlight and walking stick in annoyance all the way down the driveway. The brazenness of it all—the children missing, his truck's tires slashed, Kobus Kok's truck stolen and now, as an encore, they'd taken his motorcycle. This was not something Alice Lenshina's followers would do, neither could he believe the local government would attempt it. The political fever in the country was mounting as they approached the proposed October date for independence, as the clash in Fort Jameson showed. But this was something different ... or was it?

The *Amisionni* in general, especially the group in Madzi Moyo, were absolutely apolitical—at least on the surface. What was busy unfolding this evening surely had to be someone smaller, someone with a personal vendetta perhaps. But Ulrich was dumbfounded. They didn't have enemies on the Station. In all these years amongst the Chinyanja people, he had experienced only deep respect and acceptance from the local community, even from the local chiefs. He went through every household on the Station in his mind. Could it have been someone from the Madzi Moyo community? He realized the risk they took by appointing new people from outside the local community of Chinyanja's, but the work on the station had to be done; they needed willing hands.

Several men stood on the steps of the church, holding flashlights. Ulrich greeted them. "Patrick," he said to the Evangelist, "please ask your son to stop ringing the bells. He can join us."

He walked over to where Kobus Kok was getting off his bicycle. "Thank you for coming, Kobus, and sorry about your truck."

"I can't believe that we didn't hear the truck being driven away," Kobus said.

"There must be more than one person involved," Ulrich said as they joined the rest of the men. "They could easily have pushed it some distance from the house before starting it up."

"Gentlemen," he addressed the group, "the individuals who stole Kobus's truck and slashed my truck's tires, as a special gesture, rode off with my motorcycle, only minutes ago!"

Some of the men laughed as if they were embarrassed. "*Bwana* Wessels," one man said, "we're terribly sorry. I saw that motorcycle. It was dark already, though, so I couldn't see who was riding it! I thought it odd of you to come flying out of your driveway like that, almost losing your footing. But the driver did wave before he disappeared down the road toward the hostel."

Ulrich gave a feeble laugh. "How could you have known?"

The men had questions. "What is going on Ulrich? Where are the children?" "Did you phone the police?" "Do their parents know?" Everyone tried to get a question in.

He held up his arms in defense. "Whoa, whoa guys! One question at a time."

Ulrich Wessels cleared his throat. "Rianna Vermeulen, Lukas Ferreira and Anthony Benade are officially missing. Yes, I phoned the police in Fort Jameson; they promised to send out a unit."

"And the parents?"

"I have not yet phoned their parents, I was hoping we might find the children on the Station first, but things are becoming complicated. We have been stranded here—you have just heard about the two trucks and my motorcycle. This does not look like the work of an amateur."

Evangelist Miyanda held up his hand. "*Mbusa*, I don't think everybody is here."

"Sorry? Patrick, who's not present?"

Patrick Miyanda looked around, counting quickly. "Mbusa, almost everyone is here, except for Mavuto, Mapopa, Charles Chombe and Doctor Brown."

Someone coughed behind them.

The men turned around and cheered. Doctor Brown had silently appeared at the top of the stairs. The old physician leaned on his cane, catching his breath and waved at them with his flashlight. "Reporting for duty, sir!" he hollered. Everybody laughed.

"Welcome, Doctor Brown!" Ulrich said. "I originally thought we could divide into three groups and search the Station with the trucks and the motorcycle, but that's not possible anymore. When was the last time that the three men were seen? That might shed light on who—"

"Daddy! Dad!" There was no mistaking it; the alarmed voice belonged to his daughter, Barbara. It came from the dark outside the glow of their flashlights. Moments later and he could see her cycling up. She jumped off without stopping and ran, holding the bike, the rest of the way.

"Dad," she said, "Adam Kok's mother just phoned! She said someone was outside their house on a motorcycle." Barbara took several deep breaths and continued. "She heard the engine, but thought it was you. But it didn't turn off, so she went outside to see what was going on."

"Who was riding the bike?"

"She wasn't certain, it was too dark, but she did tell Mother that it definitely wasn't you. This person was twice your size!"

Some of the men laughed nervously. Ulrich Wessels smirked.

"So," Barbara continued, "Mother told me to come tell you and to suggest that perhaps everybody should come over to our house." Barbara took her second breath.

"Thanks, Barbara—we're coming."

He turned around. "Everybody, please come along. I need to make some urgent phone calls, before we can start with a search of the Station. It seems as if Mavuto, Mapopa and Charles Chombe can all be culprits, but we don't know that for certain."

"*Bwana*, and the church?" Evangelist—always the practical one.

"Oh yes. You and Peter should turn the lights out and lock up, then come over to our place as well. Please."

The men took off, some on bicycles, with Ulrich Wessels in the lead; their headlights and flashlights played over the uneven road and against the trees, throwing strange long shadows over their path. Barbara cycled slowly alongside Doctor Brown, who had to lean heavily on his cane as he followed in the cool evening. The wood doves had called it a day, but several cicadas, still unwilling to accept the arrival of night, continued their penetrating wing-song.

30

Fort Jameson. July 29, 1964. 6:45 p.m.

Constable Pillay sat still at his desk. The only things moving were the ceiling fan and his right hand, playing with a pencil. One of these days he would manage to roll the pencil round his index and thumb without dropping it onto the table. "I don't like this. I don't like the sound of this at all!"

Constable Pillay often talked out loud when he was stressed.

He had no problem at all with the white people in the land, but the *Amissionni*, always added a degree of complexity to any issue. *Just imagine, missing children—and for that matter, missing white children and to make it even worse, missing white Amissionni children!*

Now he would have to phone the station commander. Sergeant Rangarajan was going to be very unhappy with him. *Rangarajan probably just made himself comfortable on his back porch behind his mesh screens, sipping a martini.* Second Constable Babu Pillay did not want to make waves. He was hoping to be promoted to First Constable as early as next month. Now this. *Inconceivable.*

Rangarajan will act as if it was all due to my negligence that the Missionary children disappeared. Why can't the missionaries keep an eye on their own offspring?

So be it then—I have to phone the man. The mbusa Wessels from Madzi Moyo sounded quite alarmed.

Pillay put the pencil down and, very slowly, dialed.

"Hallo, could I please speak to Sergeant Rangarajan?"

"Speaking!"

Constable Pillay jumped. Why did the sergeant always sound like his wife? He had met her several times. She was beautiful and plump but had a masculine voice. "Sergeant," he said, "terribly sorry to bother you, but Madzi Moyo just phoned—the Station chairman, *Mbusa* Wessels. Three of the boarding-school children have disappeared, vanished, apparently abducted. They requested that a unit be dispatched there as soon as possible. Preferably tonight."

The line went silent.

"Sergeant?"

"I am thinking, Pillay."

Pillay rolled his eyes. Sergeant was *thinking*. He jumped again when the voice roared, "Pillay!"

"Yes, Sergeant?"

"Get things organized. Immediately! I'm coming over. Who's with you?"

"Bisa, Sergeant."

"Right. Call Constable Juma in. He can hold the fort. Bisa and you will accompany me to Madzi Moyo."

The visit to the mission station would at least brighten up his boring twelve-hour shift. "Rifles, revolvers and the whole emergency kit, Sergeant?"

BE SILENT

"Yes, you idiot. We're not going to a cricket match!" Babu Pillay informed Constable Bisa and phoned Juma. Then he unlocked the rifle safe and took out four automatic assault rifles with two hundred rounds each. He pressed the one rifle to his nose. *I love this clean gun-oil smell. So invigorating!* He pulled out flashlights, some lengths of rope, handcuffs, a compass, some flares, emergency rations, a first aid kit, sleeping bags and water bags and started stacking the items on the one desk before stuffing it all into a large duffel bag. *We all wear our .38 S & Ws on our belts anyway,* he thought. Next he hauled a hand axe, a spade, more blankets and rain ponchos; *I probably need another duffel bag. No need to fret too much, Sergeant will find something I forgot anyway.*

He sent Bisa to fill the Land Rover's gas tank. Their other vehicle, with four officers, had been summoned to Chinsali, a few days earlier. No reason had been given. He sat back down at his desk. He was ready. Perhaps he could quickly see if he could pull off the index-thumb-pencil thing. He would concentrate harder.

The phone rang. Constable Pillay slipped halfway off his chair. One of these days he was going to suffer a heart attack from the unexpected ringing of the bloody phone. His grandfather died of a heart attack, his father suffered a heart attack—he had better be careful.

"Fort Jameson Police Station, how may I help you?"

It was the same *mbusa* from the Mission. This time he *really* sounded upset— distraught, even. Could more children have gone missing? If Constable Pillay recalled correctly, there were twenty-two of the brats on the Mission.

"Yes, *mbusa*, what's wrong this time?" he said. "More children gone missing?"

He could tell that *Mbusa* Wessels was not amused by his lightheartedness.

"Constable Pillay, I'm afraid not. It's quite possible that the person or persons who stole the truck were also involved in kidnapping the children. The theft of the truck and the motorcycle, the slashing of the second truck's tires and the disappearance of the children all took place between five-thirty and six-thirty. If they have left the Station, they could have turned either way on the T4, but we have reason to believe they may have turned north toward Fort Jameson, and are coming your way."

"*Mbusa*," he said, "it's almost seven. If they drive fast they would have reached us already, and could be on their way further north on the M12."

"Constable, there must be *something* you can do," the *mbusa* pleaded. "A roadblock perhaps?"

"*Mbusa*, Sergeant Rangarajan is on his way. We're probably too late for a roadblock, I'm afraid. We'll send a unit to the Mission. A description of the vehicle again please, and the license plate. I also need the names of the children who are missing."

Constable Pillay was still taking down the particulars when Rangarajan stormed into the office.

"Pillay, fill me in!" He paced the room until Pillay finished talking to the *mbusa*.

"Let's try again," he said. "Fill me in. Now!" He glanced at his wristwatch as the young Pillay spoke: 7:01.

"Sergeant," Pillay finally finished, "one of the missing children is the ten-year-old son of *Mbusa* Ferreira, who lives in the Mission Rest House just up the hill!"

BE SILENT

"Thanks Pillay—just to make things even more complicated for us. Bisa!"

"Sergeant?" Bisa said.

"Get the stolen vehicle's particulars from Pillay. Phone Lusaka, Chinsali and our border post with Malawi. The border post is the closest of the three. Start there!"

He turned back toward Pillay. "Too late for a roadblock. Anyway, I've lost half of our manpower. Let's see what you got in these bags." He rummaged through them.

He looked up at the constable. "Somebody has been paying attention. Excellent work, Pillay. Rifles? Ammunition? Vehicle? Gas?" Each time Pillay nodded with satisfaction.

Constable Juma barged in. "Sorry, Sarge, I was on the outskirts of town!"

"Never mind Juma—gallivanting again with the young ladies, I am sure. You are *very* late. Pillay, please brief the man. We need to be on our way. Bisa, let Juma do the phoning. Pillay, take this stuff to the vehicle."

7:11. The three men were ready to leave.

"Juma!"

"Sergeant?"

"You understand your orders? We are taking the Rover to Madzi Moyo."

"Yes, Sergeant. I am presently in charge of this station, sir! First thing is to contact the border post, then Lusaka and then Chinsali. I have my rifle, my Smith & Weston, both with the appropriate ammunition. The police radio is on; I have verified the correct frequency. I will keep listening and stay in touch, sir!"

31

Fort Jameson. July 29, 1964. 7:00 p.m.

Louis Ferreira was still in the office outbuilding, busy preparing the machine and waxed paper to print their next newsletter, when Maria appeared in the door. She had to raise her voice above the clatter of the old printing press; he only looked up once he heard the panic in her voice.

He turned the power off and dropped the sheet of waxed paper and ran to her. "What's wrong, Maria?"

"It's Ulrich Wessels, from Madzi Moyo … Lukas …" She started sobbing.

"What happened?"

She pointed toward the house, "He's … still on the line …. Ulrich."

He ran down the few stairs, and along the gravel path to the house, with Maria a short step behind. "What about Lukas?" He called back over his shoulder.

"Ulrich will tell you, Lukas has disappeared—"

"Disappeared?"

"Three of them, late this afternoon or early evening."

They reached the small back porch off the kitchen, Louis slipped on the red polished floor as he ran, windmilling with his arms before regaining his balance and running into the house to the waiting telephone.

"Ulrich!" he yelled into the phone.

"Hello, Louis, I am very sorry my friend …"

Louis sat down on a chair, catching his breath. Maria pulled a chair closer for herself, and took hold of his free hand.

"Ulrich," he said, "what happened to Lukas?"

Ulrich briefed his friend and colleague in detail about everything that had transpired since they'd made the discovery about the three children.

"But how did that happen?" Louis asked. "How could no one have seen the children when they were taken?"

"Louis, you *know* the children have reasonable freedom to move around on the Station as long as we know where they are. They *only* have to be back for supper at the hostel."

Louis Ferreira moaned. He dared not look at Maria. He was the one who waved her legitimate concerns earlier that year. He, of all people, called Madzi Moyo a pearl in the jungle.

"Do you know where the children went?" Louis pleaded. "Didn't they tell?"

"No, and this is not the first time that they took off without telling anybody," Ulrich answered.

"But you have twelve adult men on the Station and all the female staff to keep an eye on them! Good heavens, Ulrich, they are only children! Little boys!"

"Rianna is not a little girl anymore!"

"They are still children! Do we know for certain that the three are together?"

"We don't, but it's reasonable to assume that."

"So basically we only know they disappeared. Everything else is guesswork?"

"Hang on, my friend. This all happened barely an hour ago. We believe they left or were taken off the Station between six-thirty and seven. It is now seven-thirty. I just spoke to Fort Jameson for the second time. They're sending a unit as we speak."

Louis Ferreira went quiet. He realized he was looking for someone to blame. The signs had been visible all around them—throughout the country. And he had chosen to immerse himself in the Mission's work and play with his printing press.

He looked at Maria who kissed his hand. "I am sorry, Ulrich, but I am afraid I'm not thinking clear. Do you have any idea who was responsible for this?"

"Two or three of our own staff may have been involved in the theft of the truck and the kidnapping. Possibly an inside job."

"How is that possible, Ulrich! I thought we select and interview the workers on the Station!"

"We do, but there was no indication that this could happen—"

"Don't we do background checks anymore?"

"Louis, you *know* we don't really. This isn't the Secret Service. The Station has always been peaceful, low profile. "

"Whatever, Ulrich. I'll be there shortly. Good night!" He slammed the receiver down.

Maria's eyes were big, "That was very rude of you, Louis!"

BE SILENT

"No, Maria. Is it too much to expect that they would keep an eye on children? The whole country is on edge, especially here in the Northeast. How could they not have taken precautions for the safety of the children?"

She tried to hug him but he gently pushed her back.

"Sorry, Maria. I have to find out for myself what is going on in Madzi Moyo. I'll see if Mphatso or Nixon or one of their wives can stay with you and the girls until I get back. I'll drop in at the police station for an update too."

He planted a kiss on her cheek and gave her a quick hug after all, then ran out the backdoor, flashlight in hand. One had to be careful—this time of night the snakes started moving, looking for food.

Minutes later, after organizing with the house boy, Nixon, and his wife to stay with Maria, Louis Ferreira was impatiently stuffing a few items in a bag, including his lever-action Marlin with telescopic sight and two boxes of ammunition.

Maria could not believe this. "Louis Ferreira!" she said. "Are you now turning into a man hunter? Are you not a missionary, a man of peace?"

He paused, looking at her with a drawn face, "My dear, I am not starting a war. It is for self-defense. I want to bring our son—the children—back. The Lord knows, I hope I don't have to use it."

He first kissed her lips, then the tip of her nose, then each eye and held her for a long time before he disappeared into the night.

She heard the gravel being kicked up as the Opel flew down the hill toward the police station. He had not, she was sure, left on a peace-finding mission.

32

Fort Jameson. July 29, 1964. 7:15 p.m.

Louis Ferreira pushed the heavy door of the police station wide open. A single officer stood behind the counter. Where was everybody?

"Good evening, Constable."

"Good evening, *Mbusa*." Juma recognized the missionary—his son was one of the three children who had disappeared.

Louis Ferreira scrutinized his nameplate. "Constable Juma, I need to speak urgently to the station commander. It is in connection with my son and the other missing children." His knuckles were white as he grabbed hold of the counter.

"*Mbusa*, I'm in charge of the station at the moment. Sergeant Rangarajan has left with two men for Madzi Moyo—"

Louis leaned over the counter. "When did they leave?"

Juma stood his ground, their faces inches apart. "About five minutes ago, sir. He instructed me to keep you informed if there

BE SILENT

was any news about the children ... Sergeant was hoping you would stay home, then we could contact you when—"

"Did he expect me to go home and sit down and *wait for news?*" Louis said. "You are not serious, Constable! Are there only four policemen in all of Fort Jameson? I don't believe this!" He rested he head in his hands for a moment, then looked up again. "Shouldn't the sergeant at least have sent someone toward Lusaka, and someone toward Chinsali? Constable?"

Juma felt great sympathy for the man—he was a father himself. "*Mbusa*, we have only the one vehicle at the moment. Those were my orders. This is a small station. Where can we get hold of you, sir?"

Mbusa Ferreira was already standing in the doorway. "I'm going to Madzi Moyo myself! Goodnight, Constable!"

"*Mbusa*, wait!" The door swung back. The man was gone.

———

Louis Ferreira sat for a moment with his hands resting in his lap. How could he go home and wait? He slowly backed out into the street and drove past darkened shops and offices. At the first intersection he noticed that the lights were still on in Youssef's shop. *Youssef Khalil.* Why would he be the only one on the whole street who hadn't locked up his shop for the night? Louis pulled the Opel over in front of the shop and double-checked that he locked it.

There was no doorbell, so he knocked, hesitantly, and waited. No response. He knocked harder. Still no response. He knocked a third time with more force and called out, "Youssef!"

There was movement inside now—latches were opened, then a pause followed. "Who is that?"

"Youssef, it is Louis Ferreira!"

A long pause. Why would the missionary be calling at night? Youssef opened the door wide and stood back, perplexed. He'd known the man for only seven months, and then merely as a customer, especially Friday afternoons, when he brought the boys. But he'd never seen him this agitated. Something serious was amiss—the *mbusa* was not there to buy ice cream.

"Come in, *mbusa*, come in." He took his still hesitant visitor by the arm and pulled him inside, locking the door.

Louis glanced around, inhaling deep. He always found this shop more pleasing to his senses than Kapoor's bazaar—the fragrances were so much gentler. "Youssef, I don't know why I'm bothering you, but I just left the police station and saw that your light was still on. So I decided to come in and talk to you. My oldest, the ten-year-old boy, Lukas, went missing this afternoon, from Madzi Moyo. You know they're in the little Mission boarding school there. Three of the children have disappeared from the Station, apparently kidnapped." He wiped over his eyes and swallowed, obviously fighting for control.

"Come and sit down, *mbusa*. Please." Youssef guided him toward the dimly lit, small office and cleared a pile of papers off a chair. He was suddenly conscious of the papers stacked on every possible flat surface, the ceiling fan turning unenthusiastically high above.

"Why don't you begin at the very beginning, *mbusa*, up to the moment you knocked on my shop door?" Youssef pushed two more stacks of paper out of the way and sat down behind his desk, the only other uncluttered chair in the room.

33

On the road toward Fort Jameson. July 29, 1964. 6:55 p.m.

"I am hungry, Rianna, and cold," Lukas said. They couldn't snuggle up now, not like in the shed, when she could get her arms around their shoulders and warm them. It was impossible with their hands still tied behind their backs.

"Lukas," she said, making her voice soothing, "Mavuto promised he would stop in a while, so we could eat something,"

"Why do you believe him, Rianna? He has evil plans. But he'd *better* stop—I really have to go to the bathroom. We need to *make* him stop."

Anthony piped in, but had to yell as the truck's tires made loud whirring sounds on the twin strips of tarred road. "He won't hear you, Lukas, even if you yell. He's mad at us, he's driving as fast as he can."

Lukas was desperate, though. Perhaps Mapopa could do something. He wiggled down the trunk bed toward Mapopa, who yelled in alarm when Lukas got next to him. He must have fallen asleep, Lukas thought.

"What do you want?" Mapopa pointed the pistol at his chest.

"Please Mapopa, I need a *chimbudzi*."

"You have to wait. There are no latrines anywhere nearby."

"I'll wet my pants if we don't stop—I've been holding it in for a long time!"

"I don't care—you can pee in your pants."

"You won't be happy! Everything will smell. You're sitting below the wind. Please, make him stop, Mapopa."

Mapopa was struggling with the call of nature himself, and, like the children, he'd not had anything wet or dry cross his lips for the last seven hours. Still he hesitated. He feared the wrath of Mavuto more than an empty stomach or the smell of soiled pants, even when he was sitting below the wind.

"No. Go sit next to the others!"

"I need a *chimbudzi, Mapopa!*"

"Go back!" Mapopa helped Lukas along with the nozzle of the pistol in his ribcage.

Lukas shuffled back until he slammed into the back of the cabin. He would get Mavuto's attention on his own. He rolled away from Rianna and Anthony, onto his back, and pushed his feet as high as he could on the back of the cabin. If he could kick with the heel of his sandal against the little window, Mavuto should hear him. But when he tried, his legs were too short. He

BE SILENT

wiggled closer and stretched farther, giving one mighty tap with his right foot. Again. Harder. And again.

"Lukas, he's going to kill you!" Rianna said.

"Isn't that what he's planning on doing anyway?" Lukas said. "I'm hungry and I need to pee." He tapped again, harder still.

Mavuto stepped on the brakes and swerved off the road. A door slammed. Mavuto's brisk steps sends gravel flying. The children waited for his head to appear under the canvas flap.

Rianna was right—he was upset. He roared as his head appeared, "*Ma ku funa chiyani?*" What do you want?

"Mavuto," Rianna said sweetly, "we need a *chimbudzi* and we're hungry and thirsty. Please let us rest."

Mavuto looked at Mapopa who pulled up his shoulders. "Okay. At the first side road we come across."

The truck's body shuddered as Mavuto slammed the driver's door.

He did not switch the engine on immediately, though. Instead, he reached into one of the backpacks and pulled out a bulky radio contraption. He had almost forgotten—just as well that the pesky little boy had squealed for a bathroom break. He turned it on and fiddled with the dials; he had to find out what the police and government forces were up to, especially now that he had the children. He couldn't afford to be apprehended, to not reach his destination. There was only static, no voices; that was good news as far as he was concerned.

One mile farther down the northeast-bound road, his headlights fell on a smaller gravel road to the left—he slowed down

153

and followed the smaller road to a clearing, where he pulled off, next to a large tree.

Fort Jameson was not so far now. Perhaps he should continue on this gravel road northwest, which ran almost parallel to the main road, and slip past Fort Jameson that way, avoiding any roadblocks or police. They had food and water and gas; they didn't need civilization for a while.

34

On the road toward Fort Jameson. July 29, 1964. 7:15 p.m.

Mavuto got out but walked to the front of the truck, where he leaned against the fender and peered into the night, resting his throbbing leg. It was not a luxury he allowed himself often–introspection. He was a man of action who despised talking and philosophyzing, but today's events justified a brief pause. Too many things had deviated from the plan he originally had in mind. *Get your act together, Lisulo*, he chastised himself as he walked to the back and unlatched the canvas flap and dropped the rear lid.

Mapopa immediately jumped to the ground and stretched his cramping limbs. Mavuto started rummaging through the box with canned food, then looked at the children. They were still sitting in the back.

"What are you waiting for? Get out!"

They required no second invitation. Mere seconds later, they were standing with their backs to him, holding their tied hands for him to see.

"I'm sorry," Mavuto said, "I forgot your hands were still tied." He untied the knots without another word.

The moment Rianna's hands were freed, she hissed, "You did *not* forget and you're *not* sorry!" as she rubbed her wrists.

She stepped toward the front, away from Lukas and Anthony and faced Mavuto. "You guys stay behind the rear end of the truck for your toilet break. I'm going to the front."

She looked at the two men. "Do *not* try and follow me."

Mavuto snickered. "Don't try and run away, *mwana*. If you do, I *will* shoot the boys before I come after you and shoot you too." He swung an automatic rifle over his shoulder.

"Mavuto," Rianna called out. "You're a very brave man to scare three unarmed children, standing there with your AK-47! Aren't you ashamed? The *Amisionni* trusted you. We did nothing wrong, other than discovering your stupid hiding place. Now you threaten to shoot us because we ask for a *bathroom break*?" She swung around and walked to the front of the truck. Mavuto glared after her, clenching his fists.

Lukas couldn't wait any longer and ran for a small tree nearby to relieve his bursting bladder. There was no water; the best he could do was to wipe his hands on the sides of his pants afterwards. Anthony had also run off to find some privacy behind a tree. Lukas waited on his friend and together they approached Mavuto—Rianna was still tending to her own business.

"Do you have any water that we can drink, Mavuto?" Lukas asked. "We're very thirsty. Please?"

Mavuto returned from the front with the two canvas water bags, and handed one to Lukas. "The three of you can use this one. Mapopa and I will take that one."

The bag was large, heavy and clammy. Anthony helped him hold it and wiggle the cork stopper out of the short spout. A thin string attached the cork to the neck. It was hard to lift the heavy collapsible canvas bag and drink; if he lifted it too high, he felt like he was going to choke in the abundance of water. The water was cool; it smelled of the wet canvas, and it tasted like an old gunnysack. But his thirst was stronger. They decided each of them could only take three small gulps. Anthony had just pushed the cork back into the spout when Rianna joined them.

"Water, Rianna?" he said. She took the bag. She was strong and managed to drink without any help from the two boys to hold the bag.

"Only three gulps, Rianna."

She nodded, sealed the spout with the cork and wiped her mouth. "Let's go find some food."

Mavuto held out a single can of beans to her, already opened. "The three of you can share that, we have to ration our food."

She looked at him, incredulous. "Thank you, Mr. Kidnapper. What do we eat it with? Do you have a spoon?"

"Apologies, your ladyship, that the service is not to your liking." He laughed. "Use your fingers or go hungry!"

Mavuto called after her as she swung around. "*Mtsikana*, what do you know about AK-47s?"

Rianna glared at him. "You're not the only one who pays attention, Mr. Lisulo."

The children clambered onto a rock next to the bigger tree, and first took turns to inhale deeply from the open can—they were so hungry—hoping it might double their pleasure of enjoying the beans. Scooping a few beans at a time out of the can with their fingers was hard—they couldn't dare cut a finger on the sharp rim, or drop any of the precious food on the dry earth. While the can did the rounds, there was ample time to lick their fingers clean, savoring the delicious red sauce for a third time.

Only a few stars were visible in the dark sky—it was too early for the moon to light up their night. Lukas became aware of his trusted companion on his shoulders—his backpack—and remembered his promise to Rianna. He turned around to face the men, who were leaning against the rear end of the truck, eating. "Rianna," he whispered, "if you untie just one clip, you can slip your hand into the backpack and take out the pocketknife. Mavuto won't be able to see right now. Do it quickly."

Her agile fingers required only seconds for the task. "Lukas, look, my fingers also found a piece of chalk. Perhaps we can write a message on this rock." She slipped the knife into her dress pocket.

Lukas and Anthony took a short step forward and Rianna scribbled on the rock.

Mavuto righted himself next to the truck. "Time to go! Come on! "Bring your empty can along—we'll leave no sign for the bloodhounds."

BE SILENT

They were bundled into the back, this time without their wrists tied. Mapopa jumped in and Mavuto closed them in. He returned a moment later and threw a bulky roll in their direction; it was a thin blanket.

Rianna whispered, "The monster does have a heart."

35

Madzi Moyo. July 29, 1964. 7:15 p.m.

Ulrich Wessels had finished his calls to the parents of the missing children. The rest of the responses were similar to that of Lukas Ferreira's father, although not as vocal. They were all planning to drive straight to Madzi Moyo. Louis Ferreira was the closest; he could be there within half an hour, probably on the heels of the police.

Ulrich decided to divide the remaining men into only three small groups and attempt to skim through part of the Station to see if they could pick up any leads. He would not be able to just sit and wait until the distraught parents and the investigators arrived; he had to do something. Ultimately, everybody would make sure it was him who was held responsible for the children's wellbeing. He asked Doctor Brown to stay with Rina and the children.

Kobus Kok lead the group that were to start from the far side of Lower Madzi Moyo. The Evangelist and his son headed to the school and clinic to see if they could find anything in that area. They would all be back in half an hour.

Peter Miyanda reached the clinic first, with his father right behind him. The front door was locked. They made their way to the back. Peter played his flashlight over the back door.

"Look, Father!" he called out. The lock was forced open.

"Don't touch the handle with your bare hands, Peter!" Evangelist said. "Here, take my handkerchief. We don't want to disturb any evidence."

They entered, switching lights on as they went. "Wait, Peter, let me go first." Evangelist switched his flashlight to his left hand and brandished his walking stick. He could feel the hair in his neck stand erect as he moved ahead stealthily. Peter followed, crouching behind his father. No other traces of the intruder's visit were found. They left, turning the lights off and pushing the damaged door tight as best they could.

Over at the school, they circled the building once, checking for any breaking and entering. Peter circled wider and shone with his flashlight at the old tennis court, then walked in the direction of a post that reflected in the light.

"Where are you going, son? It is time to return to Mbusa Wessels' house."

"I just need to check something, Father."

Peter thought he saw some colored markings on the post, which was odd. He knew the place—he often followed the footpath next to the tennis court; the markings were new. He stepped closer. It looked like an arrow. He followed where it pointed with his flashlight; the beam fell onto the cracked concrete slab of the court.

"Peter, come!" his father called.

"No, come and see this, Father!"

Another crude arrow pointed toward the river, with a single word scribbled underneath it.

Reverend Wessels' voice came from the school grounds. "Patrick! Where are you guys?"

"Over here, *Mbusa*," Evangelist called back, "at the old tennis court!" The rest of the search party joined them.

"Have you found anything, Patrick?" Ulrich asked.

"Someone broke into the clinic, *Mbusa*, forcing the back door open. Whoever it was, left no other signs. So we walked over to the school. Peter just found these chalk writings: arrows and this single word on the slab."

So they'd found nothing, Ulrich thought. "Some of the younger ones from the school must have been playing out here. Anyone could have written *hut*. Come, let's get back to the house; the police should be here any minute." Ulrich turned around.

"*Mbusa*, please?" It was young Peter Miyanda, still standing in the middle of the cracked slab of pavement. "There is a hut not far from here," Peter said, "an abandoned shed; it's on the way to the river. Can we quickly have a look? Please?"

"Mbusa," Evangelist added, "it's possible that none of the missing children wrote this today, but why don't we walk there, just to make sure? I remember now, it is not so far from here, tucked away amongst the trees. It hasn't been used in years."

"Then let's do it *quickly*—we don't want to make the police wait," Ulrich said.

BE SILENT

The men left their bicycles next to the school and fell into a single file, sweeping with their flashlights as they walked; Peter Miyanda jogged ahead. A group of hyenas barked in the distance and closer by a large animal grunted—was that a lion? The men quickened their pace. Even with only the feeble light from the flashlights, Ulrich could now see the new footpath that had been trampled open near the entrance of the hut. They rolled the rock aside and entered the little structure. Ulrich took the lead, stepping into all the dark corners of the long narrow room to peek and probe, ready to air his disappointment. The bad odor was discomfiting. As he turned around to leave, his light danced over the wall behind the door.

"Gentlemen, have a look!"

They all stepped back. Written on the wooden wall in the same colored chalk, but by a different hand, were several words. Ulrich spelled it out loud. "It looks like *Help. Rianna. Lukas. Anthony. Mavuto. Map ...*"

"What is Map?" Kobus Kok asked.

"Mapopa perhaps, if the writer didn't have time to finish?"

"Gentlemen," Ulrich said, "we've seen enough. The children were definitely here. We have to get back to the house—the police are probably waiting on us!"

This time everyone was jogging on their way back to their bicycles.

One the way, Evangelist called out, "Mbusa Wessels, one name that was missing from that list is Charles Chombe. Do you think ... ?"

Ulrich Wessels was short of breath, he seldom ran anywhere. But he managed to get out, "The writer ... possibly didn't have ... time ... to finish writing!"

As they grabbed their bicycles, Kobus Kok turned to Ulrich, "Do you think one of the three men guarded the children in the shed, waiting there for the other two to go steal the truck and the motorcycle?"

They were already riding up the little hill when Ulrich responded, "That's a splendid suggestion. Isn't it unbelievable, Kobus, them sitting right under our noses, and we didn't know it."

The men pedaled harder, their bicycles' headlights bobbing ahead into the night.

36

Madzi Moyo. July 29, 1964. 7:55 p.m.

"Slow down, Bisa, or you'll miss the turn-off to the Mission!"
"Don't worry, Sergeant, everything's under control. I know this road."

Constable Bisa geared the old Land Rover down as they left the tarred twin strip to turn at the sign for Madzi Moyo. He geared further down, to second, but in the dark misjudged the amount of loose sand at the junction, which lay much lower than the main road. The sand grabbed the front wheels and spun the tail far out.

"Bisa! You, idiot!"

Bisa kept his cool and counter-steered, slowly bringing the swerving tail back to the center of the smaller gravel road.

Sergeant Rangarajan was sitting on the left-hand side of the long front bench, with Pillay sandwiched between them, but the momentum had flung Rangarajan out against the door and glove compartment. He yelled, suspecting he had just cracked a rib.

He leaned behind Pillay and gave Bisa a firm slap behind the head. "Constable," he hollered, "what was all that about? Do you want me make you stop and stand you against a tree and shoot you? I have a witness!" He was convinced now Bisa often drove that reckless and slapped him again. "We're on a rescue mission and you almost killed us!"

"Sorry, Sergeant, but these *Amissioni* don't look after their roads."

"Bisa, don't talk through your neck. It hasn't rained for weeks and the earth is dry—nothing to do with the missionaries. Now slow down!"

"How far do we go, Sergeant?" Bisa asked. "Down to the school?"

"No, idiot, don't you pay any attention? Drive slower and continue up the hill; you'll pass the hostel on your left and then go all the way to Upper Madzi Moyo until you reach the church, where you'll turn right to *Mbusa* Wessels' house."

"Yes, Sergeant," Bisa mumbled, almost remorseful. "Sorry again, Sergeant, and sorry, Pillay."

Pillay only laughed. He continued to be impressed by his superior. Even though the sergeant was of small stature and had a high-pitched voice, he showed considerable guts in slapping the colossal Bisa behind the head. Fortunately for the sergeant, Bisa was a *gentle* colossus—he would save the life of an ant given the opportunity.

Pillay was glad it wasn't him who had skidded in the loose sand; he could have bidden his promotion farewell. He ignored his own discomfort, beeing squashed between his two colleagues, and the unrelenting odor as they perspired in the tight cabin.

BE SILENT

As they approached the church, the Rover's headlights fell on a haphazard group of people on bicycles, reflecting off the fast-moving, gleaming black frames. The next moment the cyclists disappeared, swallowed by the darkness.

Constable Bisa squinted. He knew the windshield was covered with dust, but did his eyes deceive him? How did the cyclists disappear? He slowed down.

"Why are you stopping Bisa?" the sergeant yelled at him. "Keep going! We're almost there."

"Sergeant, those cyclists—they worry me. How did they all suddenly disappear?"

Sergeant Rangarajan laughed, "Bisa, that was the *Amissioni* with some of the Mission staff; they probably went searching for the children and just returned to meet with us–they had turned off toward the *mbusa*'s house."

Bisa slowed down as they turned onto the little path leading to the house.

Pillay looked at his companions. He liked Bisa even more than earlier that evening. Bisa was young and irresponsible; he made Pillay look so much better in his superior's eyes.

37

*On the road, south of Fort Jameson.
July 29, 1964. 7:30 p.m.*

Youssef Khalil glanced at his companion as they turned south onto the road to Madzi Moyo. The faint light of the last street lamp momentarily stroked Louis Ferreira's face; his eyes were closed, his face a mask. He had not said a word since they had packed Youssef's truck with provisions for their unplanned trip, after he had poured out his anguish in Youssef's office. Youssef looked down at his passenger's hands, the knuckles blanched from clutching his rifle. Poor man. He wondered if the *bwana* was praying. He smiled, thinking of Miriam, his wife.

She had been troubled when he told her of his plan. "But where will the two of you go, Youssef? Where will you even start looking? The children probably aren't on the Station any more. You're not the police. Neither of you are investigators, either. And why are you taking your rifle, my husband?"

BE SILENT

His reassurance that it was only for protection against wild animals did not quiet her. "Youssef, promise me you won't kill."

"Miriam, no one is going to get killed. I'm a father helping another father who came to me in the night, asking for help. We'll take my truck. The children and you will be safe here in town. I have to hurry. Don't wake the children. Hush now. Goodbye, my love."

Miriam, like himself, had been born in Egypt. Their parents had met on the riverboat down the Nile, as they left their country with their immediate families. It was early in 1938; he was four and Miriam three. After the boat trip, they traveled by train for several days. The two of them became playmates. His father was a staunch nationalist, unwilling to remain in an Egypt that could not receive full independence from the Crown. The British troops withdrew from his country only when Youssef turned twenty-two.

Youssef always wondered why his father chose Northern Rhodesia, for it would also later fall into the hands of the Queen. It seemed, his father was destined to serve Her Majesty. He himself had never returned to his fatherland, but it was one of his dreams, a dream that Miriam shared. They had saved almost enough money for the trip. Miriam was a good mother: she would be able to look after nine-year-old Salma, eight-year-old Yasmin, and little Omar who had just turned three. Omar was his *oogappel*, the apple of his eye.

"*Bwana*," he asked his passenger, "is everything all right?"

Louis Ferreira relaxed for a moment, laughing nervously. "Thank you, Youssef. Yes, I think I'm okay, only worried about the children. Can you drive a little faster?"

A convoy of four military trucks steamed past them in the opposite direction, their wake shaking his truck ever so slightly. The *bwana* was so preoccupied he probably didn't even notice the trucks. Youssef wondered about those large vehicles in such a hurry, in the middle of the week, after dark. He accelerated.

He recalled the many times he had seen the *bwana's* Opel, disappearing in a cloud of dust around corners in town; the man seemed to always be in a hurry. He couldn't put his finger on what had made him offer to become involved in the missionary's business tonight. The man was, in essence, a complete stranger. Buying ice cream once a week did not make you a family friend. Ferreira hadn't even really asked; he'd only needed to share his heartache with someone after he left the police station—another man, a father to listen to his sorrow.

Perhaps it was the combination of being intrigued, honored and humbled that had persuaded Youssef to come along. He smiled again. What would the imam say if he could see the two of them off on a road trip, a trip with an unknown destination?

Youssef could clearly hear his father (God rest his soul), who had taught him the basics of planning and risk management and running a business, say, "Youssef, it alarms me to see you make these impulsive decisions, without thinking them through. How can you forget everything I taught you? Have you thought, even for a second, about any of the risks? Have you given any thought to the consequences—for your business, your family, your reputation, yourself? Who do you think will open your shop tomorrow morning, after you and the *bwana* (just imagine, *a bwana,* of all God's creatures!) go driving blindly into the night?"

BE SILENT

Youssef shrugged his shoulders, peering into the darkness beyond his truck's headlights. The *bwana's* little Opel would definitely not have made the cut if they had to outride whoever took the children, follow them into goodness knows where. Miriam would manage quite well with the shop. Salma and Yasmin have already learned to perform several smaller tasks in the shop; Mirriam would not be alone.

Youssef was well prepared too. His truck always had four extra jerry cans of gasoline, a small water container, basic camping utensils and dehydrated food. This practice had been born out of his frequent travels to Lusaka for scarce provisions and shop supplies that the regular trucks didn't bring through. He and the *bwana* could survive for a few days if need be.

The bwana must have fallen asleep; the cabin was dark, the only sounds the soft growl of the engine and the hum of the tires on the thin, tarred strips. Youssef's thoughts had just drifted back to his three children when the *bwana's* voice jolted him in the dark.

"Which road would you have taken Youssef, if *you* had just kidnapped three young children in Madzi Moyo?"

"*Bwana?*"

"Would you flee south to the capital, to the north, or east, across the border?"

"Do we know who took the children ... your son?" Youssef asked. "That might help us figure out where they would go."

"We suspect three Chinyanja men employed on the Station. Which road would you have chosen?"

"*Bwana*, Mister Ferreira ... I might choose only to get off the Station and then go into hiding, bunker down in a safe house."

"That is a possibility Youssef, going into hiding." Louis said. "But, if you *do* decide to run, and rather use the eleven hours of darkness to your benefit, to put some distance between yourself and your pursuers, which route do you choose? You've lived here for many more years than I ever have. *Which route do you choose?*"

Youssef laughed softly. "*Bwana*, I see you want me to run. Okay. I won't go toward Lusaka—reinforcements could be dispatched within minutes, so that would be foolish. I would run southeast, for the closest border post."

"And if you don't have accomplices in the border-control office, how will you get across?"

"I'll bribe them, *Bwana*."

"They might take your money and still report you."

"That's true. If I expect that, I will run northeast instead, to Chinsali."

"Thank you, Youssef. We will go to Madzi Moyo, find out what we can, and then take the road northeast." For the first time that evening, as he cradled the rifle against his chest, Louis Ferreira gave Youssef a convincing smile.

38

On the road toward Fort Jameson. July 29, 1964. 6:55 p.m.

As he accelerated down the T4 toward Fort Jameson, Charles Chombe wished the circumstances were different, that he could have asked to borrow *Bwana* Wessels' riding goggles. The warm wind made his eyes tear, forcing them into narrow slits, and he strained to see into the darkness beyond the headlight's reach. The *bwana* would only have laughed at this request, though. He was probably going to find himself without employment once they discovered he took the motorcycle, if not behind bars.

But he could not let harm come to his little friend, the *Mthunzi*—or to his friend Anthony, or even the girl with the impudent mouth.

At least there were the thin parallel strips of asphalt, which made it possible for him to push the motorcycle hard, without enveloping himself in suffocating dust. The asphalt was a blessing. And the kidnappers had at most five minutes' advantage on him, maybe only three. The missionaries, Charles was sure, had discovered the children's disappearance only minutes before he had borrowed the motorcycle—when they started tolling the church bells. No pursuit would be expected from Madzi Moyo; the kidnappers knew that the only other truck on the Station was neutralized. Charles hoped that would have made them complacent, anticipating only a potential confrontation coming toward them from the police force in Fort Jameson.

But the police would require at least twenty to thirty minutes to put a task force together, Charles thought. He was friends with the big constable Bisa. There was always only one officer on duty after sunset at the police station, he knew; that would give the kidnappers ample time to disappear into the night. If he, Charles, had been the kidnapper, he would have stuck to the paved twin tracks until just before Fort Jameson, and only then turn off onto one of the smaller roads on the outskirts of the game reserve, and slip past the town, before getting back onto the main road heading north.

He struggled to make sense of the events of the past half hour. But he was certain it had been *Bwana* Kok's wife, Magda, who had called to him outside their house, ten minutes earlier. For a brief moment when she opened the kitchen door, her shadow had fallen on the ground next to him, the light behind her throwing long shadows into the night, her silhouette showing she was with child. He wiped the tears from his eyes with his left hand. He cursed the wind.

He was still surprised that he had turned away at the last second, without telling her what he had discovered. For all he knew,

BE SILENT

he was now also counted as one of the kidnappers, he had become a wanted man.

Being impulsive has cost him dearly in the past, he knew. As he wiped his eyes again, he regretted not spending that one extra minute to brief *Amayi* Kok about his plan to try and apprehend the kidnappers. He was concerned about her—old Doctor Brown had been saying that he wanted her to deliver the baby in Lusaka in three months' time. It would be safer for the mother and baby, something about her blood pressure, he said. But Charles dared not speak to her. She would have insisted that he first discuss using the motorcycle with *Bwana* Wessels and Evangelist Miyanda, who both would have persuaded him not to attempt the impossible, if they even would have allowed him to take the motorcycle in the first place.

No, he would not have been able to force his plan on her. It was not possible to force *anything* on her. She was petite and meek, which made people misjudge her, but life had armed *Amayi* Kok with a surprising double helping of determination. One look at him with her turquoise eyes and he would have surrendered. He had learned over the past year, as she helped him prepare to complete his high school diploma by correspondence, that those eyes could melt rock.

He smiled as he thought of her young son, Adam, his young friend. Over time he had become an older brother to the boy. Helping with minor repair and maintenance jobs around the house, had turned into being around when the bwana was away and then to her helping him with the English-language section of his correspondence course. They had all spent more and more

175

evenings together. Adam reminded him of a scared little tortoise that would, at the slightest provocation, pull back into his armored shell. *Bwana* Kok's absences, often with Mission commitments in Lusaka and Ndola, did little to improve his son's lack of assertiveness.

Only a few evenings ago Adam had asked, "Charles, why is Daddy never here?"

Charles had been busy fixing the wooden frame of the screened-in veranda on the side of the house, "*Mwana*," he answered, "Mission business often takes him to the city and to bigger towns."

"Then I don't like Mission business," six-year old Adam had said.

"It's his job—he has to do the work."

"No, his job is to be here and be with me and Mother and fix this veranda. I wish he was as tall and strong as you," Adam said.

Charles had chuckled as he sent the boy on his way. Adam's father was small, like his wife.

Charles lowered his head, leaned forward as he pushed his bottom out in an attempt to lessen the wind resistance. For a moment he saw a flicker of red far ahead of him on the road. Was that a vehicle or a campfire or his imagination? He blinked and pushed the motorcycle harder.

39

In the vicinity of Fort Jameson.
July 29, 1964. 7:55 p.m.

Mavuto slowed down, swerving slightly as he leaned across the long front seat to reposition the police radio, which had toppled over. He adjusted the dials, keeping one eye on the winding road and one on the dials, as the radio crackled to life. He couldn't get rid of the static completely.

"Seargent ... Sergeant Rangarajan ... Do you hear me?"

Mavuto smiled—he recognized the caller: Constable Juma. He and Juma had gone to high school together. Mavuto had become a soldier, a reservist in the Northern Rhodesia Regiment, and Juma had gone for police training. Yet in spite of all his years in the service, the poor man still had not mastered correct radio procedures.

"Foxtrot Juliet, this is Sierra Romeo, over." That must be the local smart-ass police chief.

"What? ... Sorry, Sarge ... this is Foxtrot Juliet ... Have you reached Madzi Moyo ... I mean Mighty Mike ... I repeat—Mighty Mike?"

Mavuto laughed in spite of the throbbing of his thigh. *The idiots.* The vehicle swerved on the twin track, between his listening to the conversation and fiddling with the dials.

Mighty Mike! Mike Two would have sufficed, Mavuto thought.

"Positive, Foxtrot Juliet. We have reached Mike Two. Over."

"Any sign of the ... ah ... vulture and missing chickens, over?"

Mavuto called out, "Me ... the vulture? At least the man is original, though he remains an idiot!"

"Negative, Foxtrot Juliet, we are inside Mike Two. I will keep you posted. Over." The radio went dead.

Missing chickens, Mavuto thought. *I'll make sure they don't get the chickens, at least not until we reach our destination. I must prevent the Lumpa people from derailing the independence plans—They have to be stopped. The government gave them ample time to return to their original villages, to leave their fortified settlements behind, but they declined. They can't disobey the government like this. I'll prove to my superiors my intuition was correct.*

Mavuto had not made up his mind which of the Lumpa villages he would go to first. It was ironic that he and Mapopa had grown up in the village of Paishuko, in the very same area that Alice Lenshina and her Lumpa church had moved to, his mother included, and now he was planning his own private offensive to stop the church. He did not hate the church—his mother brought him up too well for that. He hated what they represented, what

BE SILENT

they threatened to become; they had become a spike in his flesh, in his country's flesh. He loved his mother, but he was a staunch African nationalist and had recently become a UNIP supporter: The Lumpas had to go.

The church followers' safe villages were scattered throughout the triangular Northeastern Province with the towns of Kasama and Isoka at its top corners, and Mpika at the bottom point. Chinsali, where his mother lived, was almost halfway between Kasama and Isoka. He decided to make Chinsali his first point of call; perhaps he could convince his mother, this time, to leave the Lumpa church, or at least leave the so-called safe village and come home with him.

His last contact with the UNIP office had informed him that the prime minister's office had issued a formal statement earlier that month, declaring, "Lumpa Church villages which are not authorized by the government, must be destroyed." At the time, weeks earlier, he was convinced his mother would be safe in Chinsali—the prime minister had lived there once, and would spare it—but he wasn't so sure any more. Rumors were circulating that huts had been burned down, that Lumpa villages were being destroyed, and that some church members and even policemen had been killed. He did not believe it—rumors; dirty, rotten rumors, anything to embarrass the new African government. But Alice Lenshina and her followers were fanatics who had succeeded in placing his mother under their spell. He had to go and rescue her.

However, his mother, *Fatsani Lisulo*, had a gift for disarming him. Even his strongest arguments could seldom hold water for

179

long when he was in her presence. That was why he often avoided her. He thought back to their last conversation.

"Mavuto, why do you hate the church?"

"Mother, I've never hated the church, but Alice Lenshina is teaching you people to despise the authorities and to not pay taxes."

"Son," his mother said, "our first responsibility is to be obedient toward God."

"Mother, there can never be peace if the church teaches its members not to follow the rule of the land!"

"Mavuto, we didn't feel safe in the villages the prime minister wants us to live in."

"Mother *Fatsani*, then come stay with me, I beg you—I can protect you."

He had never been more serious in his life. His mother had only laughed.

40

*In the vicinity of Fort Jameson.
July 29, 1964. 8:00 p.m.*

Rianna pulled the two boys tighter against her sides. Lukas was slender, much like her nine-year-old brother, P.J. She suddenly missed P.J. and her much younger brother, Casper, who was still at home. She closed her eyes. It was so dark in the back of the bouncing Chevrolet truck, it made little difference whether they were open. She was thirteen, almost fourteen, but felt much older than the three and a half years that separated her from Lukas and Anthony.

She had overheard her mother tell her father the other day, "I don't know where Rianna gets this from, but she sometimes makes me feel like I am the daughter, and she the parent. She sounds so old, so wise." She never understood exactly what her mother meant, especially when she thought about how hard she had to fight her mother for "foundation garments," for proper ladies' underwear. If her mother thought she was so mature, then why the hassle to obtaining proper lingerie? Perhaps it was lack of money combined with Mother's unwillingness to see her first-born grow up too quickly.

Weekend nights, when she was back home in the quiet house in Katete on the Station, she was often awakened by her parents' urgent voices. They never fought, never yelled at one another: it always remained a civilized affair. Her father was so patient—she had never even heard him swear—but he could become whole-heartedly upset. He would let her mother talk and talk, but only up to a certain point, when he would defend his position. It was often about the same subject, money, and the lack thereof, and the church's role in their situation.

Her mother's voice, coming from their bedroom, the door of which was often left ajar, would gradually rise, "Phillip, how can you defend the church for paying you—us—only a stipend?"

"Anna, dear, it's not a stipend, it's a formal salary. We don't go to bed hungry. We have a roof over our heads." Her father would laugh and add, "A roof with a wrap-around veranda, Anna!"

That would only make her mother's voice rise further, "Phillip Vermeulen, the house with a veranda, doesn't belong to us, and never will. This church, which you defend so hard, has enough money to let you men build new church building after new church building here in the African interior, but it has no money to pay its missionaries a fairer salary, a living wage?"

"Anna, we have everything we need."

Her mother's voice would eventually soften. "Phil, I'm worried about Rianna, about sending her to the South at the end of the year. Yes, it is about there never being enough money, but I am also worried about what is happening here. I hear what the cooky and the house boy talk about every day—things are happening. They forget that I understand Chinyanja."

Rianna could hear her father kiss her mother–kiss her protest away. "In the South she will be safe. We should however be concerned about our other children, who will stay behind when Rianna leaves. But they will at least be with us."

"I fear for all three of them at the moment," her mother said. "What's going on in the Northeastern Province, with the Lumpa villages and the police raids and the NRR being deployed?"

He kissed her again, louder this time. "Hush, my dear. Kaunda's government supports a *no violence* policy. They were only warning the Lenshina church not to overstep the boundaries of propriety, to be law-abiding citizens. Everything will work out in the end—you'll see."

Her mother sighed and then laughed softly; she had surrendered. Rianna wondered whether her parents were so absent minded that they forgot to close the bedroom door. She couldn't believe her parents would let her hear all this on purpose. She dared not tiptoe over there and close the door; then they would know that she had eavesdropped. It was too late. This was how their heated discussions usually ended; the agitated voices would drag on and on into the night, until the fire in them had died down, and a soft rain would then cover the earth.

Adrianna draped her pillow around her head, covering her ears, to shut out the sounds from her parents' bedroom. She blushed. This was not the first time she'd had to listen to her mother's soft gasping and the rhythmic squeaking of bedsprings. She rolled onto her stomach, the pillow still around her head, thinking, *At least they love us, and love each other. Everything will work out in the end.* Then she listened to her parents make love in the quiet house before she drifted off into a deep slumber.

Rianna realized that they'd been traveling slower since Mavuto had turned off the main road. They had traveled north, and very fast at first, but then changed direction. She had a sense for direction. He must be timing his arrival at a particular place, she thought. A rock in the gravel road made the truck jolt, sending shockwaves through her. Mapopa cursed from the far end of the truck bed. The boys woke up and pulled free from her arms.

"Rianna, what's going on?" Lukas called out. "What's happening?"

She laughed. "There was a bump in the road, that's all."

For Lukas, the novelty of riding in the back of a truck at night had worn off. It was almost time to go to bed and he was still hungry. "Where is Mavuta taking us?" he asked Rianna from his dark corner. "What is his so-called plan?"

Mapopa yelled, "Shut up! No talking!"

Rianna ignored him. "I don't believe it's so much Mavuto taking us somewhere, as it is him still pursuing his original plan, dragging us along, because we discovered his stupid rifles. I think he didn't want us to run off and tell the adults, who would certainly have gone to the police and brought an end to his scheme."

BE SILENT

Lukas had been pondering their experience since they were captured. "Rianna, what do you think Mavuto will be able to do with two machine guns and two pistols? Even if Mapopa helped him?"

"I'm not sure. A very small war, perhaps? That's the first thing I'm going to ask him at our next stop."

"I don't think he'll tell you," Anthony whispered. "We must be in his way now. He might have to kill us *first*, before he could implement his plan, don't you think Rianna?"

Rianna laughed gently. "Come on. I don't think he'll kill us. He's a soldier, not a killer."

"How do you know he's a soldier?" Lukas asked.

"I don't know for certain," Rianna said. "but something was always strange, out of place, when he was tending to the gardens. Didn't you notice how poor his gardens looked, compared to the other garden boys' gardens? He's no farmer or gardener. And haven't you seen how muscled he is? He looks so comfortable with the rifle and the pistol. He *must* be a soldier."

"Then why don't we try to escape?" Anthony asked.

A frustrated Mapopa tried to threaten them again. "No more talking!"

Rianna yelled, "*Choka* Mapopa, *choka!*" Go away!

She pulled the boys closer and whispered what she had in mind. Anthony's idea to escape was an excellent one, she agreed. It was dark in the back of the truck, there were three of them and they had the element of surprise on their side. Mapopa was alone, and although he had a handgun, she was convinced he had never used it—he looked too uncomfortable with the pistol. He would

185

hesitate, she was sure, giving them a chance, and since the truck made so much noise, Mavuto wouldn't hear or see a thing.

"So, boys," she whispered. "This is what we're going to do. Listen carefully. *We have to get it right.*"

41

Madzi Moyo. July 29, 1964. 8:00 p.m.

Sergeant Rahul Rangarajan instructed Constable Bisa to pull up in front of *Bwana* Wessels' house, right in front of the wide stairs leading up to the veranda with its polished red floors. There was no sign of the men, who, only minutes before, had headed up to the house. Their bicycles were neatly stacked against the stair posts.

Bwana Wessels appeared at the top of the stairs just as Sergeant Rangarajan walked around the Land Rover with Pillay and Bisa a step behind him. Bisa turned back to lock their vehicle; they had their handguns on their person, but had left the rifles in the Rover. Besides, enough vehicles had disappeared for one night. Rangarajan recalled Commissioner Subramanium's prophetic comment to him earlier that year about the unrest brewing in the land: "Rahul, it's all your imagination! Perhaps you should cut back on all that curry you eat, hey?"

Rahul knew, being needed here tonight was *not* his imagination—he was convinced that what was happening here would eventually be linked to the unrest in the Northern Province. He only had to prove it. But he didn't expect much sympathy from the commissioner once Subramanium learned about the missing children.

The sergeant climbed the stairs with an extended hand. "Good evening *Bwana*," he said.

"Good evening, Sergeant. Thank you for coming." Ulrich Wessels shook his hand and acknowledged his colleagues. "Constable Pillay, Constable Bisa. Please come in."

The missionary's ability to remember people's names, even after having met them only once, always amazed Rahul. *Yes Rahul,* he told himself now. *Do not underestimate the man.* They followed *Bwana* Wessels to the large living room, where the rest of the Station's male staff was gathered. Rahul scanned the room: nine men, including *Bwana* Wessels, if he also counted Peter Miyanda, the Evangelist's son. There were also two females in the room, the missionary's wife and oldest daughter. She must have sent the other children to bed; he could still hear their soft chatter coming from adjacent rooms.

He greeted Mrs. Wessels, *"Mwachoma banji, Amayi."* Good evening, madam.

"Good evening, Sergeant." Rina Wessels nodded in his direction and pulled Barbara tighter against her side, adjusting her other hand on the barrel of the hunting rifle she held securely. She clearly had no intention of parting with it for the time being.

Sergeant Rangarajan found it ironic that the men were all armed with a sturdy walking stick and a flashlight while the *amayi* sat there with the bolt-action Remington.

BE SILENT

"Good evening, gentlemen!" he said to the rest of the room. The men responded in a chorus, "*Moni,* Sergeant!" Hello! Ulrich Wessels filled Rahul in on what had transpired since one-thirty that afternoon, after school let out, until the point he made the first call to the police station and spoke to Constable Pillay.

At the mention of his name, Babu Pillay raised his hand and smiled his most professional smile. Him handling this assignment in a proper fashion may just seal his promotion, he thought. The sergeant looked in his direction and nodded, *Yes, Pillay did a good job,* it said.

Ulrich Wessels continued to recount the theft of the truck and motorcycle and the slashing of the other truck's tires. Sergeant Rangarajan cleared his throat. "Anything else you discovered, *Bwana*? I noticed your group on bicycles when we arrived."

"Yes, Sergeant," Wessels said. "We quickly combed the Station to see if we could find anything. Three of the men employed on the Station are unaccounted for; the clinic had been broken into, and it appears that the children spent some time in an old abandoned shed behind the school, before been taken off the Station."

Sergeant Rangarajan looked at his wrist. "*Bwana*, it is eight-fifteen. I have only the one police vehicle, with these two men. Do the parents of the missing children know?"

"Yes, Sergeant, they do," Wessels answered. "They are actually all on their way here. But what happened to your second police vehicle and your other men?"

Rangarajan swallowed before answering. His face was drawn. "I received instructions from the commissioner to send the vehicle and four men to the Chinsali District, days ago. I have one man left in Fort Jameson at the station. What you see is what we have."

Kobus Kok raised his hand. "Can't Lusaka help us, Sergeant? At least with more vehicles, manpower and rifles? These are three young children we're talking about, and it's dark out already. What about a helicopter? Time is of the essence!"

Sergeant Rangarajan laughed apologetically, "Mr. Kok, I would have loved to be able to put up at least three road blockades—one north, one south and one east—and comb the entire district. But with unrest brewing in the Northern Province my hands are essentially cut off. There won't be reinforcements."

"But we only have bicycles left, Sergeant!" Kobus said. "You saw them parked outside! Didn't the government purchase four Alouette helicopters from France in February? One of *them* could be made available to help us."

Ulrich Wessels got up and turned toward his friend. "Kobus, allow the sergeant to explain his plan to us."

Rahul Rangarajan had feared that moment; his options were so limited. Where would one even start searching with one vehicle and three policemen? The kidnappers have almost an hour and a half head start on them. Would these men be willing to form volunteer search parties and help the police? Alouette helicopters! He wanted to laugh.

He cleared his throat, "*Bwana* Kok, none of those helicopters will be available to us I'm afraid. I'll phone Lusaka immediately and report the missing children. I'll insist on speaking to the commissioner personally, explaining the need for man—"

The rest of his words were drowned by the sound of a vehicle speeding toward the house and skidding to a stop on the gravel outside. Doors were slammed and people rushed up the veranda stairs, yelling. A voice bellowed, "Ulrich! Ulrich, where are you guys?"

Louis Ferreira, who had convinced Youssef to switch places with him halfway to Madzi Moyo, so they could drive faster, barged into the living room, rifle in hand.

42

*In the vicinity of Fort Jameson.
July 29, 1964. 7:15 p.m.*

When Charles Chombe pressed his chest flat against the gas tank, his chin touching the handlebars, it added three to four miles an hour to his speed. The needle would just touch the seventy mark, then drop back to sixty-five. Never before had he ridden so fast on a motorcycle. He had to give the throttle some slack; he could feel the bike drifting, trying to leave the narrow tarred strip onto gravel, which could certainly kill him at this speed.

Yes! There it was again, a distant red flicker, perhaps two, close together—it had to be the rear lights of another vehicle. If it *was* a vehicle, it was traveling as fast as he was, too fast for the road and the time of day. He wondered how he could confirm that this was indeed the stolen truck with the three children in it. He relaxed a smidge on the throttle, keeping the needle at sixty-five, increasing

BE SILENT

the distance between them; he was gaining too much and too fast on the other vehicle. After a minute he allowed the distance between them to shrink gradually again, until he could see better. It was a truck!

I'm so stupid! He thought. Ten to one, the driver is armed, and there has to be at least two men to have been able to cover the Station so quickly, stealing one truck, immobilizing the other and keeping the children locked away until the truck was ready. *What were you thinking, Charles Chombe, when you stole Bwana Wessels' motorcycle? What are you going to do with your hunting knife against two men who are probably well armed? How will you convince them to surrender the children, unharmed? Idiot!*

Charles went over every person on the Station again in his mind, men and women, trying to come up with someone who would have done this. *Why would you kidnap three white children, three months ahead of the long-awaited date of independence for Northern Rhodesia, when it will finally become the republic of Zambia?* If a stranger from outside the Station was responsible, he would have been noticed and been picked up by the staff. It had to be someone from within their own ranks, an insider.

And if the kidnapper was an insider, he must have known that the children's missionary parents were as poor as church mice, they don't even own the old mansions they live in, and neither their local church nor even the mother church from the Republic in the South have any money to pay a ransom.

What was the motivation then? Revenge? *The children were harmless*—although the girl could use a guard for her free tongue. Their parents were respected members of the local community who did good and harmed no one. A political scheme, then? No, that was ludicrous.

Suddenly the truck's driver slammed on the brakes and pulled to the side of the road. Charles almost lost his footing. He couldn't afford to let them see him. He geared down as fast he could while braking.

He was still going too fast. He turned the headlight off and desperately tried to gear down further when the rear tire left the asphalt and swung out to the left, throwing him, with the motorcycle, onto its right side. He skidded to a standstill into the soft sand on the side of the road. The engine cut out. Charles remained on his side without moving a muscle—he was too dazed. His heart pounded as wave after wave flushed through him—the adrenaline continued pumping into his system. For a moment he was certain he was dying.

Don't move, Charles Chombe, don't move. Play dead.

The driver had walked to the rear of the truck and glanced in his direction—for three agonizing seconds. Then he turned and opened up the back. It was definitely *Bwana* Kok's truck. But it was too far away and too dark out for Charles to identify the driver.

The driver was furious with whoever was in the back, but Charles couldn't hear the words. Some yelling took place, the back was closed up again, a door was slammed and then silence followed for thirty full seconds. Suddenly the truck pulled away, gravel flying in all directions, taking Charles by surprise. *That is one unhappy kidnapper!*

Charles wiggled out from under the motorcycle and, limping, pushed it back toward the tarred strip as fast he could. He

BE SILENT

had to spit several times in an attempt to rid his mouth of the sand grinding between his teeth. Something burned on the inside of his calf. *Probably the blooming exhaust.* Too bad, he thought: he could not afford to lose that truck. The engine sputtered and refused to take on the first try. He jumped on the kick-starter again and cautiously played the throttle until the engine turned and stayed on. The truck's red lights disappeared in the distance.

He had been following the truck for another mile when it slowed down and turned left onto a smaller gravel road. They were not too far from Fort Jameson, Charles realized; the kidnapper must be avoiding the town and any form of civilization. He slowed down. This was becoming tricky. The chances of the driver seeing him on the smaller, narrower road was so much greater; he would have to increase his following distance.

Charles stopped at the turn-off and waited for the truck to disappear into the night on the smaller road. How could he alert the search parties from the Station and the police, who would, he was sure, be following him, thinking him to be part of the kidnappers? They will easily miss this turn-off. He rummaged through his knapsack. His hand found the only extra piece of clothing he had brought along: a white shirt. He dismounted and had taken a few steps back toward the main road to find a tree or post to tie a piece of the fabric onto, when he heard several large vehicles approaching on the main road. He dropped down, out of view, in the deep shadows and peered at the road.

Four large military trucks, with an identical following distance between them, rumbled past. The starlit night sky made it possible to see into the backs of the trucks: he thought he saw soldiers—men in uniform, holding automatic rifles. The men were shouting and laughing.

Charles hesitated a moment—it was one of his better shirts—then cut and ripped the shirt apart with a moan and tied a piece to a tall post, right at the turn-off, which looked like it had once had a road sign attached to it. He grabbed the hunting knife again, this time using the handle and wrote large words across the road surface. He'd better hurry, he knew: the kidnappers would get too far ahead.

He started the motorcycle and raced down the smaller road without headlights until he could see the truck's red lights, then followed more cautiously. Just as well—barely two miles on, *Bwana* Kok's truck pulled off the road next to an enormous *mopani* tree. The driver did not turn off the headlights. Charles killed the engine, pushed the motorcycle off the road and parked it behind some tall scrubs. He took the knife from his knapsack and snuck closer, taking great care where he placed each foot–he dared not announce his presence.

He got closer, then froze, exhaling slowly. He could see the truck in its entirety now: the back was down, the canvas cover thrown open; people were moving around and talking. He could clearly hear a girl—it was definitely Miss Rianna—but he could not see her. She had to be over in front of the truck. Two men came into view. *Mavuto and Mapopa!* Charles's jaw dropped. *The bastard Mavuto! Mapopa could at most only be his sidekick.* The men paraded up and down next to the truck with AK-47's over their shoulders. The rifles look brand-new. *But why were they not on one of those military trucks, if they wanted to play soldier?*

BE SILENT

Charles pulled further back into the dark shadows of the trees when Lukas and Anthony appeared mere feet away from him, and started peeing. For a second he considered drawing the boys' attention, but stopped himself. He might startle them, alerting Mavuto, who looked trigger-happy.

Think carefully, Charles Chombe! You have one hunting knife; they have two automatic rifles.

He was not interested in doing the math. He waited until everyone was back in the truck and the engine had been started before he ran back to the motorcycle. As he slowly steered around the curve, giving the kidnappers time to put distance between them, his headlight fell on a large rock next to the clearing. Something was written on the rock, in color. Charles slammed the brakes, killed the engine and ran to the rock. Colored chalk. He smiled—that must have been Lukas's doing.

He leaned closer: *July 29. 7:15. Help. Ria. Anth. Luk. Mav. Mapo. 4 guns.*

Something in the dirt caught his eyes as he played the flashlight over the area. He bent forward and carefully scooped it up, inspecting it in the light—brought it to his nose—definitely canned beans; they were still moist. He realized how hungry he was.

Charles cut another long strip from the white shirt and tied it to a small flat rock. This he put on top of the big rock, draping the fabric down, and tied a smaller stone to the tip of the cloth so the wind would not blow it sideways. Anyone coming down the road, would, he hoped, see the strip of cloth in their headlights—and find the scribbling.

43

Madzi Moyo. July 29, 1964. 8:05 p.m.

"Hello, Louis. I'm sorry about Lukas. I want you to meet Sergeant Rangarajan from the Fort Jameson Police Department." Ulrich Wessels' calming words brought the distraught Louis Ferreira to a standstill.

Louis took several deep breaths. He was not known to be a vocal man. "Hello, Ulrich. Sorry about the outburst … and thank you … I have met Sergeant Rangarajan." He nodded in the policeman's direction, also acknowledging the other people in the room, who waved back.

Rina Wessels jumped up, handed Barbara the rifle, ran to Louis and hugged him, careful not to knock the rifle from his hand. She kissed him on the cheek, whispering, "How is Maria? We're going to find them, Louis." She hugged him again.

"Maria's fine—she stayed behind with the girls. Thank you, Rina." Louis turned around, gesturing Youssef into the room.

BE SILENT

"Ulrich, meet Youssef Khalil," he said, "a friend of mine. He's also from Fort Jameson." Youssef stepped forward as Louis added, "He has a good truck and offered to help with the search for the children."

Ulrich Wessels' eyes met those of the Fort Jameson shopkeeper, and held fast. *Yes, Ulrich, he is a man like you, a father who has empathy for another's plight, even though he wears a long cheesecloth tunic with a skullcap and a long beard.* "Welcome, Mr. Khalil," he said. "Thank you for helping us. Please have a seat."

Sergeant Rangarajan cleared his throat; he was pulsing with impatience. "Pardon me, *Bwana* Wessels," he said, "but may I quickly use the phone in your study? I need to speak to the commissioner in Lusaka." He nodded his gratitude and added, "Why don't you brief *Bwana* Ferreira on the latest?"

Wessels and Kok gave a matter-of-fact summary of what they knew to Louis Ferreira.

Louis had difficulty hiding his disappointment. "I cannot for a moment believe Charles Chombe is one of them! Lukas, and even little Wouter, talked about him every Friday afternoon when I picked them up for the weekend, almost as much as about their school friends. He sounded like an older brother they wished they had. Mavuto and Mapopa, well—I didn't know them at all."

"Louis," Ulrich said, "they're the only men on the Station unaccounted for, as of late this afternoon."

"It is 8:05 already!" Louis said. "Youssef and I are leaving now—there's no other way to catch up with those criminals. Just imagine what they can do to the children, especially to Rianna! Is any one else coming along? Constable Pillay, Constable Bisa, what did the sergeant say?"

Youssef Khalil got up, along with the constables, but Ulrich jumped ahead of them. "Louis, my friend, just hold on! Where will you go? Where will you start looking? They could be *anywhere!*"

"I can't stand around while the sergeant has a chit-chat with his pal in Lusaka."

"Louis, we have to join forces," Ulrich said. "We need a plan before we scatter in too many directions. According to the sergeant they probably won't receive additional manpower. Let's hear what the commissioner in Lusaka had to say. Perhaps he changed his mind. If we can find an extra spare tire, we can get my truck up and running in a few minutes. Then we at least will have three vehicles to use."

"Sorry, Ulrich, but I'm leaving." Louis's voice broke. "One of those children is *my son.*" He moved toward the door, his knuckles white as he clutched the Marlin, with Youssef on his heels.

Sergeant Rangarajan swept into the room. He held his hands up. "People, listen! Please. Bwana Ferreira, one moment please. Why don't you all sit down? I'll be quick, I promise."

Louis Ferreira turned back, but remained standing.

"Commissioner Subramanium in Lusaka has been informed about the kidnapping. He sends us his best wishes but cannot spare us any manpower, not for at least the next forty-eight hours. He had received ministerial orders to deploy his force elsewhere, his hands are both tied. So—"

"No reinforcements for two days!" Louis called out. "Sergeant, that's an insult! By that time the kidnappers can be in Dar es Salaam with the children and sell them as slaves!" He moved purposefully toward the door.

BE SILENT

"*Bwana*, wait! I know your son is one of the children, but I heard what Bwana Wessels suggested about borrowing a spare tire. It's an excellent idea. The more vehicles we can get on the road the better! I don't believe the Land Rover's spare will fit on the Chevy, though." He turned toward Youssef, "Mister Khalil, would you have a spare tire that we could use on *Bwana* Wessels' truck?"

Youssef stepped forward, "Actually, Sergeant, I always carry two spares in my truck." He laughed, as if embarrassed. "I often have to travel to Lusaka, and experience with punctured tires has taught me many lessons. He can certainly borrow one."

Sergeant Rangarajan was all business again; he would not allow Lusaka's ineptness to ruin any chance they had to rescue the children. He thanked Youssef and spun around to face Bisa, who was twice Pillay's size; he would be able to complete the task in record time. "Bisa, go with Mr. Khalil and *Bwan*a Wessels, get his truck up and running, then report back. You have ten minutes. Go!"

Then he pulled out a map and looked in Mrs. Wessels' direction, "*Amayi*, may I use this coffee table to lay the map on? I want to show everyone what I had in mind."

Rina Wessels cleared the large coffee table and the sergeant spread the map out.

He knelt down at the low table to allow the others to look over his shoulder, and, with a red pen, drew a small circle around the black dot for Madzi Moyo. "Right, gentlemen. The kidnappers had three options to choose from"—and he indicated the possibilities—"southwest toward Lusaka, directly east toward

Malawi—the shortest route—and north toward Isoka, Chinsali and Mwenzo, if they wanted to get into Tanzania." He looked up at Louis Ferreira and smiled, "And we have to catch up with them before they reach Dar es Salaam!"

Louis Ferreira grimaced, "Exactly, Sergeant! Are we sending out the vehicles in all three directions?"

The sergeant stood up. "That's what I thought of doing. How many able bodies do we have?" The hands flew up. He did not count Peter Miyanda or Doctor Brown.

"And how well are we armed?" he added. "Gentlemen, who has a rifle or handgun? Pillay, help me keep count."

He turned to Rina Wessels again. "*Amay*i, do you and *Bwana* have any emergency rations? Water bags, blankets, dried food, anything else of use? We won't have time to pick up stuff from each house on the Station. We have to be on our way in fifteen minutes at the most."

Rina and Barbara Wessels disappeared to the kitchen.

"Sergeant," Louis said, "how many police radios do you have? How will we communicate?"

"We have two extra," the sergeant said. "Pillay, fetch the radio from the Land Rover and tell Bisa to finish up. We need to go very soon. We'll leave some of the men with rifles on the Station to protect the woman and children."

Bisa, Ulrich and Youssef came back in, and Bisa called out, rubbing his hands, "Mission accomplished, Sergeant! Third vehicle is ready for immediate use, sir!"

Gravel crunched outside and several doors slammed, followed by many urgent feet running up the veranda stairs. "Ulrich! … *Bwana* Wessels!"

BE SILENT

Four strangers barged into the already filled-to-capacity living room of *Bwana* Wessels, forcing Sergeant Rangarajan and his two colleagues to step aside to make room. Rangarajan wondered what it was with the missionaries, being so boisterous. He had always been under the impression it was not part of their culture, to be outspoken.

Ulrich Wessels hugged each of the newcomers and said, "Sergeant, allow me introduce the parents of the other two missing children: Etienne and Hester Benade, Anthony's parents, and Phillip and Anna Vermeulen, Rianna's parents." He quickly added, "Sergeant, I think we may have a fourth vehicle at our disposal!"

44

*North of Fort Jameson.
July 29, 1964.*

Rianna tapped the boys' shoulders, whispering, "Here we go, guys. Lukas, you know what to do?"

"Yes, Rianna."

"Anthony, you still want to go ahead?"

"Sure, let's do it," Anthony whispered back.

It was reckoning time for Mapopa.

The children shuffled slowly toward the far end of the truck bed where Mapopa sat, with Rianna in the lead, the boys remaining in the deeper shadows. Lukas and Anthony had opened the blanket and were holding it halfway up, pulling it behind them. They had to be so careful not to make a sound or lose their balance as Mavuto drove carelessly on the uneven gravel road. Rianna touched Lukas's and Anthony's heads and the boys halted; they were in position.

BE SILENT

The plan was simple. The children were praying for a big bump in the road.

Rianna shuffled forward again and appeared unannounced next to Mapopa, barely twelve inches separating them. Mapopa jumped backwards against the tailgate, knocking his elbow, which spun the pistol from his hand, and he called out, "*Jesu Christu, mwana*, what do you want?" A vicious bump in the road followed and they were all knocked off balance. Rianna yelled at the boys as she lunged forward, crashing into Mapopa, who was still grasping in the dark for the pistol on the truck bed next to him.

Mapopa fell backward, as the girl's arms locked around his upper body. He smashed into the tailgate a second time, this time head first, and yelled in Chinyanja.

Rianna yelled in panic, "Anthony! Lukas! The blanket! Throw the blanket!"

She held her tight grip around the Chinyanja man's slim body as the boys knocked into them, pulling the blanket over the furious man's head. For a brief moment the nausea washed over her—the sudden intimate proximity of their reeking bodies was unexpected. Mapopa continued swearing and yelling in English and Chinyanja, delivering vicious kicks as he tried to free himself from the triple onslaught.

Anthony cried out when one of Mapopa's boots struck him in the groin, and he let go for a few seconds.

Rianna realized that their window of opportunity to overpower the man was fast closing, as he wiggled more of himself free. *He will kill us if that happens. I am not planning to die at thirteen.* She screamed in her blood-chilling Rianna-voice right in his ear, "You are *not* going to kidnap us much longer!" Then she quickly readjusted her grip and smashed into him a second time, all the time screaming in his ear, grabbing more blanket and wrapping it around his head and down his torso.

She was terrified. *What was I thinking, that we could overpower the man?*

"Lukas, the rope!" she yelled. She had forgotten that the rope was still with Lukas. "Get me the rope from your backpack, Lukas! Anthony, help me hold him down!" Rianna and Anthony had the poor man lying partially on his stomach, with the blanket over his head, smothering him, pulling it down to his waist.

Anthony avoided the thrusting boots as best he could. The pistol was still somewhere on the truck-bed next to them, he knew, but it had to wait.

"Quick, Lukas," Rianna called out, "I can't hold his arms much longer! I hope you can make proper knots!"

"Hold still, Rianna!" Lukas protested.

'*Mwanas,*" the man yelled, "I'm going to kill all of you! You bastards!"

"No, Mapopa," Rianna said, "*you're* the bastard! We did nothing to you or Mavuto. Nothing!" She yanked Lukas's knot tighter, grabbed the knife from her dress pocket and cut the excess rope.

"Anthony, Lukas, grab his ankles!" She tied the kicking ankles, slipped the knife back into her pocket and felt around on the metal floor for the handgun. Desperate, she started crawling on all fours, until finally her hand knocked against the pistol. *Mapopa's going to kill us if he gets hold of this gun!* As her fingers

BE SILENT

closed around the cool metal, they were once again thrown sideways, this time as the truck's brakes were slammed on. Mavuto must have smelled a rat. All she could smell now was urine—one of them, in the consternation, must have had a bladder slip-up. The truck skidded to a standstill on the side of the road.

Mapopa was still lying partially on his stomach. Rianna grabbed the pistol around the nozzle. In the semi-darkness, she could just make out form and shape. She hit the blanket where she saw the back of his head. *Oh Lord, don't let me kill him!* He cried out and she hit him again, harder.

"Lukas, your backpack!" She shoved the pistol into the bag, slipped the straps over her own shoulders, and headed back to the tailgate, whispering, "Boys, positions!"

They could hear Mavuto's boots crunching on the gravel next to the truck. "You bloody idiots!" he swore. "What's going on in the back? Mapopa, what's your problem?"

He unhooked the canvas straps and dropped the tailgate, calling, "Mapopa?" Mavuto, Rianna noted, didn't have the rifle with him, only a flashlight.

Rianna and the boys didn't hesitate. They dove at him, screaming, "Mavuto, you horrible kidnapper!" as they struck him in the chest, sending them all crashing together into the soft gravel next to the road. The flashlight rolled away, its beam shining into the brush that towered above them.

45

North of Fort Jameson. July 29, 1964.

Charles Chombe followed the faint red light of the stolen truck cautiously, keeping a fixed distance between him and it. He turned his headlights on sparingly, only when the surrounding *mopani* trees formed too dense a canopy across the road, blacking out the young night sky.

He was distraught and puzzled. Even more, he was disappointed with his own poor judgment of character. How many times had he talked with Mavuto, especially early in the year, during the elections? Both of them had been enthralled by the election of the thirty-nine-year old African nationalist Kenneth Kaunda as prime minister.

What was Mavuto doing now, kidnapping the missionary children he interacted with every day? He knew about Mavuto's military training, and about his being a passionate nationalist, a firm supporter of the "Queen and her crown must go"

BE SILENT

campaign—like Charles himself. Mavuto had told him his concerns about his mother, who had become a dedicated follower of Alice Lenshina, so much so that she'd moved north. Mavuto had aired his antagonism to the church, especially his concerns that they might interfere with independence, scheduled for October.

How could I not have seen this coming? Being a garden boy was only a cover-up all along—but for what?

Charles had never given much attention to the younger Mapopa, who had remained, literally, in the shadow of his sturdy foster brother. Mapopa was a shy and withdrawn young man who became known on the Station for wearing long sleeves and long pants, day in and day out, even during the excruciating hot summer months, all in an attempt to hide his albino skin. His being part of the kidnapping must have been Mavuto's doing. What immense power did Mavuto exert over his foster brother?

Charles geared down and braked when he noticed that the truck had slowed down. *Don't let that jackal Mavuto see you, Chombe. Keep your distance!*

Charles let go of the handlebar and throttle for a second when the thought struck him. *Why did Mavuto bring the children along?* The motorcycle swerved dangerously, and he grabbed the handlebar in panic, bracing himself for a fall.

Before the night is over, Mavuto might be the death of me, Charles thought as he once more came to an emergency stop, following the example of the truck ahead of him, which had just rounded a curve in the road only to skid to a halt against a sandbank on the side of the road, its headlights still on.

What is it this time?

Charles killed the engine, pushed the motorcycle out of sight behind some shrubs and jumped back onto the side of the road. Mavuto was yelling at the occupants in the back of the truck as he busied himself with loosening the canvas straps and tailgate, a flashlight in his one hand.

The moment the tailgate dropped, clattering against the fender of the truck, three obscure objects darted from the truck bed, hitting Mavuto in his chest, crashing with him into the ground. *The children! Oh Christu! They were attacking Mavuto. They must have overpowered Mapopa. Mwanas, what are you thinking—the men will kill you!*

Before he knew it, Charles was flying down the dark gravel road, his knapsack bouncing on his back, knife in his right hand.

———

Mavuto had recovered with lightning speed, his injured leg in spite. He bounced back onto his feet, grabbing one of the boys by the arm as the girl snatched his flashlight and the other boy by the hand and started running, yelling, "Run, Lukas, run!"

Mavuto reached the passenger door, still dragging the one boy by the arm, limping with his bandaged leg, and ripped the door open. A second later he had the rifle in his hand and fired a salvo into the air, hollering, "*Mtsikana*, stop! Come back! I will *shoot* your little friend!"

Mavuto raced around the back of the vehicle, dragging the boy by the arm.

He yelled into the night a second time, "*Mtsikana*, I *will* shoot your friend!" Mavuto followed that with a second salvo of rounds into the brush to the side of the road the children had run to.

He only heard the gravel flying behind him as Charles launched himself for the attack, a knife in his outstretched arm. Mavuto spun around, but the momentum of his assailant was too much and they crashed to the ground, releasing his vise-like grip on the boy. The pain in his leg hampered his movements.

Anthony jerked his arm free and scampered to his feet, away from the struggling men. Rianna and Lukas, Anthony saw, had turned back, and stood by the hood of the truck. Rianna was clenching the flashlight in one hand, the other grasping the backpack's shoulder strap. None of them moved or said a word, their faces that of ghosts.

The next moment Rianna unfroze, jumped forward and hollered, "Charles! Watch out!"

46

Madzi Moyo. July 29, 1964. 8:15 p.m.

Sergeant Rangarajan and Ulrich Wessels briefed Rianna's and Anthony's parents on the current state of affairs. Rangarajan paced as he gave instructions: time was of the essence, he had to get the teams going. He could hear Louis Ferreira pacing outside on the red veranda floor.

If it was my son or children who were abducted, the commissioner, for one, would have had more than an earful. I would turn every stone upside down. The whole world would learn of my plight! I wouldn't only pace outside on the veranda, I would hunt the kidnappers down.

He had almost choked when the commissioner remarked, "Very unfortunate about the children, Rahul, very unfortunate. But the timing couldn't have been worse. Tonight is not a good night for tracking down lost children, not a good time. Actually, Rahul, I can't help you for the next forty-eight hours. You and your men will have to sweat it out in Fort Jameson. Make me proud, my man, make me proud ..."

Such an asshole.

Focus, Rahul! Between them they had three police radios and four usable vehicles. One radio had to remain in Madzi Moyo, which would function as their temporary base. Constable Pillay would be ideal to man it. He knew the man was working hard toward a promotion.

"Pillay," he declared, "you are going to be our man with the radio here on the Station. Go fetch your rifle and kit from the Land Rover."

"But, Sergeant, I was planning on helping catch—"

"Pillay! This is how you will help us apprehend the kidnappers. This posting comes with great responsibility. If the *bwana* and *amayi* agree, we will make *Bwana* Wessels's house the temporary base?"

The *bwana* and *amayi* nodded their consent and Pillay was on his way toward the Rover.

"Listen, everybody!" the sergeant announced to the room. "Here's a quick run down of the vehicle teams, as well the Station teams that will remain behind."

"Vehicle 1, with Bisa and myself, in the police Land Rover, will take the smaller T4 route northeast, through Fort Jameson, passing Lundazi and Chama, all the way to Isoka, approaching Chinsali from the northeast. We'll take the second radio."

"Vehicle 2, with Louis Ferreira and Youssef Khalil ..."

Rahul peeked his head through the door and hollered toward the front porch, "*Bwana* Ferreira!"

The moment Louis Ferreira joined the group the sergeant continued, "Louis and Youssef will be in vehicle 2. They will also head northeast on the T4, but only as far as Fort Jameson, where they will turn northwest to join the Great East Road at Serenje, and then turn northeast toward Mpika and Kasama, approaching Chinsali from the west. They have two rifles with them, and they will take the third radio. Correct, gentlemen?"

The men nodded.

"Vehicle 3, with Ulrich Wessels and Phillip Vermeulen, will also head north toward Fort Jameson and then southeast toward the border with Malawi at the *Mchinji crossing—*"

Vermeulen jumped up. "Sergeant, the border post closes at six. It's almost nine. And don't we need passports, visas or special permits?"

Sergeant Rangarajan sighed, but smiled. "The border post already knows about the abduction of the children. Constable Bisa over here will contact them again as soon as we leave and give them your names. There's someone on duty after six. Don't worry. Mchinji crossing will contact us by radio once you've reached them, depending on what happens in the meantime."

Phillip Vermeulen still wasn't satisfied. "Sorry, Sergeant, but are you now officiating us to become deputy sheriffs, with the power to arrest, with handcuffs and all?"

Mr. Vermeulen, you are testing my patience, Rahul Rangarajan thought. "This is an emergency; as I told everyone, Lusaka cannot help us. Yes, Bisa will give each vehicle team two pairs of handcuffs once we're out—"

Louis Ferreira interrupted. "Please, Philip. We need to leave. If you catch them, make a citizen's arrest!"

The room erupted in general applause.

BE SILENT

Sergeant Rangarajan smiled and cleared his throat. "Thank you, gentlemen. Vehicle 4, with Mr. Benade and Evangelist Miyanda, will head south on the road to Lusaka. They have one rifle with them. Correct, gentlemen?"

The two men signaled their agreement.

Rahul Rangarajan noticed the disappointment of young Peter Miyanda. "Peter," he said, "I want you and Doctor Brown to join forces and help us look after the people at the hostel. If Mrs. Vermeulen would take their car, which is not being used in the pursuit, and help bring all the remaining people from Lower Madzi Moyo to the hostel and those in Upper Madzi Moyo to this house, it would be a great help."

He established eye contact with the boy and Anna Vermeulen.

"Oh," he added, "and Doctor Brown will also take his rifle with him."

Another hand was waving. "Apologies, *Bwana* Kok!" the sergeant said, coughing to hide his embarrassment. "Seems to me I had written you out of our evening. I would be much obliged if you and the *amayi* could also go stay at the hostel. And bring your rifle along, will you?"

"Please?" he added.

Kobus Kok smiled and signed. The next moment he stood up. "Pardon me, Sergeant," he said, "but my wife, Magda, has a doctor's appointment in Lusaka this Friday at noon." He turned toward the doctor. "Dr. Brown arranged it. She is to see a doctor of … obstetrics." Kobus Kok blushed. "But my truck was stolen, as you know, and my wife is more than six months' pregnant. There are concerns about the health of the baby; they were even talking about having her deliver in Lusaka."

"I understand, Mr. Kok. And?"

"Well, do you think there might be a way of helping us get there on time?"

Rahul Rangarajan sighed deeply, but silently. "Mr. Kok, I hope that before dark tomorrow we will have located the children. Many things will then be possible. But for now, we really have to leave."

He faced the rest of the room. "Okay, people, let's go! Bisa, come!"

Sergeant Rangarajan was halfway out the door when he remembered one more thing, *"Amayi Wessels,"* he said, "thank you very much for opening your house to us tonight." He touched his forehead in a gentle salute in the direction of Rina Wessels.

"Pillay," he continued, "I want proper radio procedure. You have to do better than Juma. Do you copy that?"

Pillay straightened up. "Copy that, sir!"

Ulrich Wessels called out, "Friends, let us pray before we leave." Everyone from the Mission gathered around him and bowed their heads. The police officers and Youssef Khalil went out to the veranda and waited there.

47

North of Fort Jameson. July 29, 1964.

The panic in Rianna's voice was unmistakable as she repeated her warning, shrieking, "Charles, watch out! Behind you!"

She stopped short of diving at the figure crouched behind Charles, preparing to strike him with a rifle butt.

"Charles!" "Mapopa! No!"

Mapopa hit Charles across the side of the head and when the latter slumped, struck him a second time.

Rianna heard the sickening thwacks.

How is this possible? Rianna thought. I made double sure the knots around his wrists and ankles were tied so well! How did he even manage to get out of the blanket? Was he some kind of Houdini? She looked uncomprehending at the pieces of rope that was still attached to one wrist and an ankle as Mapopa threw the rifle toward Mavuto, who had scrambled to his feet, as he called, "Catch, Mavuto!"

And here I was afraid I was going to kill him when I struck him through the blanket. Next time you have to hit harder, Rianna Vermeulen!

Mapopa stooped and the next moment had a pistol in his hand. It must have slipped out of the backpack Rianna had put on. He brandished the gun at the three children, commanding, "Come and lie down over here. Do it *now*! I'm going to shoot *all* of you, but I'll kill the *mtsikana* last!" And he glared at Rianna.

Mapopa had taken command. He gave Charles's motionless figure a vicious kick in passing as he approached the children. "Down! Lie down! Now!" He fired a single round into the gravel next to Lukas. Both boys jumped sideways as dirt flew past their legs. Both were whimpering now, clutching their wet groins—urine and fear made for a heady aroma.

Rianna gasped at the wild look in the young Chinyanja's eyes, reflecting the soft glow of the truck's headlights. *I have started his madness. He's going to shoot Lukas, then Anthony and then me. He's really going to shoot us this time. He's not trying to scare us anymore.* Tears ran down her face. *Oh dear Lord, be with Mother and be with Father and with P.J. and with little Casper.* And *dear Jesus, be with my two friends here next to me and please, please, we don't want to die.*

She was looking into the soul of a madman. She shuddered and grabbed the boys' hands, squeezing hard. *What does it feel like when a bullet rips through your body, rips the life out of your insides? How much does it hurt when you die from a gunshot in your chest?*

"Mapopa! *Gwirani!* Stop that! There will be no killing!" It was Mavuto. As the stricken children crouched down in the dirt in front of Mapopa, Mavuto had found his voice. He shoved his younger stepbrother out of the way, firmly placed his hand on Mapopa's hand with the gun, and forced it down and away from the children.

Rianna held onto the boys with dear life, pulling them farther down beside her, willing them to lie still. *These men are both mad. There's evil in their hearts. I can see it in their eyes.* She repeated her prayer for her two young friends, then remembered Charles Chombe. *And dear Jesus, please don't let Mavuto kill Charles, Lukas's friend. Although, I am still mad at Charles for what he has done to Adam Kok's mother. Amen.*

She stopped praying when Mapopa shouted back, "Mavuto! I told you the children should never have come along! I *will* shoot them! At least the girl—she almost killed me!" And he jumped past Mavuto with his pistol again drawn on Rianna.

"Mapopa, I told you: there will be *no* killing!" Mavuto knocked the pistol from Mapopa's hand, picked it up and stuffed it in his belt. He snarled at Mapopa, "They wouldn't have overpowered you if you didn't fall asleep in the back. So stop your shit! There's work to be done. First we'll handcuff Mr. Chombe. Come, Mapopa, hold the flashlight. Now!"

Mapopa swept the flashlight over the children, who were still lying on the gravel road on the spot he had told them to, still holding hands.

Mavuto took the light from him and warned the children, "Don't try and run away, *mwanas*. I'll shoot your friend, Charles Chombe first, and then we'll catch you and shoot you one after the other. Yes, I know I told Mapopa, 'no killing.' But I'm willing to make an exception."

He threw first the rifle, then the flashlight back at Mapopa. "Guard them, I'm getting some stuff from the truck." Within seconds Mavuto was back with the other rifle and one of the large backpacks.

"Mapopa, hold the light. Let's get this big boy sorted out. There we go," he said as he rolled Charles over onto his stomach and clipped a pair of handcuffs to his wrists, behind his back. Charles moaned softly. The entire left side of his head was caked with blood.

"No ropes for him—only the proper stuff," Mavuto said, patting the cuffs.

Lukas scrambled to his feet. "Mavuto, he's hurt! Look, he's bleeding! Please don't handcuff him, he can't harm you anymore—Mapopa cracked his skull. Please. Let me clean his wound."

Mavuto laughed, "*Mwana*, your friend almost killed me. No, we're going to make sure he can't bother us. He's caused us enough trouble. He won't die from the wound—it's only a little cut."

He took the flashlight and searched the ground where he and Charles had struggled, then bent over, picked up Charles's hunting knife and stuffed it into a side pocket of the backpack.

He slowly walked over to the children and tied each one's wrists behind their backs. "Listen, children! This is my *final* warning. The three of you, and your big friend over there have been responsible for several delays and almost ruined my plans. It's unacceptable. I did say, 'no killing,' but if you keep on trying to escape, I will change my mind."

He suddenly yelled in their faces: "Do I make myself clear?"

BE SILENT

The children scudded back against the side of the truck. "Yes, Mavuto," they whimpered.

Mavuto then dragged the somewhat more alert Charles toward the truck and pulled him halfway up against the rear wheel. He kicked him in the side with his healthy leg, making Charles groan, "Chombe," Mavuto asked, "how did you get here?"

Charles only moaned, his eyes closed.

Mavuto kicked him harder.

"Chombe, where is your vehicle? Why didn't I see your headlights?"

Charles mumbled, "I won't tell you, traitor ..." He laughed through his pain, coughing, and added, "Charles has the eyes of the lion, he sees in the dark, no lights necessary ..."

Mavuto kicked him in the ribs this time, eliciting a yell from his victim as well as from the children. "You know nothing Chombe!" he shouted. "You don't know who the traitors are! 'Eyes of a lion.' Hah! Don't bullshit me!" And kicked him again.

Rianna jumped to her feet and bellowed, "Stop that, you devil!"

Mavuto laughed. "Calm down, *mtsikana*. Your friend is not cooperating, but we can't delay any longer. Mapopa, keep an eye on our prisoners. I'll have a look for his vehicle. He's no ghost—he couldn't have flown here."

Mavuto tied Charles' ankles with a piece of rope and limped off into the night with an AK-47 and the flashlight.

48

North of Fort Jameson. July 29, 1964.

Mavuto returned ten minutes later, puffing and swinging the flashlight with purpose. He walked up to Charles and kicked him hard in the ribs, shouting, "You bastard! What did you drive? Where did you hide it, Chombe?"

The children protested and Charles grimaced, then mumbled, almost singing, "He has eyes of a lion, no lights are required. Charles Chombe is a ghost, he can fly ..."

Mavuto slipped the rifle from his shoulder and shoved the barrel against the center of Charles's breastbone.

"You think you're clever, Mr. House Boy! You think nobody knows you lust after the *bwana's* wife. Your lust made you blind. I'm going to pull this trigger if you don't tell me where your vehicle is!" and he jammed the barrel harder against his captive's chest.

Charles gasped but whispered, "I won't tell you. You're no killer, Mavuto. You're a soldier. I do not understand what your

BE SILENT

mission is tonight, but I have no quarrel with you, my brother. I followed you to free the children." He paused, catching his breath. "Release the children; they have done you no harm. We won't follow you—we'll turn back, we'll go home. You don't want to do this."

"I am *not* your brother!"

"As you wish, but you can still let us go and continue on your mission. I know of a place nearby where the children and I can hide for the night. Nobody will find us there. I won't go to the police until morning. That will give you time to get away or do what you need to do."

Mapopa called out, "Don't listen to him Mavuto! The man's a snake!"

Mavuto lowered the rifle for a moment. "Shut up, Mapopa." Then he yelled as he jabbed his captive again. "I'm not stupid, Chombe!"

"I give you my word …" the injured man mumbled.

"I don't trust you, House Boy, not for a moment. No. We've had enough delays tonight. Look at the time, you idiots, it's almost nine! You're all getting into the back of the truck. We're going to gag each one of you and tie your ankles as well. I had enough of your shit!"

Without a single word more, Mavuto performed each task himself. He didn't trust Mapopa any more. But he did need help with moving the captives—his leg was throbbing too much. Together with Mapopa, he lifted the children back onto the truck bed and then struggled to drag-lift the bounded Charles as well.

Mavuto took hold of Mapopa's shoulder once the captives were stowed into the back and turned him around, forcing him to face him. "You have the pistol and the AK," he said. "Don't mess up this time, Brother Mapopa."

Mavuto jumped forward on the truck bed, brandishing his rifle. "Everybody, move back! Move!" he yelled. "All the way toward the back. Yes, Chombe, you as well! The games are over. If you try to escape, Mapopa *will* shoot you."

Mavuto swept the flashlight over each person's face. "Do you get that?"

Everyone nodded. No one made a sound.

Mapopa stepped away from the back of the truck. "Mavuto. Can I talk with you?" He gestured to his stepbrother.

"What's it now, Mapopa?" Mavuto said. "You're tired and want to go home and go to bed?"

Mapopa stepped back another two feet. He laughed nervously. "No, Mavuto, I'm not tired."

He lowered his voice to a whisper. "Where exactly are we going? You never told me. I know we're going northeast, but *where*? And, once we get there, what are you planning to do?"

Mavuto felt a pang of guilt toward the youth in front of him. Mapopa had never asked to become part of this *ulendo*, this journey. He had even suggested that they let the children go when they were still in the shed. But that had never been an option, not once the children discovered the rifles. Mavuto shook his head. *Focus, Lisulo, focus on your mission.*

"Mapopa," he said, "don't you trust me?"

The youth laughed again, nervously. He stepped closer toward his brother. It was impossible not to hear the "*umph-umph*" coming from the forest behind them—that was not a hyena—the lions must have moved their prowling session to the early evening.

BE SILENT

"Mapopa, when did you last see Mother *Fatsani*?"

"Mavuto? I think it was many months ago. Not long after the elections."

"Do you know where she is now?"

Mapopa shook his head. His stepbrother wasn't thinking clearly anymore. That fall to the ground when Charles attacked him must have knocked his head against something hard. And he had a wound above his knee—he is limping, he must also have lost some blood.

"I received a letter from her only last week saying she was moving to *Paishuko*."

"Paishuko?" Mapopa asked. How was it possible that his stepmother would have made this decision out of her own free will? He wasn't superstitious, but something strange was happening.

"Yes, my brother—the place we grew up in."

"But there will be Lumpa people there! You don't like the Lumpas. I know *that* at least."

"Yes, Mapopa, that's true. I was originally afraid the Lumpa mobilization would prevent independence taking place— that's why I got the AKs. I was willing to stop them with force, if necessary. That was my original mission. Strange, but at present, I fear mostly for Mother."

He coughed, as if embarrassed. "From the time the children jumped on me, trying to escape, I have experienced this overwhelming concern about her. I can't shake it. I have to go find Mother Fatsani *first* and bring her home. Once she's safe, I'll reconsider my original plan."

He turned around. "Come Mapopa—enough talking. Get in the truck. Let's go get Mother *Fatsani*."

Mapopa still paused. He had little experience with thinking things through, but this was news. He had no taste for the idea of confronting the Lumpa people in Paishuko, or anywhere.

A dark shadow moved across Mavuto's eyes. "Mapopa! Just because I opened up to you, gives you no liberties. Get in the truck! And don't let the ten-year-olds overpower you a second time!"

Mavuto slammed the tailgate shut and yanked the canvas ties tight, behind the young man. The driver's door was closed even harder.

49

Madzi Moyo. July 29, 1964. 8:30 p.m.

Louis Ferreira had to restrain himself from grabbing the handcuffs and police radio from Constable Bisa when they reached the vehicles. But the moment he got them, he realized he had, in any case, snookered himself when he'd parked in his obsessed haste, mere inches from the police Land Rover and Ulrich Wessels' truck. Now that the other parents' vehicles were here too, he was neatly boxed in.

"Thank you, Constable Bisa," he said anyway.

"*Mbusa,*" Bisa said, "can I quickly show you how to operate the radio?"

Louis laughed. "Thank you, Constable, but I'll manage. I have played with these before. I only need the frequency." Bisa gave it to him and he wrote it down. He then helped Wessels and Vermeulen stuff their things together into Ulrich's truck, and offered to act as guide so they could carefully back up and get past the other two vehicles behind them.

The sky was still moonless and none of them had the heart to overstep the boundaries of the driveway and trash Rina Wessels' well-kept garden. The night was a mixture of sweetness: sugarbush, wisteria and frangipani—and, in the distance, beating drums. The message of the missing children was being sent into the world, as had been done over the centuries.

Once the Wesselses' truck was out of the way, there would be room for Louis and Youssef to wriggle their vehicle out. Youssef had insisted, the moment they stepped off the veranda, that Louis does the driving.

"*Bwana*, take the keys," he had said.

Louis had protested half-heartedly—"But, Youssef ..."

"*Bwana*, I will drive too slow for your need tonight. My eyes are quite good and our team needs an alert navigator as well as a sentinel—I will perform those tasks."

It was a done deal.

All four vehicles paused at the Madzi Moyo–T4 junction. Sergeant Rangarajan jumped out and reiterated, "Gentlemen, all the best with your respective missions tonight. May we soon find the children. If you have any news, get in touch with me, with Pillay in Madzi or with Juma in Fort Jameson!"

Louis Ferreira required no further invitation. He had kept the big old Chevy's engine running and simply slipped it into gear and stepped on the gas pedal, making for the twin tarred strips of the main road. He looked into his rearview mirror. *Tonight we'll see if Constable Bisa has what it takes to keep up with a distraught Ferreira*, he thought.

BE SILENT

Youssef turned to his designated driver, who was in the process of testing the limits of his old workhorse, "*Bwana*, so we stick to the T4 until we reach Fort Jameson, right? No turn-offs?"

Louis did not take his eyes off the road. "You're the navigator, Youssef. You heard the sergeant."

They both thought about what the sergeant had said.

"*Bwana*," Youssef said, "how old is Lukas?"

Louis took his time before he answered. "Ten. My boy is ten." Then he added, "He's such a mature boy for his age. I can't understand why he would be gallivanting in strange places late in the day, why he stepped into some sick person's trap."

"Ten is still very young, *Bwana*. They're children. They play. That's what they're supposed to do. Some schooling, and then play."

"How old are yours, Youssef?"

"Yasmin is nine, Salma eight, and Omar three."

The consequences of his acceptance of Youssef's offer to accompany him on the search started to dawn on Louis. "Who will open your shop tomorrow morning, Youssef?" he asked.

Youssef laughed. "Miriam will, *Bwana*. There is no one else like her, not in all of Egypt or the rest of Africa, for that matter." He added with even more pride, "As soon as they return from school, both Yasmin and Salma will go help their mother in the shop. Miriam has and older auntie who looks after Omar during the day."

Louis smiled. "I thought you said ten-year-olds still need to play. So, if they're eight and nine, they need to do so even more. They can't play in the shop. It's serious business in there."

Youssef chuckled. "See, Bwana, I also sometimes don't practice what I preach, " he said. "No, they usually play in the courtyard between the shop and the house after school. We teach them

229

to help us in the shop a little bit over weekends. And tomorrow they'll be doing it to help a young friend whom they yet have to meet—for a very special cause."

Louis turned toward his new friend, "Thank you, Youssef."

Both men were quiet now as the truck sped along. Louis could barely make out Bisa's headlights in the rearview mirror.

The road had started the gradual drop toward Fort Jameson when Youssef tore Louis from his thoughts. "*Bwana*! Slow down! Slow down, I think I saw something!"

Louis slammed on the brakes. "What's going on, Youssef? What did you see?"

He scanned the night around him as he pulled the truck to the side of the road. There was nothing that he could see—no vehicle, no man-made object or animal or anything else out of the ordinary.

"Youssef?" he asked.

"*Bwana*, please back up," Youssef said. "We just passed a small gravel road on our left-hand side. I saw something back there."

Louis backed up until the headlights illuminated the turn-off. "Youssef?" he asked again.

Youssef jumped out. "There's a piece of white cloth tied to that post over there!"

Louis left the lights on, killed the engine and followed Youssef. "So?"

Behind them, the Land Rover with Sergeant Rangarajan and Constable Bisa in it, pulled off the road and parked behind Youssef's truck.

Youssef, his flashlight in his hand, reached the post. "*Bwana*, look!" he called out.

50

On the way to Lundazi, north of Fort Jameson. July 29, 1964.

Mavuto realized what had happened the moment he felt the tugging on the rear of the truck, the tail swinging ever so gently, and an unhealthy whirring sound coming from the undercarriage. For a few seconds he continued driving in denial, but the whirring worsened, with every rotation of the wheels, making it impossible to compensate for the swaying of the truck, not with the load he was carrying. The truck started to bounce.

Damn. Shit. Damn. A flat tire—tonight—on the night of my mission, with four prisoners and an unwilling assistant who was on the brink of mutiny. Damn the gravel roads of Northern Rhodesia. Damn the colonial rulers from across the water. And damn the Lumpa Church for stealing Mother Fatsani from me!

He slammed the brakes and pulled to the side of the road. *I hope Bwana Kok keeps his spare tire in good condition.*

He swore as he assessed the damage in the weakening beam of the flashlight. The truck stood level, in spite of the road's sloping to the side. The right rear tire was flat, irreparable—a long, deep gash on the outer sidewall. It must have been a sharp piece of rock, not a nail. He slapped the canvas side. "Flat tire, everybody out!"

As soon as Mavuto loosened the straps and dropped the tailgate, Mapopa jumped to the ground and stretched.

Mavuto swung around and slammed the edge of the truck bed. "I *said* we have a flat tire. Everybody out! Now!"

There was still no more response from the back of the truck. No movement, no sound.

Mapopa cleared his throat. Again the nervous laugh. "Mavuto, you tied their hands and feet and gagged them yourself. I think they can't move or speak."

Mavuto scowled, and jumped onto the truck bed.

"Sorry guys," he mumbled, then turned and yelled, "Come help me, Mapopa!"

It was easy enough to pull the children out, but they had more trouble with getting Charles down and pull him up against the sand wall next to the road, along with the children—Mavuto stepped back involuntarily. Stewing in the back, his prisoners had accrued a peculiar smell—they reeked—must be the boys who peed themselves.

He pulled the gags from his captives' mouths, but left the circular cloths hang around their necks, and made no attempt to even loosen their legs. The moment the gag came out of Rianna's mouth, she hollered, "You beast! I thought you were only a big bully. I was so wrong. You're a *sadist*!"

BE SILENT

"I said I was sorry, *mtsikana*."

Rianna cried out, snorting. "Sorry? Don't make us laugh, Mavuto Lisulo. You're a liar on top of everything else! How many years to you think you are going to get for *this*?"

"I'm helping to liberate my country, *mwana*."

"So you think you're a hero, who'll be docorated for doing this. You must be a very desperate man!"

Mavuto ignored her and started lowering the spare tire.

Rianna watched him for a minute, before asking. "We need water and food as well as a *chimbudzi*, Mavuto."

He sneered at her request. "Oh, and now you're pleading. Later. Perhaps." Then he turned around. "Mapopa, help me with this jack."

The spare was in a reasonable condition. As soon as the two men started putting the tools away, Rianna tried again. This time she sounded almost sweet. "Mavuto, can we please get a *chimbudzi* break. I'm sorry I yelled at you. We really need some water. And we have to tend to Charles's wound. I think it's still bleeding."

Mavuto only glared at her and finished putting everything away. He halted in front of her and pulled her to her legs, his AK slung across his chest. His face was drawn. "Okay, *mtsikana*, you go first. You will all go, but *one* at a time."

He bent down and undid first the ankle ties, then the wrist ties. The next moment he stepped back and pulled his pistol from his belt and fired a single round into the ground between her feet.

Rianna recoiled, tears running down her cheeks. The boys also started crying. Charles swore in Chinyanja, bewildered, rocked himself up onto his feet, arms still tied behind and tried to bounce with bound ancles in Mavuto's direction. Mavuto gave him a single shove and the big Chinyanja toppled onto his side, into the sand wall. Mapopa stood at a distance, snickering.

Mavuto stepped closer. "I'm dead serious, *mtsikana*. If you don't come back, I *will* shoot them all. Understood?"

Rianna found it impossible to avoid his piercing eyes, mere inches from her tear covered cheeks—his breathe told her he too had beans for supper, and like the rest of them, wrapped in an unwashed odor. She nodded through her sobs and ran around the truck, soon swallowed by the night.

Charles hollered at their captor, "What are you doing, Lisulo? She's only a young girl! Stop this madness!"

"A young woman with a sharp tongue who needs to be taught how to show some respect!" Mavuto retorted.

"You idiot!" Charles said. "That round could have ricocheted, hurting anyone of us! Because she has *bere*, you think she's a grown woman. You poor fool; they're only children."

Mavuto hit Charles on the chest with the rifle butt. "Shut up, House Boy. I know what I'm doing!"

Rianna returned within two minutes and drank from the big canvas water bag before Mavuto tied her back up. The boys barely needed a minute each to do their business and drank even more thirstily from the bag. Mavuto had to pull the bag away from each one, saying, "Slow down, *mwana*, we have to ration the water!"

Then Mavuto looked the house boy in the eye. (Charles's other eye was swollen closed from the wound and dried blood.) "Chombe," he said, "you know what will happen to them if you

BE SILENT

do not return," and he washed the light over the three dirt-covered, tear-streaked faces.

Five minutes later, the two men had Charles Chombe bound again, along with the boys and shoved all four prisoners back into the dark and reeking hull of the truck. Mapopa jumped on board and Mavuto clipped the tailgate in place but left the canvas straps untied.

The moon had crept out from behind the trees, big and yellow, casting a pale light over the forested landscape. Nearby, a pack of hyenas laughed into the night. The children heard the scavengers' call and huddled against Charles. The next moment, the shrill tjirr-tje-tje-tjirr! of guinea fowl made the children literally jump on Charles's lap. Something must have startled the poor birds.

The children only gradually calmed down as the truck swayed and bounced down the uneven dirt road, mile after endless mile.

Each one of the five occupants in the back could hear Mavuto cursing in the front, as the tail of the truck suddenly rocked sideways, followed by the telltale whirring noise of a damaged tire. The truck skidded to a standstill. The driver's door slammed close, shaking the entire vehicle.

"Chombe!" Mavuto called out as he rounded the truck. He ripped the canvas ties further apart. "Chombe, I need you!"

He dropped the tailgate with a clatter and searched the inside with the flashlight, fixing the beam on Charles's swollen face. "How's that for luck?" Mavuto called out. "We have a second flat tire. How far is that place that you said you would have taken the kids to for the night, before going to the police in the morning?"

51

In the vicinity of Fort Jameson.
July 29, 1964.

As Youssef Khalil untied the white cloth from the post, Louis Ferreira contemplated the wisdom of accepting the help of the shopkeeper in his search for the missing children. *The man's lost it—that much is evident.*

"Youssef!" he called out. "We can't afford to lose any more time. It's just an old rag that the wind swept up. Let it be. We've got to go!"

"*Bwana*, wait." Youssef studied the piece of fabric in his hand with the help of the flashlight, rolling it between his fingers, then brought it to his nose. "I recognize the material, *Bwana*. This has been cut from a fairly new shirt, a clean one—I can still smell the shop and the detergent. It was cut with something very sharp, like a knife, not a pair of scissors. I'm sure it's a shirt that I carry in my shop."

BE SILENT

Sergeant Rangarajan called out, "What's going on, *Bwana*?" The two policemen had stepped into the glow thrown by Youssef's flashlight.

"Youssef saw the piece of white cloth tied to the post over there, as we sped past," Louis explained. "He *made* me stop to have a look."

"Sergeant," Youssef said, "this piece is *definitely* from a shirt and was cut with a knife and tied to this post. I am convinced it was done to draw our attention."

Louis laughed. "Youssef, please!"

Rahul Rangarajan cleared his throat. "Mr. Khalil—"

Bisa shouted behind them. "Sergeant! Come have a look! Careful! Step back and shine your flashlights over here, gentlemen. Here, onto the road."

The men squinted and looked closer.

Rangarajan voiced their concern. "Bisa, I see only a dirt road ... What's that? ... An arrow and a few letters?"

"I think so, Sergeant! Look! There's this arrow," Bisa pointed at it, then moved to the first letters. "There's a 'MAV' and then an R and an A and an L."

"Bisa," Sergeant said, "are you quite sure?"

Not waiting for an answer, Louis unceremoniously took the flashlight from Youssef and stepped closer. "Let me see ... Yes ... With some imagination it *does* look like single letters. Perhaps Mavuto, Rianna, Anthony and Lukas?"

He returned the flashlight. "Sorry, Youssef, for grabbing this and for not trusting you. You were right." He mumbled, "And *I'm* the idiot" as he turned back toward the policemen. "Sergeant, *this* is the road we have to follow. I'm convinced Mr. Khalil's hawkish eyes did not deceive him. And he's not a bad detective either!"

Youssef laughed. "You see, Sergeant, I sell only quality shirts in my shop. It takes a big, sharp knife to cut good fabric like this."

The men patted Youssef on the back and ran to their respective vehicles, Rangarajan calling out, "*Bwana,* Bisa and I will take the lead, if you don't mind."

Louis and Youssef waited a few seconds for the dust of the Land Rover to settle before they followed it down the smaller dirt road with the arrow drawn onto it.

Louis mumbled, "Of course we mind. What does the man think? This is what I call 'lack of gratitude!'" He tapped Youssef's shoulder gently. "Great job back there, my friend. I missed it completely."

Youssef only laughed softly.

Louis continued. "The sergeant is, of course, afraid we're going to steal his thunder. Pathetic."

He was quiet for a minute. "Youssef," he finally said. "You're the smart one. Who tied the piece of shirt and wrote in the dirt?"

"A second party, following the kidnappers," Youssef offered.

"Okay, but who? Kobus Kok's truck gets stolen. They trash Ulrich Wessels' truck's tires and steal the motorcycle. Three men and three children disappeared. Between them they have two vehicles."

Both men quietly digested the facts as they followed just behind the dust column of the police vehicle.

Like one, then, Louis and Youssef called out, "The motorcyclist is not one of the kidnappers!"

"But who's riding it?" Youssef pondered.

"There's Mavuto, Mapopa and Charles Chombe," Louis said.

"Which name did *Bwana* Wessels say wasn't written on the shed wall?" He answered his own question. "Charles Chombe. I am certain of it now. I am so glad—I couldn't believe he was involved with all of this!"

"Slow down, Bwana!" Youssef called out.

The Land Rover had pulled off the road ahead of them and stopped halfway under an enormous *mopani* tree. Louis Ferreira followed suit and skidded to a standstill behind the policemen's vehicle. The sergeant and Bisa were already walking toward a large rock that was visible in the headlights.

Louis jumped out and ran after the policemen with Youssef two steps behind him.

Sergeant Rangarajan was kneeling in front of the rock, studying the colored chalk writing. He turned with half a smile toward Youssef, "Mr. Khalil—or shall I say, Special Investigator Khalil—what is your professional opinion of *this* piece of white cloth, dangling from this small boulder?"

Louis Ferreira stepped closer and read the chalked words. Even he could tell: the same sharp instrument had cut the strip of material—it came from the same white shirt.

52

On the way to Lundazi. July 29, 1964.

"Chombe, I'm speaking to you!" Mavuto had the light trained on his captive's swollen face.

"What do you want from me?"

Mavuto dropped the beam slightly. "Don't play games with me, House Boy! You said there was a place—a safe place—nearby, where you were planning on taking the children for the night. Do you have that short a memory?"

"I've not forgotten, Mavuto, but I have no idea where we are at the moment."

"Chombe! Stop your bullshit!" Mavuto hollered as he leapt onto the truck bed. Mapopa jumped sideways, making room for his upset stepbrother.

Charles was exhausted, struggling with a throbbing headache and an eye he couldn't see much with. He realized he was dealing with a dangerous man, a man whose whole plan was disintegrating around him. Mavuto was desperate, and this desperate man was well armed and aided by an even more unstable youth. *Play it safe, Chombe. Now is not the time for heroics. Your time will come. Pacify the man. You saw how easily he pulls a trigger.*

"Mavuto," he said, "if you help me get out of the truck and let me see my surroundings, perhaps with some kind of map, I'll find my bearings."

The two men dragged Charles out of the back and Mavuto undid his ankles. Charles noted that the moon had lightened the night around them; a few stars flickered between the overhead branches. He stretched his legs, bending his back, his arms still bound behind him with the cuffs.

"So, Chombe," Mavuto said, "*now* do you know where you are?"

"The children," Charles said, "Let them out first."

"House Boy, you are in no position to make demands!" Mavuto called out.

Charles ignored his remark. "Get the children out of the back and untie their legs."

"Chombe, you're trying me!" Mavuto laughed and gave the rear tire a vicious kick. "Get on with it, Chombe!" He jabbed his captive in the ribs.

Charles groaned and looked up at the night sky. "What time is it, Mavuto? Ten?"

Mavuto sneered as he looked at his wrist. "Not bad for a house boy." He became more serious. "Yes, Chombe, it's about ten. We passed Fort Jameson about an hour and fifteen minutes ago. We left the T4 just before reaching Fort J—that's where we first turned off—then I followed the smaller side roads, parallel to the T4. Once we passed the town, I shadowed the M12 northbound; we're working our way toward Lundazi.

"So, an hour fifteen past Fort Jameson on the M12?" Charles asked.

"We didn't go very fast."

"What was your average speed?"

Mavuto sneered again. "Hah! As if you don't know what slowed us down. With all the interruptions, we barely managed thirty-five miles an hour."

"Well," Chombe said, "the place is an old farmhouse, about a mile from the road, well hidden by trees. The turn-off is exactly sixty-two miles north on the M12."

"How do you know it will be safe?" Mavuto asked.

"I grew up on the farm," Charles said. "We lived there for many years. My father worked for the farmer and his wife. They have no children. For all the years since I grew up and left, we've kept in touch. I was there only a few weeks ago. The old man died last year, but the wife refused to leave; I visit her from time to time to make sure she's okay."

Mavuto laughed. "You're hoping she'll make you her beneficiary when she dies?"

Charles shook his head. "No, everything's going to a local orphanage and the church. But she wouldn't mind if I stayed there with the children tonight."

"That must be about four or five miles from here," Mavuto said. "Come Chombe, let's get you into the back and go find the place. We're staying there tonight."

"I'm not sure the old lady would want you and Mapopa there, Mavuto," Charles said.

His captor laughed, "That's your problem, Chombe. You convince the lady—we have invited ourselves." He snapped his hands. "Come, Chombe, jump in!"

The prisoner was loaded into the back, this time with only his wrists tied. The children remained hushed, drawn far back into the dark corners—their fearful eyes absorbing everything.

The going was painfully slow now; Mavuto dared not ruin the tire completely. If the flat jumped off the rim, he would be forced to abandon the vehicle and that would be fatal to his plan. The chance that he and Mapopa would then be apprehended was simply too big. Perhaps there would be an old vehicle on the farm, or at worst a spare wheel of some sort they could use. He would get an hour or two of sleep and start moving before sunrise, see if he could reach Chinsali by early morning.

It took them almost half an hour to complete the three miles to where the dirt road ran back onto the M12. If Charles Chombe's facts were accurate, Mavuto reasoned, they still had about two miles to cover to the farmhouse. He stopped the truck and walked to the back, opening it up.

"Chombe," he said, "I need you to come sit in the front. We can't be too far from the farm."

Mavuto gave the flat tire another kick before moving the two backpacks off the front seat and shoving Charles in. The tire was on its last legs; they would be lucky to make another mile on it. There was no side road for the next several miles, as he recalled; they would have to take the M12.

As they limped along, keeping to the side of the road, Mavuto turned to Charles Chombe. "This place—does *this* road look familiar?"

The moon was higher now, lighting up the *miombo* woodlands around them. Charles nodded, "Yes, it looks kind of familiar. Yes ... Down the curve in the road, there's a narrowing where the low-water bridge is. A hundred yards past it, is the turn-off to the farm."

The clapping and whirring of the tire became deafening as they crossed the little bridge and staggered up the incline.

"Mavuto," Charles said, "look out for the name Orange Grove. The old couple originally thought they could make a fair income with growing citrus fruit, but had to switch to mixed farming. They never had the heart to change the name."

When the sign appeared, Mavuto turned the headlights off—the moon was sufficient now—and they turned onto a narrow two-track dirt road as it wound toward the farm buildings.

As the homestead became visible at the top of the little hill, clustered amongst trees, Mavuto mused, "Chombe, are there any dogs? What about other farm workers?"

A thought struck him and he slammed the brakes on. "Chombe, if this is a trap, you *will* be the first to die. Do you understand that?"

Charles laughed through his pain, "Mavuto, you've lost your mind—you're so paranoid. I've been following you guys the whole night. There's been no time to notify anybody. I had no plan to come inconvenience this old lady who has only showered my parents and me with kindness. I'm here because of you. You have a gun to my head."

The truck still didn't move. "Chombe, are there any dogs?"

Charles smiled. "Yes, she has a boxer, but she keeps him in the house at night. She also has a rifle. She may be seventy-eight, but she can hit a food tin on a fencepost at a hundred yards. I wouldn't go into the house if I were you."

"How will she know who we are, Chombe?"

"She doesn't need to know. I'll go to the house, though, and tell her I need to stay the night in my usual room in the back of the barn, and that I have to leave early in the morning. She wouldn't mind."

Mavuto cut the engine and both men stepped out. Charles remained at the passenger's side.

"Chombe?" Mavuto hissed as he stepped closer.

"Well Mavuto," Charles said, "you have to untie my hands, I can't go like this to her door. Then she'll definitely phone the police."

"She'll ask millions of questions about your injured face!"

"I'll stay in the shadows at the back door, where she can't see my face. She'll recognize my voice. It'll be fine."

Mavuto unlocked the handcuffs. "Chombe, listen carefully," he said. "Try anything clever like sending a warning, or making an alarm—I mean *anything*—and the children will surely die. You've seen me; this is not an idle threat." He pushed his captive in the direction of the farmhouse.

As Charles's figure faded into the moonlit night, Mavuto called after him, "You have fifteen minutes to get back, Chombe!"

53

In the vicinity of Fort Jameson.
July 29, 1964. 9:30 p.m.

Louis Ferreira reread the scribbling on the rock. *July 29. 7:15.* He looked at his wrist as he straightened up. "They're two hours and fifteen minutes ahead of us, Sergeant. How do we catch up?"

"*Bwana*," Rangarajan answered, "it will be tough, but once we depart from here, we'll push much harder. We need a few minutes, however—Bisa has to contact Pillay in Madzi Moyo, and Juma in Fort Jameson. Why don't you guys go stretch your legs? This won't take long."

Louis paced back and forth next to the vehicles but stopped when he overheard Bisa make contact with Fort Jameson.

"Foxtrot Juliet, this is Sierra Romeo, come in," Bisa said.

Static and radio noise and bleeps followed, then Juma's voice, "Hallo Sarge ... I mean Sierra Juliet, this is Foxtrot Juliet, over ..."

Sergeant Rangarajan, standing next to Bisa, cursed and mumbled, "Confounded Juma—will the idiot never learn how to radio-talk properly?"

"Sierra Juliet, any sign of the vulture?" Juma again.

"Negative, Foxtrot Juliet, but we found the trail. Repeat, we are pursuing the vulture."

"Copy that, Sierra Romeo, over."

"Foxtrot Juliet, we're moving. Over."

Bisa had barely ended the connection when Louis Ferreira exclaimed, "Sergeant, didn't the commissioner make you dispatch half your task force to Chinsali?"

"Yes, he did."

"But don't you see, Sergeant?" Louis said. "That's where we're heading, but we're two hours behind the kidnappers. If your other men come south on the M12, we have a chance of apprehending them!"

"I'm afraid I can't call on their support tonight, *Bwana*."

"Sergeant, we're talking about three young lives that hang in the balance!" Louis insisted. "Why can't you contact the commissioner again?"

"I can communicate only with Fort Jameson and Madzi Moyo at the moment, *Bwana*. Those were my instructions. I'm sorry."

Louis was furious and ran toward Youssef's truck. "Come Youssef!" he called out, and, turning again, added, "Sorry, Sergeant—then our ways are parting. You aren't serious about apprehending those criminals. We'll hunt them down ourselves!"

Youssef was still slamming his door shut when Louis pulled out, sending gravel flying, leaving the two surprised police officers behind in a cloud of red dust.

Sergeant Rangarajan ran after the truck waving his arms. "*Bwana*, we should proceed together ..." All he saw were the two red taillights bouncing down the dark road, soon swallowed by the night and a column of dust.

Louis seethed. "Youssef! Can you believe it! Those two were giving us a demonstration of radio-talk, instead of contacting Lusaka and Chinsali for reinforcements! Why can't he override the commissioner and send his team south to catch the kidnappers?"

"*Bwana*, he has his orders. He did tell us there would be no additional support for forty-eight hours."

"But that's boloney, Youssef! Bogus!" Louis drummed his fingers on the steering wheel as he fumed. "Youssef, get us the police radio telephone set up. Please."

"*Bwana?*"

"It's okay, I'll do the talking. Here's the frequency." He passed a slip of paper to his navigator friend.

As Youssef fiddled with the radio, static noise filled the cabin, mixing with the growling of the engine and the drumming of Louis's fingers on the wheel.

"The handset, please, Youssef."

Steering with one hand, Louis grabbed the handset. "Foxtrot Juliet, this is Lima Foxtrot, come in."

BE SILENT

Static followed.

"Foxtrot Juliet, this is Lima Foxtrot. Come in!"

"Lima Foxtrot, this is Foxtrot Juliet. Over ..." Constable Juma's voice was stronger than it had been on Bisa's call.

Louis whispered to Youssef, "What do I call Lusaka in radio lingo?"

Youssef laughed, pulling up his shoulders. "*Bwana*, I have no idea. Big Lima, perhaps?"

"Foxtrot Juliet, I am chasing the vulture. You need to get Charlie in Big Lima to send a team south on the Mike Twelve. Do you copy that?"

"Lima Foxtrot, message unclear. Repeat ..."

The radio went dead.

Louis Ferreira cried out, "The incompetence of these people! Did he just cut us off? Are they unwilling to help save a few children, three insignificant children!"

Try as they might, the radio remained dead. Louis muttered a prayer. Youssef had to strain to hear him whisper, "Lukas ... I'm coming my boy ... Please hold on."

The canopy of trees above them opened up for a few seconds as they raced down the dirt road and a narrow band of moonlight fell into the cabin. Youssef could see two wet trails down his friend's cheeks.

54

Orange Grove farm, near Lundazi.
July 29, 1964.

The moment Charles stomped off to the farmhouse, Rianna turned to Lukas and Anthony, who were still huddled in the back along with her. She could see Mavuto standing outside, mumbling to himself, clasping the assault rifle, which hung over his shoulder. He appeared haggard. Mapopa sat on the edge of the truck bed, resting his back against the metal side, smirking, watching them all like a hawk.

She whispered in Afrikaans, "*Is julle ouens nog oraait?*" Are you guys still okay? "Charles went to the farmhouse to ask permission for us to stay here the night." She had lost hope of them escaping these two men, but this was a brand-new situation, with new possibilities—perhaps …

"Silence! Not a word!" Mapopa snarled as he threw a handful of gravel at them.

"*Choka,* Mapopa!" Rianna snapped back. Go away! She turned back to the boys. "With the second flat tire, Mavuto is stranded, and he knows it. Look how worried he is. See?"

The boys peeked at their captor, his face visible in the moonlit night. Lukas found that he was not comforted by the knowledge. He whispered, "But it isn't a good thing if he's mad. You've seen how easily both of them can pull a trigger."

Mapopa glared at the boys. "What are you peering at, *mwanas*?"

"Oh shut up, Mapopa," Rianna retorted.

"If Mavuto feels cornered," Anthony said to her, "aren't *we* going to pay for it?"

"No, not yet," Rianna's confidence had returned. "He has to get the tire fixed and he doesn't want to be stranded out here," she continued. "He knows the police will find them if they stay here." She watched as Mavuto slowly stepped back under the cover of the acacia, becoming one with the tree. His watchfulness had returned, she realized.

"Rianna," Lukas said, "what did you and Charles talk about? How did he find us?"

She told them about the motorcycle and the white shirt that Charles had cut into strips and placed along his route, in the hope that their rescuers will find them in time.

"Isn't he clever, Rianna?" Lukas asked.

"Only a little," she said. "He got himself caught by these two idiots."

"I think he only got caught when we tried to escape and jumped Mavuto," Lukas said, defending his friend "Didn't he show himself only then, when he realized we were in trouble?"

"He should've been more careful, Lukas," Rianna said. "Look at the trouble we're in now. Charles is of little help to us now!"

"Why are you so mad at Charles?" Lukas asked.

"Because he allowed himself to get caught."

"That can't be the entire reason," Lukas insisted. "It must be something you were mad about *before* today—before we got kidnapped. *Wha*t is it, Rianna?"

"It's nothing, Lukas. You're imagining things. Didn't you hear me yelling, warning him, when Mapopa attacked him with the rifle?"

"I know, Rianna. And we're glad you did. But I can see the way you look at him. You're mad at him about something else."

"Stop it, Lukas."

You're only a little boy of ten. How can you know what I feel?

"I need to know," Lukas pleaded now.

Rianna sighed. *What if I shake his blind faith in his African friend—wouldn't that be a terrible thing to do? They're still so young. I don't think even Anthony will understand why I am mad about what Charles has done. They don't know his secret.*

"Lukas," she said, "I will tell you, one day."

"So you can't tell me because I'm too little!" Lukas's voice had an edge to it. "Is that it?"

"Silence, *mwana!*" Mapopa hurled another handfull of fine gravel at the boy.

Lukas pulled away into a darker corner, trying to make himself more comfortable. It was impossible—not with his hands still bound behind his back. The ropes had grazed their skin. Anthony shuffled over to comfort him, casting a hurt look in Rianna's direction.

BE SILENT

She shuffled in their direction, careful not to lose her balance on the tilting truck bed. "Lukas, I'm sorry," she said. "Please look at me."

I feel as old as Mother. Dear Lord, how do I tell him about Charles and Amayi Kok? He didn't understand what Mavuto was yelling at Charles, after he had bound him. Accusing him of lusting after Adam's mother. We've all seen it. And now they're sending her away to Lusaka, to have the baby there. They don't want us to know. How do I tell Lukas that?

"Lukas, I will tell you one day," she said again. "I promise. It's about Adam's mother. She—"

Mapopa jumped off the truck bed, rocking the truck slightly, making the three children bump into one another. Rianna groaned as she heard the muffled voices of Charles and Mavuto next to the truck.

Mavuto's head appeared around the canvas top, fixing the flashlight on their dirt-streaked faces. "We're driving up to the farmhouse. Charles will walk ahead of us. Not a sound from any one of you. Understood?"

They all nodded.

"Do I have to gag anyone to ensure cooperation?"

They shook their heads emphatically. He clipped the metal tailgate in place but left the canvas lid flipped open, thrown onto the canvas roof.

Mapopa followed behind the slow, limping truck, his AK-47 slung loosely over his shoulder, the moonlight cradling his haunted boyish features. Rianna peered, but could not see any of his albino skin. The night had granted him temporary clemency.

253

55

Orange Grove farm. July 29, 1964.

Orange Grove's outbuildings were tucked between an old circular stonewall, which was falling apart, and a cluster of *mopani* and *miombo* trees. The homestead, quiet and dark, stood a hundred yards away, shielded by scattered mango and citrus trees, with a flower garden out front.

This time Mavuto took greater care when he let the tailgate down. No reason to broadcast their presence to the world. For a brief moment he let his guard down. He felt like an old man in need of a cane, the weight of his endeavor smothered his spirit—he was so tired. He wondered about the children, about Charles and Mapopa, and especially about Mother Fatsani. *Enough of this, Lisulo,* he thought. He herded the children in a neat row behind Charles, who led the way into the cavernous barn, through a small side door—fertilizer, engine oil and maize flour wafted at them from the vast darkness.

BE SILENT

Mapopa tailed them, his assault rifle at the ready. The children's wrists were still tied and they stumbled along down the poorly lit passage, following their Chinyanja friend to the living quarters at the far end.

Mavuto bundled the children into the first room Charles showed them and made them stand against the far wall. The room was sparsely furnished: a naked bulb gave light, a single metal-frame bed with a bare coir mattress stood in the one corner and a teak table and chair was pushed into the other. Five feet above the floor a narrow rectangular window adorned the third wall.

"Turn around, all of you." Mavuto bent down to untie the children's wrists and stuffed the pieces of rope into his knapsack. He had slung his rifle's strap across his chest; the rifle dangled down his back, keeping his arms free. He tossed the same blanket the children had used on the truck onto the mattress and held the canvas water bag out to them.

"Come, drink some water."

The boys and Rianna thirstily gulped down a few mouthfuls each until he pulled the bag away, capped it and slung it over his shoulder.

"*Zikomo*, Mavuto," Rianna said—thank you.

Mavuto remained impassive. "Mapopa will guard you. He'll sit in front of the door. Get some sleep. Remember, no tricks. He'll shoot first and then ask what you're up to."

He gestured with the pistol in Charles's direction. Charles stood motionless in front of the window. "Come, Chombe. Let's go fix that tire."

Rianna called after him, "Mavuto, can we have more blankets? One is not enough. It still gets cold at night. Please."

"I only have one more," he said. "Mapopa, keep an eye on them."

Mavuto returned two minutes later and tossed the second blanket at the girl. He grabbed the chair and carried it outside, followed by Charles and Mapopa, who closed the door behind them. Mapopa then made himself comfortable outside, sitting in the chair, facing the bedroom door.

Charles and Mavuto continued into the barn, where they rifled through the place. A John Deere tractor stood in the middle of the barn floor, with an assortment of engines on tripods and pulleys surrounding it. An array of plows and planters took up half the remaining floor space. An open area, just the right size for a vehicle, stared them in the face. Against the one back wall, scores of car, truck and tractor tires were piled in neat stacks, according to size.

"Chombe, where's the old lady's truck?"

"She often parks it on the side of the house," Charles said. "I believe that's where it was tonight. It was dark out—I couldn't see well."

"Who's working on those engines?"

"The old lady. She does everything. She has just a few farmhands left. She farms, she cooks, she shoots and she drives the tractor and the truck. And, she's about this high." Charles held his hand below his breastbone, the same height as Rianna, about five foot six. "But she's scaling back—her ambition has gone since the old man died."

Mavuto poked around the pile of truck tires. He felt no desire to confront the fire-spewing, rifle-toting pioneer lady who ran this little farm, not in the middle of the night, flanked

BE SILENT

by a well-trained attack dog. He would rather leave her truck untouched where it was, next to the side of her house.

Mavuto found what he was looking for. "Give me a hand, Chombe," he said. They took two tires from the pile. Mavuto had learned his lesson. The state of the roads demanded a spare or two. Fifteen minutes later, *Bwana* Kok's truck sported a fresh rear tire. As Mavuto tossed the second tire into the back, his injured leg snapped under him and he grasped the rear end of the truck to steady himself.

"*Oh Jesu!*" he whimpered. He could feel a sticky warmth running down his leg. The wound must have pulled open and started bleeding again. He moaned as he limped to the passenger side, keeping the pistol fixed on Charles Chombe. He handed him the two backpacks.

"Take that, Chombe. Let's go join the others." He noticed the light in his captive's healthy eye. "Yes, I'm injured," he said, "but don't try anything. I'm very, very trigger-happy. Don't test me."

He limped behind the house boy, who carried the two large backpacks into the barn.

"Chombe," he said on the way, "we need water to clean with." He added, "If you behave, we can clean your wound as well. Perhaps."

Mapopa jumped up from the chair upon their arrival, but Charles ignored the youth. He brushed past him and disappeared through another doorway. Mavuto limped behind.

"Mavuto!" Mapopa called out. "Where's the man going? What's going on?"

"Shut up, Mapopa, keep an eye on the children," Mavuto snarled as he disappeared down the short hallway, following Charles Chombe.

257

Minutes later, even the children could hear Mavuto's whimpering, as he cleaned his own wound with the disinfecting alcohol from the clinic. He screamed softly as he put a fresh suture in the wound, close to the first one, approximating the gaping sides better, before pouring iodine on it. They were in the little kitchen; he had placed the pistol next to him on the counter.

"Let me help you," Charles Chombe insisted, ignoring Mavuto's gesture of dismissal. He took the bottle with iodine from Mavuto's shaking hands, capped it and put it down on the table. Then he took a clean dressing, covered the wound and wrapped the bandage deftly around his captor's leg.

All this time Mavuto's eyes darted between Charles's hands, busy with the bandage, and his pistol on the counter. His training and instinct clashed head on, making him bite on his teeth. He struggled not to slap his captive's helping hands away—he wasn't sure he could afford such proxcimity of the man—being so vulnerable made him uncomfortable and he edged away.

"Thank you, Chombe," Mavuto said. "I see you've done this kind of thing before … I need something for the pain …" He struggled with the amber bottle, his hands still shaking: he tilted a few aspirin tablets out onto his palm, shoved them into his mouth and took a few gulps from the canvas water bag. He wiped his mouth with the back of his hand, pulled his pants back up and pulled the only chair in the kitchen out from under the table.

"Sit down," He said brusquely. He patted the backrest of the chair. "Let me have a look at that wound of yours." Mavuto avoided eye contact.

BE SILENT

Charles hesitated only a moment, then sat down. It was his turn to whimper and complain softly as his captor cleaned the cakes and crusts of blood and dirt from the side of his face. There was a laceration from his eye to his ear and a second deep gash behind the ear. The wounds both started bleeding again once the crusts were cleaned away.

"Damn it, Mavuto! It's bleeding again!"

"Shut up, Chombe, you sound like a little *mwana*! Bite on your teeth—I have to put in a few sutures."

Afterward, the two men, Charles now sporting a bandage around his head, returned to the hallway where Mapopa still sat, outside the bedroom door, guarding the children. The youth staggered upright. It was unclear whether he had dozed off.

"Mavuto, what's going on?" he repeated.

"Nothing is going on, Mapopa. I cleaned the wound in my leg."

"And what about him? Why did it take that long?" Mapopa couldn't place his finger on it, but he was aware of a shift in the dynamics. What had happened in the kitchen?

"*What* about him?" Mavuto barked at his stepbrother. "It took long because I'm not a doctor, and I had to operate on myself without anesthesia. Are you happy now, you idiot?"

Mavuto fiddled in a side bag of one of the backpack's, took a deep breath, and knocked on the bedroom door before he opened it. He motioned for Charles to go in ahead of him.

"Sit down, everyone," Mavuto said. "Move over to the edge of the bed. Yes, you too, Chombe."

Mavuto had four pairs of handcuffs in his hands. "I'm not going to tie your wrists, but I will clip these cuffs in place."

He clipped cuffs around the children's ankles without a word of protest from them, but when he tried the same on Charles's ankle the latter snarled at him. "Idiot. These were made for wrists, not ankles."

"Suit yourself, House Boy," Mavuto said, and he grabbed one of Charles's wrists, snapped the cuff on and clipped the other half to the bed frame.

"We're going to sleep for a few hours," he announced. "Mapopa and I will be taking turns standing guard outside this door. We'll all leave before sunrise."

"Mavuto, we're hungry," Rianna pleaded in her sweetest possible voice," and we need a *chimbudzi*. Please."

"Sorry, *mtsikana*. You'll have to hold it. Remind me first thing in the morning."

"You're a sadistic monster, Mr. Lisulo!" she hollered after Mavuto, who only shook his head, saying, more to himself, "You're so wrong about that, *mtsikana*."

He tugged the string for the light and pulled the door close behind him.

Mavuto paused outside the bedroom door. "It's eleven o'clock, Mapopa. I'll take the first watch until one-thirty. You'll take the next two and a half hours' duty. Then we can get everyone up by four and be on our way long before sunrise."

"Where do I …?" Mapopa began.

"There's a second bedroom with a bed next to the kitchen. I'll wake you at one-thirty. Now go."

56

On the way to Lundazi. July 29, 1964.

Louis Ferreira slammed the brakes of Youssef's truck as they rounded a curve to avoid a discarded wheel, lying near the side of the road. The truck's tail swung out several times before it righted itself.

"Idiots!" he yelled.

Louis slowed down and pulled off the road. Youssef looked at him. "*Bwana?*"

"The idiots who left that tire in the middle of the road! The trail has gone cold my friend. Let's wait on the sergeant and Bisa. That discarded tire might be more than it appears."

The men were standing outside when the police Land Rover pulled in behind the truck.

"I assume that's why you stopped, *Bwana?*" Sergeant Rangarajan pointed at the wheel. He noticed the slumping shoulders of the missionary, the stance of a man defeated.

"Well, yes," Louis answered, "I'm not sure why, Sergeant. I've seen abandoned tires before, but since we're trying to catch up with kidnappers on the run, and their trail disappeared into the red earth, I thought we should have a look …"

Bisa turned the wheel over. There was a big, long gash on the outside near the rim.

"Recognize the tire or the rim, *Bwana*?" Sergeant said.

Louis shook his head, as he played with his flashlight over the wheel.

"Very careless of who ever left it here," the sergeant remarked. "If it was our kidnapper friend, it could be a sign he's becoming desperate."

"Or that he was so sure of himself that he threw caution to the wind," Louis offered.

"Perhaps," Rangarajan said. "He must have been one hundred percent certain he would have no trouble finding another spare. But where would he do that? And at least he could have shoved it into the underbrush next to the road, out of view."

Louis suddenly straightened up—although it seemed that they have lost the trail of the kidnappers, the secret pursuer might still make it possible for them to reach the children in time. "Sergeant, have you given more thought to who left us the leads in the first place? Those cut pieces of white fabric?"

"Not exactly, *Bwana*."

"It *must* have been Charles Chombe," Louis declared. "He must be the one who took the motorcycle. He paused at *Bwana* Kok's house but then took off after the kidnappers. He must have thought he would be able to apprehend them or something."

"*Bwana*, I'm not so sure about that."

BE SILENT

"Who else could it be?" Louis said. "Young Mapopa is unlikely to have ever been on a motorcycle before. Charles had befriended the boys. I've met him several times. He would never harm the children."

"*Bwana*, perceptions can be deceiving," the sergeant cautioned. "Through the centuries people have been known to betray their own blood, all in the name of ideology or lust for power or money or when their own life is threatened. Chombe may be no exception."

"How else do you explain the leads and clues we stumbled upon?" Louis said.

Rangarajan laughed softly. "You may be right Bwana, Chombe was probably the hero."

"'Was,' Sergeant?"

Rangarajan was good at appeasing people. Working in the force has taught him that. The *bwana* was near breaking point—that much was clear. "The trail has gone cold," he said. "They may have captured him or killed him. It is difficult to tell."

Constable Bisa, standing next to his superior, coughed. "Excuse me, Sergeant," he said, "but I spoke to Charles Chombe quite recently. We had a long discussion about the country, politics and the nearing date of independence. We touched on the impact of the Lumpa Church—"

"Sorry, Bisa, but we need to get going. What's the point of your story?" The sergeant had righted the wheel and started rolling it toward their vehicle. It could serve as evidence.

Bisa strode ahead to open the back door. "Sorry, Sergeant, I'll be brief. Chombe told me about Mavuto's mother, Fatsani Lisulo. About her close ties with the inner circle of the Lenshina movement and how she moved recently to Chinsali and then to Paishuko."

"And Mavuto?" the sergeant said. "Where are his sympathies?" He glanced from Bisa to Ferreira, to Khalil and back. To think, all these years, he had thought he understood, at least partially, the Chichewas, the East Indians, the Egyptians and the white people. He suddenly wasn't sure anymore—what does Africa *do* to its people?

"He's a staunch African nationalist," Bisa said. "He loathes the church. Chombe shared how very concerned, even upset, Mavuto was about his mother's dedication to the church. He apparently tried unsuccessfully to get her to move back with him to Madzi Moyo. He was especially concerned about the escalating friction and clashes between church members and the authorities—with the police and the military. He told Charles that he feared for her safety."

"You think he's *not* trying to flee the country?" Sergeant Rangarajan said.

"No, I don't," Bisa said. "It may be an explanation for the route Lisulo has taken. He's on the way to Chinsali—to Mother Fatsani."

"Come on, Bisa!" Rangarajan called out. "Chinsali?"

"Yes, Sergeant, maybe even Paishuko. I think he wants to go and 'save' his mother."

"You mean forcefully remove her and take her back home?"

"I'm sure that's what he's planning." Bisa said.

"Then why on earth did he take the children?" Louis said. "To use as a human shield? He knows we don't have money to pay a ransom!"

BE SILENT

"Bwana," Bisa said, "money is not his motivation. I think the children stumbled upon something he didn't want them to see—what exactly we don't know—but he must have believed that the police would be on the scene too soon if he let them go and they ran to *Bwana* Wessels."

Sergeant Rangarajan busied himself with loading the damaged tire in the back, deep in thought. And he had thought Bisa was only all muscle and brute force–a brainless giant. Perhaps he should be promoted instead of Pillay. He turned to face the other men. "*Bwana*, I think that is where we have to go then—to Chinsali, and find the mother. This way we should find Mavuto. The trail has gone cold on us. This damaged tire doesn't tell us much. Unless you have a better suggestion?"

Louis Ferreira pulled up his shoulders. "We'll find him if Bisa's theory holds water."

The vehicles set off in the direction of Chinsali, Louis following the Land Rover. They reached it by three the next morning. Bisa knew a local Lumpa member, who informed them (after being encouraged by the visible display of his visitor's firearms) that Fatsani Lisulo had indeed fled to Paishuko only days earlier.

They finally located Fatsani Lisulo shortly before six that morning. She sat outside her house in the small garden—as if she was expecting visitors. The modest house, like all the others around it, was thatch covered. Hers stood near the village church.

Once she got up from the wooden chair, it was clear where Mavuto had received his features from—tall and strong-boned.

She, however, was plump. In spite of the poor early morning light they could see her face—fearless, almost serene.

She claimed she had not seen her son in two weeks time.

"What has my boy done, Sergeant?"

"That's what we're trying to establish," Rangarajan said. "We were hoping to find him here. We need to talk to him. If you see him Fatsani Lisulo, you have to tell him to contact the Fort Jameson police. It is urgent."

"I will tell him, Sergeant."

Fatsani Lisulo remained standing in front of her house as the four men returned to their vehicles. With her eyes open—watching the visitors depart—she prayed. She prayed for her son and stepson—and then she prayed for the two policemen who were accompanied by the white man and the Muslim man.

"Mavuto, my boy," she murmured as she entered the house.

57

Temporary police headquarters, Madzi Moyo.
July 29, 1964. 10:05 p.m.

Constable Babu Pillay was quite satisfied with how the evening had progressed, especially with the fact that Sergeant Rangarajan's team was able to get onto the kidnappers' trail so soon. *They were chasing the vulture.* He chuckled to himself. He'd never had the slightest doubt that the sergeant would be able to solve the mystery of the missing children. His colleague Bisa had better pay attention—he might not appreciate that he was working with a master.

Pillay looked at his wrist, it was five past ten, and he'd just returned from a walkabout on the Mission Rest House grounds. Everything was safe and sound. He hadn't even had to use his flashlight—the partial moon lit up the land. He would add that to his report: *Inspection of grounds surrounding temporary headquarters at 10 p.m.; found to be satisfactory and peaceful.* He could still recall his instructor in college saying, *Follow the rulebook, Pillay—follow the rule book and you'll do well.* That's what he planned to do.

He had made his temporary headquarters in the Wesselses' living room. *Amayi* Wessels brought him a camping cot and he had his own sleeping bag, although he doubted that he would be able to get any sleep tonight. The police radio had been placed on the side of the large coffee table, and he had pulled up one of the comfortable armchairs. His rifle sat on the table right in front of him, his notepad and pen between the radio and rifle. The residents of Upper Madzi Moyo who'd been instructed to come to *Bwana* Wessels' house for the night had all retired to the other rooms in the vast old house, as allocated to them by the *amayi*.

The excited chattering coming from the rest of the house was slowly dying down, the residents, Pillay was certain, realized they could afford to close their eyes while the police force did their job looking after the citizens' well-being. That was what he enjoyed most about being a police officer, a law enforcer, Pillay thought: looking after the well-being of his fellow men.

He balanced his pen between thumb and index finger, slowly rolling it over onto his middle finger, without touching the coffee table surface. *Concentrate Pillay, concentrate. You know you have it in you to do this pen-finger-roll thing. Come on, try harder. Yes … See … Careful now, roll it over … Keep going …*

The radio's red light flashed frantically, making Pillay drop the pen.

"Damn! I almost had it!"

The radio went live, "Mike Two, Mike Two … This is Foxtrot Juliet, come in."

BE SILENT

"Foxtrot Juliet, this is Mike Two, over."

Constable Juma, in Fort Jameson sounded surer of himself this time, but failed to hide his irritation. "Mike Two, I have a domestic situation, contact me on landline ... I repeat ..."

Pillay rolled his eyes. *And I was so proud of you Juma. What is it now?* "Foxtrot Juliet. I copy that ... Clarify domestic problem, over."

"Negative, Mike Two, contact me on landline." Juma sounded determined.

The radio went dead.

"The bastard!" Pillay exclaimed as he got up to find the lady of the house. "He's forcing my hand!" Pillay knew the phone was in *Bwana* Wessels' study, but it took him several minutes to track down *Amayi* Wessels. He was a police officer, but it would still be proper to let the missus know he needed to use the phone in the study.

Juma picked up at the first ring. Pillay didn't wait for him to speak.

"What on earth is it now, Juma, that could not have waited until morning?"

"Pillay! What's it with these missionaries? They can't look after their children, they can't even look after their wives, they—"

"Juma, what is the crisis?"

"I don't have a crisis exactly Pillay, but—"

"Has the Fort Jameson police station been attacked by revolutionaries?" Pillay had difficulty hiding his sarcasm.

Juma laughed, sounding embarrassed. "No, Pillay, it's this *Amayi* Ferreira, the *bwana*'s wife."

Juma had Pillay's full attention. "Has something happened to her or the two little ones at home?" he asked.

"No, Pillay, but she started phoning me on the half-hour for a status report. She started at 8 p.m. sharp. Not long after the *bwana* dropped by, here at the station."

Babu Pillay laughed, relieved, "Juma, you big baby, that's part of your job, *our* job: keep the public informed."

"You don't understand, Pillay," Juma sounded as if he was in pain. "She's phoned me five times already, every half-hour since eight! Nothing has changed, we have no new information, other than that the police are hot on the kidnappers' trail—I told her that. It's as if she didn't hear me, or believe me."

Pillay coughed. *Now I even have to play police psychologist. I think I need a raise. I'll have to tell the sergeant that once all of this is over.*

"Juma," he said, "do you have children?"

"You know I have the two boys."

"Well, imagine if it was me who phoned you five minutes ago to tell you, 'Sorry, Juma, but one of your boys has disappeared.' How would you have felt? What would you have done?"

The line went silent on the Fort Jameson side.

"Juma?"

"Sorry, Pillay. I was thinking. I would have phoned you every ten minutes and *demanded* a status report!"

"Exactly."

"I think I know what to tell her if she phones again. Goodnight, Pillay."

"Goodnight, Juma."

58

Orange Grove farm. July 30, 1964. 7:00 a.m.

In the sleeping quarters in the outbuildings on Orange Grove Farm, all hell broke loose. The sun was already higher than even the tallest of the *mopani* and *miombo* trees behind the barn. *Bwana* Kok's truck still stood on the same spot as the night before, by the small side door. From inside the barn, a person standing there could have heard yelling in both English and Chinyanja.

"I said I'm sorry, Mavuto!"

"Mapopa, you're such an idiot! I let you sleep until one-thirty. All you had to do was wake me at four. But no, you couldn't even do that. Look at the time, you imbecile!"

Mavuto was hyperventilating, his leg was throbbing again and he struggled not to draw his pistol and shoot the youth on the spot. "And now, for your information, it is seven a.m.!" he hollered.

"I am sorry, Mavuto! Okay? I was tired, I must have fallen asleep—"

"I thought so! That's enough for a court-martial—falling asleep on guard duty!"

"That's why I'm glad I am not a stupid soldier," Mapopa retorted.

Mavuto snorted as he lined the three children up just inside the side door.

"'Stupid soldier.' Yes, you would fail miserably as a soldier, Mapopa Lisulo, miserably."

"Children, Chombe," he said to the others. "I was hoping we could slip out under cover of the night. As you have learned, things have changed. We were supposed to have arrived at our final destination by now."

Rianna looked at him in surprise. Their captor even sounded as if he was sorry. She looked at Charles Chombe, who pulled up his shoulder. The children's ankles were still in handcuffs; Charles's wrists were behind his back. Rianna was reminded again that she needed to keep Mavuto to his promise of a bathroom break. *He promised.* But it was clear that it would take very little at that point to make him explode completely—he was dangerously unstable. They would have to wait and pinch harder.

"Chombe," Mavuto asked, "do you think the old lady is up by now?"

"I know she is. She's an early riser," Charles said.

"I don't want any trouble from her," Mavuto said. "I have a big enough crisis on my hands with this incompetent assistant of mine."

"I asked her last night not to come to the barn until after we left," Charles told him. "She will honor my request."

BE SILENT

"What *else* did you tell her last night?" Mavuto asked.

"Nothing. I didn't say much—only told her I need to stay over for the night with a group of people."

"What about her other farmhands?"

"They'll wait until we take our leave. Perhaps we should go now, before they see the rifles and handcuffs and things," Charles added.

Mavuto turned to Mapopa. "Give me your rifle. We'll cover both weapons with a blanket. Pull your shirt out and cover your pistol, like this."

He faced his captives. The night had otherwise been gracious to them—the children reeked much less; something of the barn must have rubbed off on them, he thought. "Listen very well: I'm going to unlock the cuffs. You will walk in a single file and get in the back of the truck, where I'll put the cuffs back on. I'll walk behind you and will have my rifle drawn on you the whole time, covered by the blanket."

He paused. "Please do *not* try to draw attention, or to escape. I don't want to shoot you, but I will."

"Do you understand me?" he suddenly barked.

The children all jumped and nodded.

Mavuto gestured with his head. "Mapopa, you go first. Open up the back so these guys can get in quickly. Move!"

Mavuto kept the side door open just at a slit, and an eye on Mapopa outside. Then he turned back to his prisoners. "Come, it's time."

The children walked single file as instructed, then jumped in, one after the other, without a hiccup. But when Charles prepared himself to jump onto the truck bed, Mavuto held up his hand.

"Change of plan, Chombe. Don't look now, but the madam is watching us from her back porch. The dog is standing next to her and she's resting a rifle across her folded arms. You will walk slowly to the passenger side and get in there. Once we're off the farm, we can change the seating arrangements. Now go!"

He turned back to his stepbrother. "Sorry that I lost my temper with you, little brother. You will sit at the back and guard them, please."

Mapopa did not answer, but mumbled under his breath.

Mavuto followed Charles to the passenger side and closed the door after him. He paused, looking at the farmhouse, then briskly walked to the back and jumped in and clipped the cuffs on the three children's ankles.

He waited for Mapopa to jump in and then closed the tailgate and canvas cover. He backed up and turned the truck around. As they followed the narrow, winding two-track drive, they passed closer to the homestead.

The farm's owner stood on the same spot on her porch with her dog and rifle. Both men in the front of the truck raised their hands to greet the old lady. She stood impassive, watching them, before raising a tiny hand and returning the greeting.

59

*Orange Grove farm. July 30, 1964.
7:10 a.m.*

Half a mile down the drive, out of sight from the farmhouse, Mavuto stopped and walked around to the passenger side. He opened the door, snapped the cuff around a submissive Charles's wrist and clipped the other half to the horizontal bar of the armrest on the door.

"Sorry, Chombe," he said.

Charles smiled. "About last night, Mavuto—you had a change of heart. Why keep up the charade? Let us go."

Mavuto shook his head. They continued down the winding path toward the M12. "I'm not your friend, Chombe," he said. "I can't let you go—not yet."

They clattered across the animal gate and reached the junction with the main road. Mavuto leaned forward to see the partially obscured main road to his right, letting the truck slowly crawl ahead to peek past the scrubs. Two military trucks steamed past them on their way north, shaking *Bwana* Kok's small truck, covering them with a cloud of red dust.

Soldiers. And both truck filled to capacity.

"Lisulo," Charles said, "what *are* you doing with *Bwana* Kok's truck? Why did you have to steal it? Shouldn't you be among those soldiers?"

"Shut up, Chombe—I am not accountable to you. I don't have to tell you anything!"

Charles tried to make sense of the past thirteen hours—he even tried the impossible task of putting himself inside Mavuto's skin. How did the undercover garden boy's mind work? This truck, the rifles, the children, him chained to the armrest, the army trucks full of soldiers—what could Mavuto ever have hoped to achieve? He, Charles Chombe, was at any moment as staunch an African nationalist as Lisulo, yearning for independence from Britain. But what was going on here? It didn't add up.

"Perhaps you do, Lisulo," Charles said. "You misjudged yourself with your stepbrother, and the one calamity has struck you after the other."

"Shut up, Chombe!"

They continued in silence, following the army trucks, which were already only a rolling dust cloud on the horizon, disappearing down the Luangwa Valley on their way north.

"Where are they going in such a hurry, Lisulo?" Charles asked.

"None of your business."

"Oh, you *made* me part of all this." Charles tugged on his handcuff. "It *is* my business now. Where are the soldiers going?"

Mavuto refused to respond.

Charles turned to face his captor. "I think you don't know!" he said.

"Don't taunt me, Chombe."

"What were you hoping to achieve, with two assault rifles and two pistols plus ... how many, a thousand rounds of ammunition? Who did you want to kill?"

"I wasn't planning on killing anybody!"

"Mapopa almost killed me."

"Served you right—you attacked me. But neither him nor you were part of the original plan. I took him along when the children stumbled on the hiding place for the rifles. I had to."

Charles chuckled; he felt a tinge of sympathy for his troubled captor. "Has Mapopa become the Jonah on this ship, then?"

"Jonah?"

"From the Bible. Jonah was a troubled man who was in the wrong place at the wrong time, and the crew had to throw him overboard to save the ship during a storm."

"So they killed him?"

"No—he got swallowed by a big fish which spewed him out onto dry land."

Mavuto laughed. "That's a fairy tale. I can't throw him overboard, I still need him."

"No, it's not a fairy tale," Charles said. "It's a parable. Mapopa will bring you only trouble. Pull over and let the children and me go. I can make up a story about what happened to us."

Mavuto laughed bitterly. "Why would you want to do that, Chombe? You don't understand. You'll *never* understand."

"Mavuto..."

"Not a word, Chombe."

"Where are we going, Lisulo?"

"You'll see."

"Aren't you concerned that the military will prevent you from completing your so-called mission?"

Mavuto exploded. "It is *not* a so-called mission! I had it all worked out! I was posted to Madzi Moyo by the UNIP office. I worked undercover as a garden boy."

"So you were a spy."

"Undercover agent."

Charles snorted. "No wonder you were such a terrible garden boy!"

"It was embarrassing," Mavuto sneered, "performing such a ridiculous task."

"So you took matters into your own hands—is that it, Lisulo? Are those AK-47s the UNIP office's idea?"

"No, but I couldn't allow the Lenshina people to derail independence. Never!"

They continued in silence down the gravel road into the valley that dissected the *miombo* woodlands on their way north. They followed forestry roads around the town of Lundazi, before slipping back onto the M12 north with the goal of Chinsali and Paishuko village.

As they finally turned onto the M12, Charles turned to his captor. "*How* were you hoping to stop them—the Lenshina people??"

"I had a plan, Chombe."

"But *how*, with only two AK-47s?"

"Chombe!" Mavuto barked. "No more questions!"

60

*Orange Grove farm. July 30, 1964.
8:00 a.m.*

By eight in the morning, Emily Harris had had her fourth cup of tea. That had never happened in the past forty-one years. Not even after Donald passed away, had she changed her routine. She always rose at five, had her first cup and would then only allow herself a second one at eight. Now she was pacing the back porch of her Orange Grove homestead. She had been unable to shake the feeling of unease since Charles Chombe had knocked on her back door late the night before.

Everything was so unlike his usual demeanor. *He stayed in the shadows, not allowing me to see his face, but I know it was he—it was his voice, his physique. He always came into the house, especially after Don passed, when he started coming out to the farm almost every month to visit.* Last night he refused to even talk, only asking for shelter for the night, for him and some friends. They would be gone before sunrise. He sounded embarrassed and he wouldn't elaborate. *Odd.*

They must have overslept. Then this morning, that was even stranger. The two men with him were both Chinyanjas. But the three children, where do they fit in? They were white—the children. And Charles marched like a tin soldier, and he had a bandage around his head. *Something is very odd.*

She put her empty cup down, took the rifle and went down the steps toward the barn for the third time since after seven, when the Chevrolet truck with the canvas canopy disappeared down her farm road. She turned back, whistled and called, "Come, Roger!" The boxer was at her side within seconds, happy to oblige.

Emily Harris was back in the house ten minutes later, telephone receiver in hand. She had made up her mind. It would be wiser to phone Fort Jameson than Lundazi, she had decided. Although Lundazi was barely thirty miles form her doorstep, they had only one police officer on duty, at any time. They would be of little help.

"Fort Jameson Police, Constable Juma speaking."

"Constable, may I please speak to the station commander? It is Emily Harris from the Lundazi district speaking."

"Sorry, madam, but Sergeant Rangarajan is out on patrol. I'm in charge at the moment. How may I help you?"

"Constable Juma, something strange happened on my farm, Orange Grove. I had visitors who stayed overnight, and they left about an hour ago." Emily Harris filled Constable Juma in.

He didn't interrupt her until she paused to take a deep breath, when he quickly asked, "Mrs. Harris, you could identify only one of the six people. And this individual, Charles Chombe, he is known to you, correct?"

"Yes, Constable. I've known him since the time he was a little boy. His father worked for my husband years ago. The family lived on the farm then."

"Could you identify *any* of the other people?"

"No, Constable. I've never seen any one of them before."

"Mrs. Harris, you are convinced one of the children was a girl?"

"Oh definitely! And she was much taller than the two boys. But as I said, they were at the outbuildings, about a hundred yards away."

Juma paused. "A hundred yards? That's very far to see clearly. How old are you, Mrs. Harris?"

"Constable? I'm seventy-eight."

"Do you wear glasses, Mrs. Harris?"

Emily Harris laughed. The constable was not going to upset her. "I don't even need reading glasses and only yesterday I practiced my target shooting. I do it once a week. I can hit a jam tin on a post at a hundred yards. I think my eyes are still in good shape. I know what I saw, Constable."

Juma coughed. "Please accept my apologies, ma'am. I have been disrespectful." He cleared his throat. "Your information will be of great help. You have no idea how we have been looking for those six! I will inform Sergeant Rangarajan immediately. I'm sorry, but I have to end our conversation, Mrs. Harris. Once again, thank you very much for calling."

"Goodbye, Constable Juma." Emily Harris chuckled to herself as she walked to her kitchen. This called for the fifth cup of tea. And it wasn't even eight-thirty. She went out to the back porch and sat down, Roger glued to her side. She brought the steaming red-brown brew up to her nose—she could never get enough of the earthy smell of the South African *rooibos* tea, which she so loved. She cautiously sipped the scalding drink—no milk, no sugar ... medicine for her troubled mind—as she regarded the features of her beloved Orange Grove.

61

*Paishuko village. July 30, 1964.
9:45 a.m.*

Mavuto decided to bypass Chinsali. He could not afford another mistake. His mother would be in Paishuko—he would find her there. The certainty of this became overwhelming and helped him relax. It was 9:45 by the time he reached the outskirts of the village. He had pushed the old truck of Bwana Kok as hard as it would go, often until the speedometer's needle bobbed against its ceiling, at a steady seventy miles an hour when the roads allowed it.

Only when he paused now at the top of a hill, scanning the landscape, did he notice that the engine had overheated: oil vapors filled the cabin. Charles Chombe had been moved into the back, once they passed Lundazi, almost two hours ago. Mavuto wound the window down and took several deep breaths.

The air outside had not changed, not since he'd grown up here; again he smelled the red earth, the grass, the sand, the *mopani* and *miombo* trees. The musky odor of moss, fern and mushrooms in the shade of fallen trees wafted toward him—it brought comfort.

Because it was so late in the morning already, his only option was to pull off the road, hide the vehicle, leave Mapopa with the prisoners and go find Mother Fatsani.

I hope Mother will be up to walking the mile and a half from the village back to the truck. It is the only safe thing to do. He would have to cut through the bush, to make the truck and its occupants disappear, otherwise, with the police and military vehicles in the area, his plan would be blown. He'd need the machete. *She had better come out of her own free will, because I don't think I will be able to use force on her.*

Mavuto slowed down until he found a small break in vegetation on the side of the road, enough for a vehicle to slip through. He accelerated and veered the truck over the low sand wall and a boulder, and bounced the truck over rotten branches and dead trees before he slammed on the brakes. He could hear the occupants in the back yelling as they tumbled around

Mavuto ran around to open up the back.

"Were you trying to kill us, Mavuto?" Mapopa screamed.

His prisoners, however, were silent, their faces drawn. Rianna stared at Mavuto. She had learned it was perhaps better to say nothing. She noticed the electrified excitement of their captor—he had seen his goal.

"No, Mapopa," Mavuto said, "I wasn't!"

"Idiot!" Mapopa mumbled, "I think *I* should drive on the way back."

"We'll see about that. I'm really sorry, my brother. Quickly help me so I can turn the truck around. There's very little space to maneuver. I need directions. But we have to hurry."

Mapopa stared at his transformed stepbrother; he was all focused and apologetic and gentleman-like. But Mapopa had learned; this was still a dangerous Mavuto, a totally unpredictable Mavuto.

A minute of maneuvering was sufficient.

"That's good, Mapopa!" Mavuto called to him. "Guard the prisoners. I have to go wipe our trail clean." And he limped off toward the road with a branch in his hand—his leg had started hurting again. He knew how not to leave telltale signs. Minutes later, *Bwana* Kok's truck and its occupants had disappeared.

Mavuto popped his head into the back. "Okay, people, here's the situation. We have reached our destination—"

"Where are we, Lisulo?" Charles Chombe sounded, even to himself, like his head felt—throbbing and dull. He was convinced the wounds on his scalp had become infected.

Mavuto laughed, "That's not important, Chombe. Now listen. I'm leaving Mapopa in charge. Do *not* annoy him. We'll only leave the ankle cuffs on—I'll leave your hands free and won't gag you—but only if you swear to cooperate. Mapopa's instructions are clear: if you try to alert outside people in any way, or try to escape, he will have to shoot you."

He paused. "Is that understood?"

The children and Charles nodded in silence.

Mapopa laughed and rubbed his hands. It sounded like a brilliant plan to him.

Rianna couldn't hold much longer. "Mavuto, before you go. Please let us each have a *chumbudzi* break. We also need something to eat and drink. Please. You promised last night."

Mapopa righted himself, hit the side of the truck and snarled, "Shut up *mtsikana*! You can wait until Mr. Lisulo returns from his mission—"

Mavuto touched his stepbrother's shoulder, pushing him away. "Silence, Mapopa. Help me to get them out, one at a time. I did promise."

His stepbrother chuckled. "You've gone soft Mavuto. You've become weak."

"You shut up, Mapopa," Mavuto said. "Don't confuse honor with weakness."

Mapopa laughed as they pulled the children out of the back of the truck, one at a time, undid their cuffs and let them disappear into the brush to relieve themselves. They didn't say a word; Mavuto only showed them the pistol. They understood.

"Honor … hah!" Mapopa muttered. "What do you know about honor, my brother?"

Rianna was the last of the children to go, and stayed away double the time the boys took. She was flustered when she returned, almost out of breath, though she tried hard to act nonchalant. She had been sitting next to Charles in the back, with only their ankles tied. They had ample time to talk. She had much time to ponder the pleading conversation Lukas had with her concerning her apparent distrust of his friend, Charles. She had been asking herself many times the last hour whether she was perhaps wrong about her assumption of the kind of relationship that existed between *Amayi* Kok and Charles Chombe.

But, *how could she be wrong?* She was convinced they had a physical relationship—no, she had proof: even one of his own, Mavuto Lisulo, had accused him in so many words of "lusting after" Adam's mother. Why would they be sending her to Lusaka to have the baby there?

She was confused. Charles Chombe was good, very good. He had told her so many things in the back of the truck. But he was too sure of himself—which in itself was a bad sign.

She tolerated Charles only because of her concern for Lukas and Anthony, because they were still so young and naïve, unable yet to grasp the intricacies of love and desire and deceit. She would act as their gateway, protect them, like she protected little Adam. Without hesitation she accepted the strips of white shirt he had offered her. "You'll know when to use it, *mtsikana*," he had whispered after Mapopa had dozed off in the far end of the truck. She had no idea where they were, but somebody from outside might still be able to help them.

Mapopa immediately picked up on her appearance. "What took you so long, *mtsikana?*"

"I had to hold in for so long, there was much to do," she shot back.

He laughed even louder. "She's been playing with herself—"

Mavuto shoved him with the rifle butt in the ribs. "Cut it out, brother! I have to leave."

He clipped the cuffs onto Rianna's ankles and lifted her onto the truck bed. "Chombe, your turn. Hurry up!"

Mavuto left five minutes later, his AK-47 strapped to his back, pistol in his knapsack, a small water bottle on his belt, his machete in one hand. He tipped his cap and disappeared between the trees.

62

Paishuko village. July 30, 1964.

Mavuto had been able to keep up a steady pace once he found his rhythm, in spite of his throbbing leg. He kept to the road's edge, in the wooded areas, taking care to remain out of sight and off the road surface. He only had to use the machete a couple of times to clear a path. His leg injury did make the going slower, but he accepted that. It was much harder, though, than it would have been during summer with more lush vegetation: he had to rely on his expertise to remain melted into the shadows.

He smiled grimly. His training was not being wasted—he would prove it to his superiors. Garden boy, *zikomo kwambiri*! Thank you very much!

He reached the first house. There were no street names—the village was informally laid out, which he loved. His mother hadn't said which house she would be staying in, but he guessed which one she would have chosen—the one in the middle of the village, next to the church. When he craned his neck he could see the low steeple between the trees.

Mavuto remained pressed against the back wall of a shed outside the first house. He wracked his brain. *Think, Lisulo. Something is the matter.* He tied the machete to his back and slipped his rifle around into his hands but stayed where he was. He sniffed the air again—a strange, sweet smell. It wasn't the forest or the maize flour or livestock that he smelled: this was different.

Even though it was the end of July and cold during the winter nights, the sun had the earth already steaming around him—and it wasn't even noon yet. Within a few hours, it would become sweltering out. He peered at the clear sky: there were three black specks. They circled lower—large birds, with massive wingspans. *Eagles? No, those are vultures.*

The silence! Where did all the vehicles full of people that passed us in the morning go? Nothing is moving here. There's only silence. I'm in a ghost town. He looked up again. There were five vultures circling now. No dog barked, no chicken scrubbed around as they always did when he had visited in the past.

He snuck around to the door of the shed, pushed it ajar and sprinted inside, rifle at the ready. The shed was empty. He did the same at the house. The front door was unlocked; but no one was home. Mavuto ran from shadow to shadow, house to house. Every single one he checked was empty.

Only at the fourth house did he encounter people. The sweet smell became overwhelming. They were all dead. There was so much blood. There was a man, a woman and a child, lying in a disorderly fashion, one over the other. Under the man was that looked like a homemade shield; he was still clutching a short spear. The blade was clean.

Mavuto carefully touched the wrist of the child, a boy, who looked as if he was sleeping. He had no pulse. His hand was cool, but not yet stiff. Mavuto stepped back. Bullet wounds on the bodies were mixed with multitudes of lacerations—deep, gashing wounds. Then he noticed the dead animals.

He ran from house to house. Some were empty. In others he found more bodies, all dead. And outside, more dead animals. The women's and girl's dresses were torn off. There was more blood.

Mavuto ran outside and vomited against a small backyard mango tree. Finally he reached his mother's old house. The front and back doors had both been kicked in. The house was empty. *The church. I have to get to the church.* He glanced at the sky again. There were more birds than he could count; they continued circling.

The church had a low wall around it. As Mavuto stepped through the front gate, he encountered bodies strewn everywhere, leading up to the doors and into the sanctuary. Mavuto was crying now, running from body to body. People must have fled to the church, hoping they could find sanctuary there.

"Mother Fatsani," he called softly. *Perhaps she's still alive—she must be inside the building. I have to work faster. Hurry up, Lisulo!*

By then he was wailing: "Mother Fatsani!"

The outside walls and doors were bullet-ridden. Some of the bodies, men and women, had sharp instruments shoved into every orifice. The majority of the dead were women and children.

Mother Fatsani lay between two pews, on her side. She was not breathing—her eyes closed. Mavuto watched her for a long time. A reposeful smile framed her now quiet face. A single bullet wound adorned her chest—there were no cuts. *Thank God!*

He lifted her into his arms and sat down on a pew, cradling her. "Why didn't you come back, dear Mother? I pleaded with you, for so long. I had an extra room prepared in Madzi Moyo. This is what I'd been afraid of. Who did this to you?"

Mavuto sobbed as he carried her cool body outside and laid her down in the shade of the only tree, an acacia, on a long wooden bench. He was amazed by her weight as he maneuvered her body—she used to be so very big. *Poor Mother, you must have starved these last many weeks. Didn't you have any food? If only I'd known.*

When he was little, only six, he had asked the bishop why they had planted the thorn tree in front of the church.

"Why one with thorns, *Mbusa*?" he had asked.

The bishop had laughed. "We did not plant it, Mavuto. It's a wild tree, it grew on its own. I think the Lord wanted to remind us what hatred does to the soul. It is like these long white thorns that enter your foot; if you don't pull it out, it will fester there."

Mavuto hadn't understood about hatred, but the thorn part was easier.

Mavuto sat down next to his mother. The bench was deep. One of her shoes was missing. He ran back into the church and found it in the pew where she had fallen. He carefully wiped it clean of blood. Once both feet had shoes on, he folded her hands onto her stomach and pulled her long dress down neatly. In her house he also found two blankets and wrapped her body in them. More birds were circling. He found two large flat stones and put one over her lower legs and one on her stomach to keep the blankets down. He found a third stone and put that on her chest. He didn't trust those birds.

Mavuto knelt down next to her, weeping without making a sound, tears streaming down his cheeks, shoulders shaking. Then he bent down and kissed her on the face, through the blanket.

"I will come back for you, Mother Fatsani," he said. "I promise. I'm going to find Mr. Chombe and show him. I need a witness: no one will believe me. Then we will bury you."

Mavuto gave her another kiss before he became one with the shadows again.

63

*Mwenzo, Zambia.
July 30, 1964. 9:55 a.m.*

It was not easy for Constable Juma to locate Sergeant Rangarajan and his three traveling companions—after leaving Mother Fatsani in Paishuko village, they had proceeded north until they reached Mwenzo, the border town with Tanzania, by eight that morning.

Constable Juma succeeded only at 9:55 a.m., an hour and thirty-five minutes after Mrs. Emily Harris phoned him. He located the sergeant at the police station in Mwenzo (Nakonde), only after the customs office at the border post, which couldn't shed any light on the fugitives, informed him of the whereabouts of his superior.

Juma had used the radiotelephone, but once he realized the sergeant was inside the police station, he insisted on switching to

BE SILENT

a landline. The radio-lingo made him sweat profusely—he always made such a fool of himself.

What I won't do to accommodate a staff member, Rangarajan thought—even *one with a heavy tongue in his mouth*. He agreed reluctantly to abandon the secure police radio.

"Juma, how long ago did you speak to her?" he asked after his subordinate described to him his conversation with the owner of Orange Grove.

"An hour and thirty-five minutes, sir."

"Constable Juma! So you decided it wasn't important enough to inform me immediately?"

"Sir, I did phone you immediately. But first I had to track you down. *No one* knew where you were." Juma started repeating every thing Emily Harris had told him.

"Thank you, Juma!" Rangarajan called out. "No need to repeat yourself—I got it. Did you get her phone number?"

"Yes, sir. You have to phone the Lundazi switchboard and ask for number 46."

"Thank you, Juma. Good job. Inform Pillay in Fort Jameson as well."

"Certainly, Sergeant. And thank you, Sergeant."

Seven minutes later, Sergeant Rangarajan was on the phone with Emily Harris. She had just finished her sixth cup of tea.

She repeated what she told Constable Juma, including her concern about the children and Charles Chombe.

"What time did they leave the farm, Mrs. Harris?"

"Around ten past seven this morning, Sergeant."

"Thank you very much for the information Mrs. Harris." He paused, then added. "One of my team members will pay you a visit either later today or tomorrow morning. Goodbye."

Following a short deliberation with Bisa, *Bwana* Ferreira and Youssef Khalil, it was decided to return to Paishuko village.

As they left the police station, Bisa asked, "Sergeant, shouldn't we go pick up the lead on Mrs. Harris's farm?"

"I thought about that Bisa—if only we had the time. But I'm afraid that's a commodity we can't afford to use more of." He added, "I'm convinced Mavuto and company got delayed on the farm, and that that's the only reason we reached Mother Fatsani before he did. We'll go back to her house, in Paishuko. It is past ten. Come, let's hurry."

They ran to the vehicles. Sergeant Rangarajan's Land Rover took the lead on the road southwest.

Once Louis had fallen in pace with the police vehicle ahead of them, staying back outside the Land Rover's dust column, he turned to his Egyptian friend. "Youssef, you know what I'm quite grateful for?"

"*Bwana?*"

"That the kidnappers didn't head to Dar es Salaam!" Louis said.

"*Bwana,* you really think there are still slaves being sold?" Youssef laughed. "This is the twentieth century, remember."

BE SILENT

"Apparently the practice has not died away," Louis said. "Let's say it has only gone underground, around the world. I think that for as long as man wields power, especially limitless power, over his fellowmen, he will abuse it and justify the abuse. And, with limitless power, he often has the means to conceal the abuse."

"*Bwana*, then we'd better find the children before the slave traders do!"

64

Paishuko village. July 30, 1964.

Mavuto realized he had to avoid the roads, or being seen anywhere else, as he made his way back, or a similar fate could befall him as did his mother. Those people in the village had been killed no more than three hours ago. He paused and listened—still the ominous silence. *Where are the people who fled? The survivors if there are any ... And where are the people responsible? How did they all simply disappear?*

His eyes were dry by the time he reached Bwana Kok's concealed truck. He steeled himself for Mapopa's response to being told that Mavuto was returning to the village immediately, but with only Charles Chombe. Would his stepbrother realize that the game plan had been overturned? He had to take the risk, though: he needed a witness, and Mapopa just wouldn't do.

BE SILENT

Mavuto appeared silently, like a ghost next to where Mapopa was sitting, a few feet from the back of the truck, and Mapopa staggered backwards, cussing.

"Mavuto, you snake!" he yelled. "What took you so long? I've had enough of their shit," He gestured in the direction of the prisoners. "They complain about everything!" He pointed up to the sky, "Look at the sun, it's right above us—we're steaming!"

Which was true enough.

"Come on, Mapopa," Mavuto said. "The truck is completely in the shade. It couldn't be that bad!"

Mapopa snorted at his stepbrother.

"Okay, everybody out!" Mavuto declared. "Time to pee again and then time for some food." Mavuto helped the children down. Charles wiggled out under his own steam.

Rianna looked at their captor with renewed interest. He continued to be a man of mystery—his demeanor had changed once again. She voiced her observation. "What's your story Mavuto? What's going on?" She watched him closely when he unlocked her cuffs, since she was having the first pee break.

He grimaced. "Nothing, *mtsikana,* I want you to hurry up. I have to go back to the village. Now go!"

She walked around the front of the truck. *He's been sweating, that much is obvious. He must have walked fast and it's warm and perhaps he even ran some. But his eyes are different.* She halted. *He cried. He must have been crying. Something happened in the village.*

Anthony and Lukas went one after the other. Charles declined the need to go relieve himself. Once the boys had returned, and

299

Mavuto had cuffed their ankles again, he handed each child a can of beans.

"Is it Christmas, Mavuto?" Lukas wanted to know. "No more rationing?" Just before Mavuto had cuffed their ancles, Lukas had taken a quick peek in the box—there were six of them, and if they had a can of food each—it would only last another three days. He was convinced Mavuto was cutting the journey shorter.

Mavuto only pulled up his shoulders, as if he was embarrassed.

Anthony was ravenous and scooped fingers full into his mouth, and added, still chewing, "What's for dessert, Mr. Lisulo? May I have a look in that box? Perhaps some canned peaches?"

His laughter was cut short when Mapopa threw a stick at him, knocking the can of food from his hands, spilling the remainder of the beans into the dirt at his feet. Mapopa hollered with mirth, folding himself double.

Rianna grabbed a stick and lashed out at the young man, hitting him across the arms, yelling, "You despicable man! He's a young boy who was eating a few stupid cold beans!"

Mavuto intervened as Mapopa pulled his pistol from his belt. "Stop that, Mapopa! Everyone, settle down!"

"The *mtsikana* will pay," Mapopa hissed. "No one hits Mapopa!" He grudgingly slipped his pistol back into his belt.

Mavuto shoved his stepbrother forcefully back against the side of the truck. "Careful, Mapopa. You will not touch her! Do you understand me?"

"Whatever, Mr. Lisulo." Mapopa glared at his brother.

Mavuto walked away from them and paced back and forth, limping. *Mapopa is so volatile,* he thought. *He's dangerous. But I have to run back to the village and take Charles as a witness. He can help me carry Mother Fatsani's body. I have no choice but to leave Mapopa with the children. Perhaps I should only leave him the pistol and take the second AK.*

"Listen up, Mapopa!" he announced. "I have to return to the village immediately. I'm taking Chombe with me. You—"

"What? Mavuto, do you have heatstroke?" Mapopa said with unconcealed contempt.

"Mapopa! Pay attention! Chombe is going to help me bring Mother Fatsani back. You have a *great* responsibility—looking after the children until we get back."

Mapopa gave a manic laugh. "Oh, now *that's* good news. Children! Did you hear that? Mapopa has been given *great* responsibility!"

He danced a victory dance and bestowed the group again with his manic laughter.

Mavuto unclipped Charles's cuffs and took the AK-47 from Mapopa's shoulder. The youth was taken by surprise and he grasped after the rifle, yelling, "What are you doing, Mavuto?"

"I need it more than you do. You may keep the pistol. The village is a dangerous place right now. If I were you, I would lower my voice and follow the instructions."

Rianna suddenly realized that their captor was planning to take them one by one to execute them. "Mavuto!" she called out. "Why are you taking Charles with you?"

Mavuto ignored her. "Come, Chombe!"

Rianna raised her voice and shrieked in cold blood, "Mavuto! No!"

Mavuto jumped at her and covered her mouth with his hand. He'd seen the fear in her eyes. He whispered softly next to her head, "I am not going to shoot him, *mtsikana*. I have to show him something terrible that has happened in the village. Children should never see it. When I return, your ordeal will be over. I promise." She relaxed against his hands.

"What is going on, Lisulo?" Charles asked now. He didn't move—he wasn't going anywhere. He didn't trust his captor's sudden change of tone.

"I'll tell you on the way," Mavuto said. "Please, we have to hurry. Here, take this." He held out a small water bottle. "We have a great task ahead of us."

He turned back to Mapopa. "Remember, brother, you may not touch the children. Do you understand that?"

"Yes, brother." Another manic chuckle followed the two men as they disappeared into the shadows.

65

Paishuko village. July 30, 1964.
12:05 p.m.

Mapopa estimated that it would take the two men at least an hour, probably an hour and a half to get back to *Bwana* Kok's truck with Mother Fatsani. Even injured, Mavuto and Charles would have made good time on their own, but Mother Fatsani, who had never been a running-around kind of lady, even when she was younger, would really slow them down. She always was plump, but in recent years had become even bigger. No, he was certain she would slow them down.

That gave him sufficient time for implementing his own plan. He chuckled. *Mavuto thinks he's the only one with a plan. We'll see. I need to get the two boys out of the way and then I can have her all to myself. Teach her a lesson or two.*

He waited fifteen minutes as he prepared a few items he would need. *Be patient, Mapopa,* he told himself while he waited, *just in case Mavuto changes his mind and turn around to check up on you.*

"Listen, children!" Mapopa then cheerfully called out as he jumped onto the truck bed. "Boys, I'm afraid I'll have to inconvenience the two of you for a while," he said as he first tied the surprised Anthony's wrists to an upright side bar, and then Lukas's, though Lukas tried to fight him off.

"Mapopa!" Rianna shouted. "Leave them alone! You have promised Mavuto you wouldn't touch us!"

"I promised nothing," Mapopa snarled. "Mavuto's head has gone soft."

The boys yelled and kicked, but Mapopa only laughed louder and tugged harder on the ropes, while he tied their wrists to the truck's frame.

Rianna flung herself at him as he was tying the last rope on Lukas's wrist. They crashed into the side of the truck, Mapopa's head smacking into the metal side. He realized his oversight—only her ankles were tied with the cuffs, leaving her fairly mobile. Mapopa roared as he rolled over and grabbed the girl from behind. There wasn't proper standing space in the back, forcing them to their knees. He hissed into her neck, "Stop it, *mtsikana!*"

"I will never stop, you monster!" she shouted and snapped her head backward, smashing it into Mapopa's nose. He yelled in pain and annoyance, then flung her down, pinning her writhing body under him as he pulled a length of rope from his pocket and tied her hands behind her back. His nose was bleeding.

Rianna hollered one insult after the other at her attacker, who wiped his bleeding nose with his sleeve and then grabbed her arm and dragged her to the end of the truckbed. Mapopa jumped off and pulled Rianna with him.

"What are you doing, Mapopa?" Lukas cried.

The man laughed at the boys. "Mapopa is going to teach the *mtsikana* a lesson. Perhaps more than one."

He dragged Rianna away from the back of the truck, yelling, "She has to be taught *several* lessons. The first lesson is Mapopa doesn't like small and dark places. So what did she do? She pulled a blanket over Mapopa's face. It was embarrassing and—"

"But we helped her! Leave her alone, Mapopa—you can teach *us* a lesson instead. Let her go!" Lukas yelled.

Mapopa only laughed as he dragged the protesting girl to a tree several feet away.

"What are you going to do, Mapopa?" Lukas cried out. "Spank her bottom?"

"One day you will learn there are many ways of teaching people, especially a woman a lesson, *mwana*," Mapopa retorted as he stuffed the gag into Rianna's mouth. He deftly picked up another piece of rope, which he had left minutes earlier at the base of the second of three chosen trees, and tied it around her wrist and then to the first upright trunk. He then did the same with the other wrist and undid the rope that held her hands together and pulled her arm out toward the third trunk, pulling her up to stand with her back against the middle trunk.

"Mapopa! Why don't you answer us? Let her go!" Lukas demanded from the back of the truck, from behind the canvas canopy.

"You mind your own business now, *mwana*. I'm busy!" he hollered as he pulled both ropes tighter, thrusting her breasts outwards, her arms pulled backwards and to the sides. He could see the fear in her eyes.

"Don't be afraid, little wild one," he said. "Mapopa won't really hurt you." He fiddled in his pocket and brought his pocketknife out. Rianna yelled from behind her gag, but only muffled sounds escaped. Her eyes were large and terrified.

"No, little one—be silent—I won't hurt you."

He cut one sleeve of her blouse open. "Ah, now what do we have here?" he said. "Pink underclothes. Let's get rid of that." He pressed the blade under the strap and cut the elastic band. Rianna writhed and pulled on the ropes, attempted to push the gag out with her tongue.

Failing, she managed, muffled, "You monster, don't. Please don't …"

Mapopa laughed as he pulled the pink cup down and touched the one breast. "It's beautiful, *mtsikana*. Beautiful *bere*."

She tried to kick at him with two tied-together feet, bawling from behind the gag, but only managed to slip sideways and fall halfway down the side of the trunk. He pulled her up again, unclipped the cuffs and quickly tied her ankles the way he had her arms. Her breasts and pelvis were thrust outward.

She is ready for me.

He cut her other sleeve open, then cut the second elastic shoulder strap and pulled the cup down. Two *bere*. She wriggled desperately as the youth cupped both her breasts, fondling them, bending forward to kiss the one.

Lukas and Anthony, in the back of the truck, whispered and wriggled. Soon after they had left the farm that morning, Lukas had asked Rianna for his backpack. It was, after all, *his* property. She didn't object too much when they made the switch. Lukas

BE SILENT

wondered now what on earth the man meant by "There are many ways of teaching a woman a lesson." He could feel that one of his wrists was almost free. *Why are Mapopa and Rianna so quiet?* He was certain he could hear them, though: they were still nearby.

"Mapopa!" Lukas cried out as he freed his one arm. "What have you done to the *mtsikana*?" Then he whispered, "Keep Mapopa busy. Say anything. I don't know what he's doing with Rianna. I have one hand free."

Anthony shouted: "Mapopa, would you like to give *us* a spanking, instead of the girl?"

The young man laughed as he kissed the girl's breast. It was so firm. Rianna screamed behind her gag, wriggling constantly.

But a moment later, the boys shook in terror: Mapopa's face appeared around the truck's canvas side, and he yelled, "Are the two of you behaving?" He had a strange glare in his eyes, as if he'd been hypnotized.

Lukas froze and prayed that Mapopa wouldn't notice his freed wrist. *Keep the man busy. Say anything. What is he doing with Rianna?*

"Mapopa," he began, "I was wondering. Aren't you hungry? Why don't you have a look in that box of Mavuto's …"

Mapopa's head disappeared. Again the manic laugh. "Thank you," he said, out of sight again, "but I have already started on dessert …"

He was enjoying himself—there was no need to hurry. He would take his time and prepare the girl properly.

"Okay, *mtsikana*," he said. "Now for lesson two. Never hit Mapopa. Never."

307

He cut the blouse open in the front and pulled the severed garments off the writhing girl. Her taut breasts thrust about helplessly—trying to escape his advances—pure white in their innocence. Next he carefully cut her skirt on the side, until it flopped to the forest earth at her feet.

"It still hurts where you hit me on my arm," he said as he touched her navel with his palm and pushed his fingers lower.

Rianna shook her head violently. "No, no, no, no!" she yelled behind the gag.

Lukas had both his hands free. Anthony's wrists must have been tied much tighter than his, he thought. He slipped his backpack from his shoulder, then remembered. *Rianna returned my backpack, but not the pocketknife.*

He slipped the backpack back on, whispering, "Sorry, Anthony, she still has my knife. I have to loosen it with my fingers."

He continued fiddling with the knots, yelling, "Mapopa, please come back!"

Mapopa only laughed. He dropped his pants and stepped closer, slowly pushing the elastic band lower, until he could see the first curls. It was red-blond after all—he sighed as he slipped his finger beneath. Rianna yelled behind her gags, shaking her head even more violently and tried to pull away from him. Mapopa was so busy he did not notice the two bouncing figures behind him.

Anthony and Lukas yelled as their tree branches rained down on the man. Lukas missed, but Anthony struck him on the side of the head. The boys were hollering for life and death, and Rianna managed at last to get the gag pushed out of her mouth and joined the screaming. The boys struck him again and again, yelling.

BE SILENT

Lukas scrambled back to his feet and lurched at Rianna's skirt, which was lying at her feet while his friend continued hitting Mapopa with the branch. His fingers found the knife in her skirt pocket. Lukas cut her ropes.

Lukas noticed several things at once: her face was wet from crying, both her breasts were naked, and Mavuto and Charles had appeared out of nowhere.

Three shots were fired in close succession. The last thing Lukas remembered was hearing Mapopa cry out in pain and surprise and then Anthony's cry before he felt the burn in his own leg. He tried to turn to see where his friend was, but by that time everything had gone dark.

66

*Paishuko village. July 30, 1964.
1:30 p.m.*

Lukas blinked several times and looked around. *Father is here. And there is Joseph Khalil.* What was he doing here? Did he bring everyone ice cream on a stick? *I am so thirsty. Ice cream would be nice. It doesn't even have to be chocolate flavor. And who was that ... Charles? But where are my friends? Where are Anthony and Rianna? Why can't I see Anthony? And where are Mavuto and Mapopa? My leg feels so cold, and it burns.*

"Father?" he said.

"Lukas!"

"How did you find us, Father?"

"The old lady from the farm where you guys stayed last night phoned the Fort Jameson police, who eventually got hold of us, so we came back here, figuring that Paishuko village was where we would most likely find Mavuto and the rest of you. The two pieces of white fabric tied to branches on the roadside nearby helped too."

Lukas looked around again. He was propped up in the front seat of Youssef Khalil's truck. Mavuto was sitting under a tree to the side of the road, with Mapopa's head on his lap, stroking the younger man's face. The two vehicles were pulled onto the side of the road.

"What's wrong with Mapopa, Father?" Lukas said.

Louis Ferreira turned away, avoiding his son's eyes.

"Father?"

"He's dead Lukas. He was hit by a bullet."

Lukas quickly counted the people he could see—there were five of them, plus the body of Mapopa.

"Then what is Mavuto doing?" Lukas asked.

"He was the one who fired the shot that killed him."

"But Mapopa was hurting Rianna!" Lukas's voice broke as he relived the minutes Anthony and he had fought Mapopa off of Rianna with the branches. She was so terrified—spread open against those trees, half naked with only her pink panties partially on—when he managed to cut her ropes. He gave a sob.

"We know, Lukas." Louis hugged his son.

"Mavuto must still have loved his stepbrother, don't you think?" Lukas whispered as he pulled free.

"I think so, Lukas."

"Father, where are Rianna and Anthony? Is Anthony okay? ... Dad?"

Lukas wondered what his father wasn't telling him. There were so many things he realized now—the adults were not telling them—thinking they were too young, too little. And see what had happened since yesterday! He implored his father.

"Lukas, Anthony also got shot, in his groin—"

Lukas jumped up to get out of the truck, then grabbed at his leg. "Where is he? Is he …" Lukas dared not say the word.

His father reassured him that his friend was not dead. He told him how Sergeant Rangarajan and Constable Bisa raced with Anthony to the small hospital in Chinsali where the sergeant managed to get one of the military helicopters to fly him to Lusaka. He had been shot in the big vessels in his leg—in his groin.

"Dad … did he bleed lots?"

"Yes, Lukas."

"What's wrong with *my* leg, Father?"

"You also got shot, but not as seriously as Anthony. From what Charles was saying, Mapopa shot both you and Anthony, as Mavuto shot Mapopa."

"What's going to happen to Mavuto, Father?"

"The authorities will deal with him."

"And Rianna? Where is she? Is she okay, Father?"

Louis smiled now at his son. "Enough questions for one day. She's still in shock and has been wrapped in blankets and is sitting in the front seat of *Bwana* Kok's truck."

"But she shouldn't be left alone! Can I go sit with her?"

"She didn't want anybody to touch her, or even be near her."

Lukas looked at his father with pleading eyes; it was hard enough that Anthony was shot so badly and had to be taken to hospital. He could not let poor Rianna sit alone in a stupid old truck—not after what she had gone through.

"Well, you can go see if she'll let you."

"Please help me, Father," Lukas murmured as he slipped off the front seat of Youssef's truck. "Just one more question, Dad. Where is Mother Fatsani—did they find her?"

"Yes, Lukas, they found her. Charles helped Mavuto carry her body back. She was killed earlier this morning in the village."

Lukas did a recount—there were six of them now plus the two bodies. "That must be why Mavuto insisted on taking Charles with him when he returned to the village. He didn't want us to see, and he had to bring her body back, I guess?"

"That's right."

"Dad … What did Mavuto see in the village? Did you go look?"

"No, I didn't go. It was difficult enough to try and save Anthony and get him to a hospital. None of us went. We know what Charles and Mavuto told us."

Lukas had more questions. He wanted to know how many villagers were killed. His father never answered the questions but instead prompted him to run along and see how Rianna was doing.

Lukas limped toward *Bwana* Kok's truck and paused outside the passenger door, waiting.

Rianna wound the window down but didn't look at him.

"What do you want, Lukas?" Her voice was hollow—came at him from a faraway place—an unknown place.

"Are you … okay, Rianna?"

"How can I be okay, Lukas Ferreira? What kind of question is that?"

He could hear the venom drip from the words and yet he persisted.

"You know about Anthony?" he said. "He got shot badly in his leg."

"Yes, Lukas, I was there. Remember? I saw when the policemen raced off with him to get him some help."

He would try harder.

"Do you ... Do you want somebody to sit with you?"

"No ... Please go away, Lukas ... Just go ..." This time there was no venom, only a little-girl voice.

67

*Lusaka, Zambia. Saturday,
March 20, 2004. 8:30 p.m.*

Lukas held onto the railing and peered at the bustling street, six stories down. He couldn't smell the woodlands and red earth, but it did smell different from home—exhaust fumes all smelled the same, but the *nshima* porridge was unmistakable, and so were the Chinyanja-chattering eddying from the streets below. The day had not cooled down yet. He continued to be surprised by Lusaka. That it would have such busy streets on a Saturday night was unexpected. For a moment it felt like being in Manhattan—not the size but the never coming to rest. *It's almost time to go down to the lobby and see Rianna.*

She had phoned him the day before, but only to tell him that she had made contact with Charles Chombe, that the two of them were having lunch today. Then she'd asked whether he would mind to meeting her for drinks this evening in the lounge, at eight- thirty; they were staying in the same hotel. *Whether he would mind.* Her voice had changed since they had spoken for the first time, two days ago.

He went inside, pulled the sliding door close and checked himself in the hallway mirror. He had lost count of how many times he'd done that in the last hour.

Lukas walked into the lounge at exactly eight-thirty. He scanned the room until he noticed her. There were twelve other people in the room. He was certain it was her, sitting by herself at a tall table to the one side, her purse clutched in front of her, her lips tight. Their eyes met and she smiled immediately and slipped off the stool as he stepped closer.

Lukas put his hand out in greeting. She took it only for a moment, then opened her arms and pulled him in for a firm hug, which took him by surprise. In all these years he had grown only a little taller than her. He was reluctant at first, then hugged her back, her breasts pressing against his chest, they were still firm. He could feel the tension drain from her burdened body as she relaxed in his arms, until he at last broke the embrace, stood back and held her at arm's length. Her mop of long hair had been cut short into a bob.

"Rianna."

"Hello, Lukas."

He smiled. "Do you know what my biggest concern was, about this meeting tonight?"

She laughed, and for a moment Lukas could see the young girl he once knew, the redhead who made life so vibrant around her wherever she went. And, he'd been right about her eyes.

She tilted her head. "That I wouldn't show up?"
He shook his head.
"That we wouldn't recognize each other!"
"Yes. When I spoke to you on Thursday, I recognized your voice, but it was ..."
"Older."
Lukas laughed and held her hand until she sat down, then he took a stool opposite her. "No," he said, "it was mature."
They placed their drink orders, then fell quiet. It was a comfortable silence.
Lukas looked up. "How did it go this afternoon, with Charles?"
The pools of fire were gone from her eyes; all that remained was sadness. "It was hard in the beginning, to break the ice. I think it was harder for me."
"You think it was easy for him, meeting with you?" Lukas immediately regretted his sharp tone.
"No it wasn't, Lukas, but it was harder for me because I had so much difficulty accepting his forgiveness." She touched his hand. "How could he not hate me for what I said back then in the sworn statement?"
"I don't think he ever hated you."
"To think I believed it all these years! That's why I carried this burden, this self-inflicted wound, so long. That's why I never tried to make contact."
"Did Charles tell you about Mrs. Kok—*Amayi* Kok?" Lukas asked.
"You mean about the baby?"

"Yes." Lukas said.

Rianna nodded. "He did." She sniffled and wiped over her eyes.

Lukas leaned forward. "I'm sorry, Rianna …If you would rather not discuss it."

She sniffled again but grabbed his hands, almost knocking his glass over. "No, Lukas, I am so grateful you tracked me down. I was upset at first—I felt you had no right … but we … Charles and I spent the entire afternoon, in the end, talking. It was almost supper by the time he left. There was so much to say ... and listen to."

Rianna pulled out a tissue from her purse and blew her nose. "Yes," she said then. "He told me the baby died three weeks later."

Lukas peered into her wet eyes. "That's what you didn't want to tell me when we were tied up in the back of the stolen truck, when I asked why you were mad at Charles. You thought he was the father."

She nodded.

"Did you ask Charles whether he slept with Adam's mother?"

Rianna laughed, obviously embarrassed. "You know me, Lukas Ferreira—of course I did."

"And he told you."

"He didn't flinch. They were only good friends, he said."

Lukas paused. "It was Mapopa who violated you. You knew that—we knew that. Why did you persist with implicating Charles as well?"

"Lukas, please … I was thirteen years old. We were innocent children who stumbled on an abandoned shed with two stupid AK-47s in it."

"And there was this innocent house boy who tried to save his friends."

"Lukas! We'd been held, kidnapped, for almost twenty-one harrowing hours, before Mapopa started molesting me. I was terrified, exhausted and, yes, very angry at Charles for going off with Mavuto to the village, leaving us alone with that maniac. And there were the things Mavuto said about Adam's mom. I wrongly felt it was Charles's fault in the end. And at that point I was convinced that Magda Kok had to go to Lusaka for the delivery because they were ashamed of us seeing her colored baby."

They finished their drinks in silence.

"Did Charles tell you that there was a retrial," Lukas asked, "twelve months later? His reputation was cleared, after Mavuto decided to tell what happened that day, and give Charles an alibi? He claimed Charles never left the truck—that he was tied up with us."

Rianna nodded. "Did you ever see Anthony's parents again after the funeral?" she asked.

"No—he was their only child, and I believe they returned to South Africa a few months later. When I left for the South, they were already gone."

"He's still buried in Madzi Moyo?" Rianna asked.

"Yes, in the same spot—"

She softly finished, "—where we buried him under the *mopani* tree with the tire swing, in front of the school."

"How he loved that tire-swing," Lukas added.

"You had a brave friend in Anthony, you know."

"No Rianna, *we* had a brave friend."

Their hands touched again.

"Charles told me this afternoon they had a proper marble headstone put on his grave," Rianna said.

"I didn't know. I thought ... after forty years there would be little left, nothing to go back to," Lukas said.

"The marble should still be there," Rianna said.

She stood up, clutching her purse. "I would like to see it some day."

Lukas got up. "I never got to say goodbye to him," he said. "Not in a proper way."

They walked to the elevator.

"What time is your flight, Lukas?"

"At seven p.m. tomorrow. You?"

"Eight-thirty p.m."

The elevator doors opened.

"When does the commission wrap up their meeting?" she asked.

"They have to be done by one."

Lukas, suddenly embarrassed, excused himself when he noticed the chairman of the T and R Commission standing in the foyer, looking like he had to ask him something. Rianna held the elevator door as it started closing. "Is there a Mrs. Lukas Ferreira?"

"There was, but I lost her four years ago to cancer. Breast."

"I'm so sorry, Lukas."

"It's okay now. The wound has healed, mostly."

"Goodnight, Lukas."

"Goodnight, Rianna."

The elevator door closed, then immediately opened again.

"Can I interest you in lunch tomorrow?" Rianna asked, blushing.

"Only if I pay!" Lukas said. "See you at one-thirty in the lounge? They serve a light lunch."

68

Lusaka. Saturday, March 20, 2004, 10:35 p.m.

Lukas sat on his hotel-room balcony, contemplating his meeting with Rianna; he had pulled the single desk chair out through the sliding door. The evening was cooling down, but the streetlife below had no intention yet of ebbing away. He was analyzing Rianna's blushing face and her question "can I interest you in lunch tomorrow?" when the room phone rang. It was Charles Chombe.

"*Bwana* Ferreira, forgive the late hour." His old friend refused to call him by his first name.

"*Zikuyenda,* Charles?" What's the matter?

"I have been thinking much since we talked earlier this week, *Bwana,* and also since I spoke with *Amayi* Rianna this afternoon. There is a letter that I want you to read, perhaps the *amayi* as well. I know it is already late, but may I come up to your room? It's important. But it shouldn't take too long."

BE SILENT

"But of course, Charles! I'm in room 609."

Fifteen minutes later, Charles handed him an envelope. Lukas took the desk chair for himself and made his friend sit on the only proper lounge chair.

"I received it about five years ago," Charles said, "under strange circumstances. I was surprised. This letter in your hand, was enclosed in a larger envelope with a short note from the warden in the penitentiary where I did my time."

"He kept it for thirty-four years?"

Charles laughed, "I believe he held onto it until he retired, then sent it to me. He had to put his conscience to rest eventually."

"To whom was it addressed?" Lukas asked.

"Open it and see."

Lukas pulled the letter out and read:

My dear Mr. Charles Chombe

Lukas lowered the letter. "Look at the date this was written," he said. "April 18, 1965! The warden really held this letter for close to thirty-three years?"

"Read it, *Bwana*, then you'll understand. The warden had to censor inmates' letters. He must have had second thoughts about doing that, and decided to keep it, then forgot about it. I don't know."

Lukas read:

My dear Mr. Charles Chombe,

Forgive me if this letter reads difficult. I am more used to writing in Chichewa, my mother's tongue. This is hopefully my final draft, but I have to send it off to you.

I have been putting this off for too long. I realize this letter comes a little late, and that I would be arrogant to ask for your forgiveness, but nevertheless, such is the case.

I also plan to inform the warden and the superintendent about what really happened on July 29 and July 30, 1964, when you became involved with the three missionary children. I will insist on making a new sworn statement and confession, specifically about your involvement in so far as the mtsikana Rianna was concerned, when she claimed in her own statement that you assisted Mapopa, when he sexually abused her. I will state emphatically that you could not have been involved in the degradation of the mtsikana, since I took you away and you were not present at the time of the crime.

I realize today, actually, I realized it the same day that Mother Fatsani and Mapopa were killed, that you and the three children (even poor Mapopa) were pulled into this whole sordid affair because of my obsession with the independence of Zambia in October of 1964 and the threat that I perceived that the Lumpa Church posed. I realize that I should have followed your suggestion to let the four of you go on the evening of the 29th, allowing you to go into hiding on the Orange Grove farm.

As conflicting as it sounds, I also apologize for dragging you into Paishuko as a witness. But I needed someone else to witness what I saw, since nobody would have believed me. Was what you witnessed that day, a site of a rebellion or of a massacre? You decide.

I also needed someone to help me carry the body of Mother Fatsani. Thank you for doing that. As you must have gathered by now, my soul died the hour I laid her body down on that bench in

BE SILENT

the shade of the thorn tree outside the church. Little did I know that I would cradle the lifeless body of my stepbrother in my lap, less than three hours later.

I never had the opportunity to ask Mwana Anthony's parents for forgiveness. I know it was Mapopa's bullet that killed him, (no surgeon can suture those large blood vessels if a person has been shot at such close range), but I carry the burden.

I also whish I had the opportunity to ask Mwana Lukas and Mtsikana Rianna (especially her) for forgiveness.

Please forgive me. I will always remain in your debt.

Sincerely,
Mavuto Lisulo.

Lukas dropped the letter in his lap. "What happened to Mavuto? Do you know?"

"I was released in July of 1965," Charles said. "Mavuto apparently died in prison the following year. One of the stories that went round was that the Lisulo brothers were responsible for what took place in Paishuko that day."

69

Lusaka. Monday, March 22, 2004

Rianna waited in the lobby, near the large revolving doors. She knew she wasn't late, and couldn't understand where the punctual Lukas could be. She hadn't seen him since after their lunch-date the day before, when they'd decided to take Charles Chombe up on his offer to drive them up to Madzi Moyo to visit Anthony's grave. She had even rescheduled her flight for three days later.

She grabbed her single piece of luggage when she spotted Charles pull up outside, timed her passage through the doors, and yelled as she exited, "I'm ready, Mr. Chombe!"

Charles had already walked around and was opening the tailgate of his Land Rover Discovery.

"*Moni, Amayi.*" Charles tipped his hat.

Rianna laughed, embarrassed. "*Moni,* Mr. Chombe. Nice wheels. Please, I'm not an *amayi*."

"Thank you. Well, you are no longer a *mtsikana*. And I'm not *Mister Chombe*."

She laughed relieved, "Yes, Charles, you're right—I'm no longer a little girl. I don't know where Lukas is," she added. "He's always so painfully punctual."

"He's over there." Charles pointed along the front of the building to where Lukas was walking toward them, pulling his two bags, coming from a bench he must have been sitting on all along, watching them.

"You're late!" Rianna insisted. "Why didn't I see you?"

"Because I am still the *Mthunzi*, the Shadow," Lukas whispered. "It is only eight a.m., as was agreed upon, Professor Vermeulen."

"Oh please, spare us that! Mr. Chombe, can we make Mr. Ferreira sit in the back, to teach him a lesson?"

"That can be arranged, *Amayi Rianna*." Charles laughed as he loaded Lukas's luggage. "Welcome, my friend. I will call you Mr. *Mthunzi*."

Charles's new 4x4 made good reckoning with the 550 kilometers to Madzi Moyo in the Eastern Province, although the going was often slowed by crumbling pavement, rough even for the off-road vehicle. The air conditioning did take the stab out of the humid late-summer day.

It was shortly after two when Charles took the turn-off to the old Mission station. His passengers had grown quiet. Neither of them had returned after they left in 1964. Charles pulled off the gravel road at the top of the hill and parked in the shade of the old *mopani*, the same one Lukas's father had always preferred.

He remained in the vehicle and waited as his two passengers got out. Then he lowered the driver's-side window, "*Amayi* Rianna, Mr. Mthunzi, you two go ahead," he said. "Walk around—you'll notice there are new hostel and school buildings, but they're closed this week since everybody is on school vacation. I'll meet you in an hour or so, down at the school. There's no rush—we're staying overnight in Fort Jameson. We'll leave early in the morning." He smiled. "Fort Jameson. It's called Chipata nowadays. It is only twenty kilometers from here, so take you time."

Rianna and Lukas wandered pensively around the hostel grounds, uncertain where to start. The mango tree that had once stood to the side of the building was gone. A bougainvillea grew as strong and lush as the old one, casting the long porch into deep cool shadows. The frangipani with its sweetness was nowhere to be seen. Lukas counted the *mopanis*—of the original sixteen, only thirteen had survived. They slowly made their way down the wide gravel path toward the school.

Miss Visagie's *rondawel* had recently been rethatched and repainted. They paused for a moment, as if to wait for the effervescent teacher to burst from her front door any moment, waving at them with one of her flamboyant hats. Then they wandered farther down, between two rows of sausage trees, the sun warm on their necks.

BE SILENT

Rianna took Lukas's hand as they walked. "Lukas Ferreira, *where* is your hat?" she said. She tried hard to imitate Miss Gerda Visagie.

"Oh, I'm so sorry, Miss, but I think *Rianna* has stolen it!" He let go of her hand. "If you'll excuse me, Miss Visagie. I'd better run and get out of the direct sun, before I'm struck down by sunstroke!" He laughed and ran the last little bit toward the new school building where he stopped in front of the *mopani* tree. Rianna joined him. There was no trace of the tire swing.

There were two tombstones, on the far side of the tree, facing away from the new school building, which sat a little farther away from the *mopani*, than the previous building had.

Rianna knelt down beside Lukas. Lukas wiped the dust from the inscription.

IN LOVING MEMORY OF
ANTHONY BENADE
May 15, 1954
July 30, 1964
*"Anthony, you were our innocent dove,
taken away too soon."*
MATT 10:16

"Goodbye, Anthony," Lukas said quietly. "Goodbye, my dear friend. You saved both Rianna's and my life that day." Lukas straightened out, touching the top of the headstone, then bent forward and kissed the marble.

Rianna paused, waiting until Lukas was ready, then walked around to the other headstone, knelt and rubbed the dirt and dust away.

"Lukas, whose would this be?" She wiped harder with her hand and then read out loud:

ALICIA MATHILDA KOK
October 17, 1964
November 7, 1964
"Can a mother forget the baby at her breast?"
ISA 49:15

"Lukas! It must be Adam's little sister."

Lukas stepped around and took her hand. He was certain she wasn't lying.

Charles Chombe found them an hour later, sitting in the short grass in front of Alicia Kok's headstone, holding hands in the shade of the *mopani,* embraced by the chorus of cicadas.

Acknowledgements:

No writer or author can exist in a vacuum—we need other people—readers and other writers. We need a community.

My thanks to Stefan Harms, the one who put me up to this. He told me seven years ago, "Go write a book." So I did. And I am still writing. So here we go!

My thanks to Stephanie Fysh for editing the manuscript.

To Victor Duarte, for being one of the faithful first-readers.

To Isabella, my most stalwart reader, and for the constant encouragement, especially when my own courage faltered.

To Toastmasters International (and in particular, Testament Toastmasters), who helped me on my journey to be more concise with words.

What would we be today, if not for parents, family, friends, teachers, writers and authors who, over the years, instilled in us the passion for reading, for learning, and for discovering possibilities?

To the following individuals, organizations and online resources that I have made use of and for verifying facts, my heartfelt thanks.

To Wim van Binsbergen. Religious Innovation and political conflict in Zambia. The Lumpa Rising. (Part I – IV)

To the hosts of Encyclopedia.com

To the hosts of behind the name.com for Chichewa names

To Robert I. Rotberg. The Rise of Nationalism in Central Africa: The making of Malawi and Zambia 1873-1964. Harvard University Press, Cambridge, Massachusetts 1965.

To the hosts of academia.edu/one Zambia many histories. Toward a history of post-colonial Zambia. Edited by Jan-Bart Gewald, Marja Hinfelaar, Giacomo Macola.

To the hosts of historyworld.net for a history of Zambia.

To the hosts of the Chichewa dictionary

And also to the hosts of Malawi.tripod.com/chichewa on how to learn Chichewa.

And finally, my sincere thanks to the new community of bloggers, writers and authors that I have met during the past two to three years. You made me realize: there is no ceiling. The possibilities are endless.

FREE DOWNLOAD

**Find out how it all started...
BE GOOD, the prequel.**

amazonkindle nook kobo iBooks
Windows *android* BlackBerry

Sign up for the author's New Releases mailing list and get a free copy of the novella *Be Good, the prequel* in the *Be Silent mini-series*

Signing up is easy! Simply go here:
http://eepurl.com/cmmGCT

Please consider leaving a review for this novel. Reviews matter. By leaving a review more readers will gain access to the novel—hence enable the author to write more.

Made in the USA
San Bernardino, CA
07 March 2017